Accolades for John H
IN A TRUE LIGHT

"A haunting story. . . . The events play out in two time frames—the cool-jazz bohemian era of 1950's Greenwich Village and the black-and-bluesy world in which Sloane currently finds himself—making beautiful music in a voice we thought we'd never hear again."
—*The New York Times Book Review*

"Elegiac and eloquent . . . John Harvey at his very best."
—Michael Connelly

"This dark and dazzling tale of crime and redemption can only enhance Harvey's reputation."
—*Publishers Weekly*, starred review

"A surprising and immensely satisfying return to crime fiction for one of the genre's true modern masters."
—*Booklist*, starred review

"Harvey is a classic Porsche that can run circles around the gargantuan SUVs that too many thrillers are today. Climb aboard. You'll feel the wind in your hair."
—*The Washington Post Book World*

"Cool, deceptively seamless, and artfully constructed . . . a pitch-perfect, pulp noir cocktail from a true master."
—George P. Pelecanos

"Harvey is brilliant at conjuring this vibrant era, and agile at the high-wire act of writing about what it's like to create art."
—*The Seattle Times*

"John Harvey's writing is beautifully nuanced, his sense of story impeccable, his characters unforgettable."
—Jonathan Kellerman

IN A TRUE LIGHT

a novel of crime

JOHN HARVEY

An Otto Penzler Book

CARROLL & GRAF PUBLISHERS
NEW YORK

IN A TRUE LIGHT

An Otto Penzler Book
Carroll & Graf Publishers
An Imprint of Avalon Publishing Group Inc.
161 William Street, 16th Floor
New York, NY 10038

First Carroll & Graf cloth edition 2002
First Carroll & Graf trade paperback edition 2003

Library of Congress Cataloging-in-Publication Data is available.

ISBN: 0-7867-1229-5

Printed in the United States of America
Distributed by Publishers Group West

'I suppose I think more in terms of colour than of line'
Jane Freilicher

IN
A
TRUE
LIGHT

1

THEY LET SLOANE OUT of prison three days short of his sixtieth birthday. Three years for deception, reduced on appeal to two; six months in Brixton, the remainder in Ford open prison. Naturally lean and wiry, Sloane walked out through the gates a fitter man than when he'd first walked in. Afternoons spent working in the gardens, cultivating everything from camellias to purple sprouting broccoli, cutting back random shrubbery, building drystone walls. Evenings he had read, sketched, exercised in his cell. Though graying at the temples, his hair was still strong and full, his eyes clear and disconcertingly blue. Strong cheekbones and lightly weathered skin. Inside, he had elected to keep himself to himself and few, fellow prisoners or guards, had tried to change his mind.

Now he stood at the center of Waterloo Bridge, the river running broad and free beneath him. To his left, St Paul's and the City; to his right, the Houses of Parliament, Big Ben. The sun pale in a blue-gray sky and the air bright with the bite and promise of spring.

That morning he had walked along the Embankment from London Bridge, Blackfriars to Waterloo Station, words and music to an old song by the Kinks accompanying him. Walked slowly, taking it all in. Open prison or not, prison was what it had been; what liberties they had allowed him, small and illusory.

Sloane breathed deeply, stretched both arms wide and, the beginnings of a smile bright in his eyes, set off for the north side of the Thames.

◆

Crossing the river: Sloane had friends way back in his early thirties who, when he'd told them he was selling up, moving south, had looked at him askance. South. South of the river. Camberwell. Peckham. Shooters Hill. You can't be serious. But to Sloane, much of whose formative years had been spent criss-crossing the Atlantic, one home, one parent to another, Chicago to London to New York to London again, the journey across the Thames failed to assume any such significance. And yet, when he looked back, it was true that few of those so-called friends had found their way south to pay their respects to Sloane in Deptford, the only place he had been able to afford the accommodation he wanted: some-where secure to live, light and large enough in which to paint. True, too, that when he himself made the journey in reverse, back to then familiar watering holes in Camden or Wood Green, all eyes would widen with amazement, as if some long-departed spirit had just walked through the door. Christ, Sloane, what you doin' here? Thought you'd gone for good.

And he had. Or so he thought. For a long time Deptford suited him perfectly. Anonymous. Poor. A shuttle of short streets and railway arches, scattered stalls selling everything from fruit and veg to knocked-off boots and jeans at stripped-down prices. When claustrophobia threatened he could stride up the hill to the broad heights of Blackheath and Greenwich Park, or cut north, following Deptford Creek to where the river curved round the Isle of Dogs.

But things changed as things must: it was in the late eighties, when Sloane returned from yet another prolonged visit to the States, that he noticed it most. The scrubbed wooden shutters that had appeared in the windows of turn-of-the-century terraced houses and the occasional four-by-four parked bulkily at the curb. Gentrification had arrived and tall skinny lattés would not be far behind. Worse still from Sloane's point of view, the growing prominence of the art school at Goldsmiths' College, west towards New Cross, was threatening to turn the whole area into a trendy enclave. Already there were two new art galleries on Deptford High Street, both exhibiting installations—perish they should show actual paintings—and more would follow. Soon, Sloane thought, take a walk to the butcher's for some lamb chops and you won't know if it's the real thing or just another piece of tired conceptual art.

It was time to change direction. Go north. North London, that is. The part of his world where he had spent perhaps his most formative years—from primary school into his early teens.

After months of searching, chasing down what seemed increasingly impossible to find, Sloane stumbled on the perfect location, half-hidden in the back streets of Kentish Town, and not so far from where he and his mother had lived all those years before. The same page of the *A-Z.*

The building was set across the end of a short, curving cul-de-sac, flat-fronted, flat-roofed, almost as broad as it was tall. Previously some kind of workshop, Sloane had thought, a small business; the brick exterior, painted white, now veiled in inner-city grime and smut. Large, squarish windows on both floors, the lower ones protected by iron bars; the heavy door padlocked fast. Both window frames and door were painted a dull blue.

To the right a cobbled alley led to the rear of an old factory, which was gradually being refitted to accommodate smaller enterprises; opposite, high fencing and overgrown shrubbery protected the grounds of a former school, the premises now rented out to minority groups and teachers of self-actualization and contemporary dance. Immediately behind and high above ground level the track of the old North London railway carried trains into West Kentish Town station every twenty minutes in the hour.

The upper floor of the building itself was no more than an open space with bare boards and roughcast walls; ample room for housing Sloane's accumulated canvases and sundry paraphernalia, room to work, his studio. It would be easy enough to tear out the partitions on the lower level, smooth and sand the floor; he would trawl nearby Junction Road for a reconditioned cooker and fridge to stand with the existing sink, a few bits of basic furniture, second-hand. A plumber could replace the cracked lavatory bowl in the extension out back and, with a little ingenuity, install a shower in the existing space.

Perfect.

A month after he signed the lease, two officers from Scotland Yard's Arts and Antiques Unit intercepted him as he left the Pizza Express at the corner of Prince of Wales Road. 'Fiorentina?' one of them asked, a slight but perceptible Welsh lilt to his voice. 'American Hot? Got to be favorite, that. Couple of bottles of Peroni. Garlic bread.' After dispensing the usual warnings, they placed him under arrest.

2

LIKE SO MUCH ELSE, it had happened by chance. Falling in with Robert Parsons, that is.

Sick of getting by on the dole and what little he could earn from selling his own paintings, Sloane had talked himself into a job at one of the main London auction houses. Nothing too demanding: packing, lifting, loading. Regular money, regular hours. Once in a while he'd poke his nose into the bidding room while there was an auction going on. Two hundred and seventy, two hundred and eighty; yes, thank you, two ninety, two ninety-five, three hundred thousand. Going for the first time at three hundred thousand pounds. The last of his own work Sloane had sold, a large canvas measuring 150 by 260 centimeters, thick swathes of vermilion and magenta overlaid with coils of crystal blue, had been bought by a former rock star, who had paid fifteen hundred pounds for the privilege of having it on the wall in his Tex-Mex restaurant. That and all the enchiladas Sloane could eat. He tried not to feel bitter and mostly he succeeded.

He was in the packing room one day, wrapping a small Matisse in folds of tissue, when one of the auction house staff came in with a visitor. Camilla, with a degree in Art History from Oxford and a diploma from the Chartered Institute of Marketing; Robert Parsons, owner of a small, conservative gallery off Cork Street, scrupulous in gray suit, pale pink shirt with white collar, public school tie. A voice you could cut glass on.

'You will treat her carefully,' Parsons said, smiling amiably in Sloane's direction. 'She's just cost me a small fortune.'

Sloane glanced down at the painting, a dancer resting among green flowers, and said nothing.

'You don't like it?' Parsons asked.

'I don't have to.' In fact, Sloane thought it lovely, delicious. The rich darkness of the green, the palpable strength of the dancer's legs, even in repose. It was Parsons he didn't like.

Sensing this, Camilla took Parsons's arm and led him off in her earnest, sexless manner, encouraging him to share whatever gossip had come his way.

Sloane didn't see Parsons again until one afternoon months later, when he was sitting in the furthermost corner of a pub in Notting Hill, enjoying a slow pint and fiddling with somebody's discarded *Times* crossword. A small group of people spilled into the bar from the restaurant upstairs, loud on their own brilliance and too much wine. Handshakes and kisses, laughter and farewells: when the rest of them had left, there was Parsons, slipping his mobile from the pocket of his overcoat and checking it for messages. Half turning, he spotted Sloane in his corner and, after only the slightest hesitation, walked over. 'Robert Parsons,' he said, extending a hand. 'The Matisse . . .'

'I remember.'

'You didn't like it.'

'On the contrary.'

'I see.' Parsons eased out a chair and sat down. 'Then it was what? The money? Not quite as obscene as if someone had turned up another dreary Van Gogh. In which case you could have objected on artistic grounds as well.' He pointed at Sloane's glass. 'Can I get you another?'

Sloane shook his head. 'I'm fine.'

'And Lord alone knows I shouldn't, but . . .' He scraped back his chair. 'You're sure?'

'Sure.'

Sloane dickered with fifteen across while Parsons fetched a white wine and soda from the bar.

'You know,' Parsons said, sitting back down, 'I sometimes wonder, people in jobs like yours, how much it matters, whether you're wrapping up fine art or so many cans of beans.'

Sloane took his time answering. Parsons's cheeks were more flushed than usual, his eyes less bright, the pitch of his voice slightly off. 'It matters,' Sloane said.

'What did you do before?' Parsons asked. 'I mean, crating up old masters, cocooning French Impressionists, I doubt you've been doing that for ever.'

Sloane shrugged. 'This and that.'

'Rumor has it you're a bit of an artist yourself.'

'Not really.'

'Camilla, she seems convinced. Apparently she saw some sketches you'd left around. Impressive, she said.'

Sloane sank some more of his beer. 'She knows bugger all about me. Or what I do.'

'Exactly. Which is why she casts around, second-guesses, speculates. She's quite fascinated, I assure you.'

'Bollocks.'

'But it's true. Our mysterious Mister Sloane. Like the hero from an Orton play.' He leaned closer. 'Paint under the fingernails, that's what gives you away.'

Despite himself Sloane glanced down at his hands.

'You should ask her back to your studio some time, look over your portfolio. I'm sure she'd jump at the chance. That and more.' Parsons sipped a little more wine. 'Always supposing, of course, that's the way you're inclined.'

The sly appraisal of Sloane's gaze made his own inclinations all too clear.

'Then, of course,' Parsons continued, easing back, 'if a professional opinion is what you're after, you need search no further.' He smiled. 'No obligation either way.'

Sloane held his gaze. 'I think I'd be wasting your time.'

Parsons took hold of the top sheet of newspaper and lifted it to one side, so that the pencilled figure Sloane had been sketching earlier was revealed in full. A woman, nude, drying herself from the bath, one hand holding the fall of thick, heavy hair. Cross-hatching at the base of the spine, the nape of the neck, curve of buttock and breast.

'Doodling,' said Sloane disparagingly.

'Degas,' Parsons said.

'My own stuff's nothing like that.'

Parsons tapped the sketch with his finger. 'Draftsmanship, control. Don't tell me that all goes out of the window the instant you pick up a brush.'

The quickest way, Sloane realized, to stop Parsons pestering him was to give in. Twenty minutes among years of stored canvases and, like other upscale entrepreneurs before him, Parsons would be excusing himself with a few choice platitudes before wiping the dust of Deptford from his feet.

Which, to a large extent, was how it was. Parsons arrived with a chilled bottle of good Chablis to celebrate the occasion and, glass in hand, moved with relative speed past the large abstracts ranged around the walls, pausing here and there to comment politely on the color, the energy of the paint.

In a corner, shelved, Parsons spotted several large sketchbooks, rimed with dust. 'May I?' Before Sloane could answer, he lifted them on to a level surface and used a scrap of rag to wipe the worst of the dust away.

The first book contained mostly pen-and-ink sketches, exercises, copies of Rembrandt some of them, faces richly detailed, heavily shaded. In the second book there was more color, more paint, attempt after attempt to reproduce a detail from a Hopper painting, *Chop Suey*, the tan overcoat hanging behind the two women as they eat, Sloane wanting to capture not only the way the sun through the window created light and shade, but the exact impression of weight, the hollowness of the sleeve as it hangs.

'I wonder if they teach painting like this any more?' Parsons said. 'Copying the masters. Learning the technique.'

'I wouldn't know.'

'And if you can paint in this style so well, so meticulously, why these?' He gestured at the canvases accumulating in the studio. 'Why abstraction?'

Sloane didn't answer immediately. 'Because it's what moves me. It's what I like.' He shrugged. 'And maybe, after all this time, I'm still trying to get it right.'

◆

Three months after Parsons's visit to his studio, Sloane lost his job at the auction house. Nothing personal, but business was temporarily in the doldrums and it was a case of belt tightening all round; as the most recent member of his department taken on, Sloane was the one to collect his cards: last in, first out. An affair he had drifted into with one of the bright young women—not Camilla but another just like her—ran aground amidst hasty threats and sundered promises, recriminations and 3 a.m. phone calls full of uneasy silences. Sloane was too old for all that. He was then facing his fifty-second birthday.

As if in bizarre celebration a storm, gleefully forecast by the Met Office, tore out several of the trees in Greenwich Park by the roots, plundered a dozen others of their upper branches and lifted slates from the roof of Sloane's home as if they were playing cards. Buckets and plastic sheets kept rain at bay but for how long?

To cap it all Sloane realized that in twelve months he had failed to sell one painting, not a single one. Several days later Parsons phoned him.

They met at the gallery after closing. A striking self-portrait by Dame Laura Knight dominated the window; in the first room were several canvases by Gwen John, studies of cats and surly girls prevailed upon to pose: at the rear a small collection of British Impressionists. Rivers at dusk in fading light; idyllic landscapes lost in a haze of longing and red poppies.

'What do you think?' Parsons asked of these.

'Competent. Interchangeable. Pleasant enough.'

'Easy enough to pull off, then. If you'd a mind.'

'I don't understand.' Although, in some way, he already did.

Parsons indicated a woodland scene, misted over, richly patterned in orange and green. Edward Atkinson Hornel, 1864–1933. 'I mean, given the right incentive you could produce something like it.'

'The incentive being?'

Parsons's smile leaked across his face. 'There are collectors in faraway places among whom these paintings have become quite prized. And for whom money is little or no object.' He was studying Sloane's face carefully. 'Whereas for those in need . . .'

Sloane looked at the color, the brushwork, the composition, imagined the money. Just one, he thought, just the one; to tide me over, to prove that I can.

It was fine while it lasted; five or so years during which Sloane slipped with increasing ease into the shoes of the mid-century dead, collectable if little known. Clausen, David Murray, William Stott of Oldham, the blotched vision of Philip Wilson Steer. Through a network of carefully preserved connections Parsons managed all of the necessary paperwork, proof of previous ownership, the forged accreditation. And he was careful, not greedy. No need to flood the market, draw attention, run unnecessary risks.

With each new commission Sloane found himself relishing more and more the challenge to his eye and his technique; so much so, he could forget what he was doing was in others' eyes of questionable morality, a crime.

The money helped. Between his work for Parsons he could devote all the time he wanted to his own painting, without having to hawk it round an unresponsive marketplace. Freedom at a price. It couldn't last.

How did he feel, Parsons asked one particularly sunny July day, about Vuillard? Sloane smiled. Parisian interiors and parks, figures caught unawares between reality and dream. Sloane had always liked his work a lot, preferred him to the better-known Bonnard. But could he capture the richness of the tapestries, the curtains and the lengths of cloth, those purplish reds and rusted browns? Sloane felt he could; knew that he would like to try.

It was one step too far. If the fake Vuillard Sloane had labored over so lovingly had remained where it was intended, pride of place in the island hideaway of a reclusive Florida property developer, everything would most probably have been fine. But once the man had succumbed to a fatal heart attack only five days after its unveiling, his fourth wife and sundry children set about his estate with the benign indifference of piranha fish coming off hunger strike. When the Vuillard made its way for valuation, in close company with half a dozen other Post-Impressionist masterpieces, it was unlucky enough to catch the eye of an expert on a good day. Luminaries from Boston, Yale and Paris were brought in for consultation and, in the course of the resulting investigation, a hazy line seemed to point via Zurich and Cologne to London. Officers from Scotland Yard's Arts and Antiques Unit took over. Robert Parsons's London flat, his Suffolk house, his gallery were all prey to the proverbial fine-tooth comb. When the findings were sifted Sloane's name shone clear. Paint samples from his studio matched those on the canvas. Parsons himself was charged but never brought to trial: Sloane and one or two lesser links in the chain took all the rap. No matter how much pressure the police put on Sloane to implicate Parsons, drop him royally in it, he kept his mouth firmly shut. 'I'll make it up to you': almost the last words Parsons spoke to Sloane before they took him away.

3

SLOANE'S MOTHER, MARTHA, HAD been a dressmaker, fulfilling individual commissions in the evenings and at weekends, while working by day as an alteration hand and dreaming of singing with a band. Which was how she came to meet Sloane's father, Al, an American tap-dancer and singer engaged on a tour of British music halls. Al was also a jazz trumpeter, a former member of the Charlie Barnett and Woody Haut Orchestras, but banned by the Musicians Union from playing officially in Britain. And one night when Al, along with a bunch of other musicians, high on weed and looking for a place to blow, descended on the after-hours Soho drinking club where Martha sometimes persuaded the proprietor to let her sing, there she was by the piano, her small but tuneful voice midway through 'Lady Be Good'. Before she could finish Al had taken out his horn and was playing along.

After which initial encounter his parents—unmarried, married, divorced, married again—proceeded to give him a very particular stance on stability. And home. Chicago? New York? Maybe London was the place he felt most himself. In Deptford, of course, and Kentish Town.

It was noon when finally he turned the corner and took two

steps along the street: far enough to see the shattered glass, spiralling graffiti on the walls, the broken padlock on the front door, its woodwork battered and scarred, daubed with names and misspelt filth.

Sloane nudged the door back with his boot and slowly stepped inside.

The stink of piss and human excrement hit him like a warm fist to the face. He coughed and swallowed bile, blinking his eyes to adjust to the low levels of light. All of the furniture, save for the low couch and the bed, had been upended, thrown aside, trashed. Someone with time to spare had found amusement transforming the couch into a sarcophagus of empty bottles and cans; heaped unevenly along the bed was a pile of dark and rotting clothing he couldn't bring himself to touch. The ashes from a succession of fires covered most of the floor in a soft gray mush that quivered when he walked through it and adhered to his legs. A viscous, yellowing rind lay thick on stale water in the sink. More graffiti on the walls, some startlingly obscene, some beautiful, one piece on the rear wall both at once. Discarded syringes lay in corners, their blunt needlepoints rusted with old blood; used condoms and soiled underwear littered the stairs.

At first he thought the damage in the studio was not as bad as he'd feared. Little of the obvious defilement that lay below. But when he looked closer he realized defilement was exactly what it was. Some canvases had merely been scrawled on, criticism of the most basic kind; others had been amended and revised, though few with understanding or with wit; one batch had simply been smeared with shit.

Sloane felt sick.

Outside, in the dubiously fresh city air, he breathed in deeply, stamped his feet. Two streets away, perched on a narrow corner, the no-name café had been treated to a lick of paint. *Breakfast served all day*, read the sign in the window, *fresh sandwiches; special today, sirloin steak and chips, meat pie and two veg.* Two workmen in once white overalls sat at one of the Formica-topped tables, relaxing with a cigarette after what looked like the steak special; a pallid youth with dreadlocks sat with both hands round a mug of tea, browsing through a copy of the local free paper; his dog, a ratty mongrel with green eyes, uncurled itself sufficiently to growl at Sloane as he passed.

The man behind the counter was no one Sloane recognized. 'Alfred?' Sloane asked. 'He around?'

'No Alfred,' the man replied. He was the same height as Sloane, maybe taller; of indecipherable age and African descent.

'Alfred, he used to run this place.'

The African showed him a fine set of teeth. 'No more. Sell to me, six month.'

'Six months ago?'

'Yes.'

The workmen called their thanks and left. Sloane had known Alfred from years back, when he had run a similarly basic place off the Wood Green High Road. Finding him here, so close to his new home, had been a bonus, an omen. Sloane had paid him three hundred in cash to keep an eye on his building, make sure the squatters and the derelicts didn't gain a toehold.

'You don't know where he went?'

'Home. Home is what he said.'

Wood Green, would that be, Sloane wondered, or Nicosia, which?

'I'll have tea and a bacon roll,' Sloane said. 'Brown sauce on the roll.'

When he brought Sloane's order to the table the African leaned towards him. 'You are Sloane?'

'Yes.'

'Alfred said you would be here.' He held out his hand. 'Dumar.'

'Good to meet you.' Dumar's grip was strong and firm.

'Your place,' Dumar said, 'how is it?'

Sloane grinned and shook his head. 'You don't want to know.'

◆

Armed with black bin bags, a borrowed shovel, a hard-headed broom and wearing thick plastic gloves, Sloane set to work. He worked through most of that night and the following day; arriving unannounced, Dumar pitched in to help with the heavier tasks, lending Sloane his beat-up Ford van to haul load after load to the waste depot near the head of Kentish Town Road. By dusk on the second evening the two men were sitting in Dumar's closed café, listening to a tape of music from Mali and feasting on a casserole of chicken and olives with rice and sweet potatoes.

In his own country Dumar had lost his home three times to the ravages of civil war; once when, after years of drought, a river burst its banks and flooded the plain. Each time disaster struck you salvaged what could be saved and started to rebuild. That was how it was.

Now the life he was building was here. He had a home, a job, a woman who read her poetry to him in bed. Dumar's face broke into pleasure at the thought. Sloane was reluctant to leave.

Back at Sloane's building the smell of disinfectant, acid and sharp, overwhelmed almost everything. Until he could arrange for the electricity supply to be restored, candles, here and there in threes and fours, provided wavering, smoky light. A sleeping bag lay unrolled on the floor. A chair from Dumar's café. A thermos of bitter coffee laced with rum. He was bundling up a pile of junk mail and old newspapers when he noticed the airmail envelope squashed down among the rest; his old Deptford address had been scribbled out and the new one written in its place; the stamps were Italian, the postmark a little over two months old. The sender's name, barely decipherable on the back of the envelope, was one he had scarcely seen in twenty years, had not spoken aloud for almost twenty more.

Jane Graham.

The last time Sloane had seen her, her face had been one of many, pale along the upper deck of the *Ile de France*, one hand raised to wave, the other clutching the rail. The kiss she had given him neither warmer nor longer than those bestowed on a dozen others who had come to wish her raucously well and bon voyage. 'Who knows? Perhaps you'll be in Paris soon yourself. You'll come and look me up.' And then she had been lost in the final clamor of goodbyes that echoed round her till she disappeared from sight, re-emerging for that all-purpose wave and smile. Just months before she had been featured as one of six exceptional young American artists in *Time* magazine. Faces to watch. Sloane watched hers until it was indistinguishable from those to either side. He was eighteen and she was twenty-nine. The first time she had made love to him he had come close to crying.

The envelope was light across his palm: how easy to have held it, forefinger and thumb, above the candle flame, waited till it caught. He slid the tip of one finger inside the flap and tore it back. The writing, blue-black on white paper, spidered haphazardly across the page: an old woman's hand.

> I wonder if you can imagine how difficult a letter this is for me to write? . . . Although I can't expect you to believe this, I have thought of you a great deal over the years, always kindly and often with sadness and regret. . . . I have been unwell now for some time . . . the doctors say the chances of recovery are slight. . . . I realize you may think I have little or no right to ask, but there are things I want to say while there is still time, things that should only be said face to face. . . .

He read it fast, then more slowly, scanning it for more than he could find. *Little or no right.* He gathered together all his change and walked to the phone box near the station. The connection was almost instantaneous, the line remarkably clear. Sloane's nerve endings anticipated the worst. In over-precise, heavily accented English, a woman who introduced herself as Valentina told him Jane was sleeping and could talk to no one. She was very weak, her condition serious. Critical. Sloane explained his delay in replying to the letter and said that he would catch a flight out the following day. After some hesitation Valentina, her voice abrupt and grudging, told him to fly to Pisa; if he let her know the time of his arrival she would meet him there.

As Sloane stepped away from the telephone, a train was passing over the bridge, gathering speed on its way west. A group of five or six Asian youths had gathered outside the late-night shop opposite, pushing one another and swearing loudly, shouting into their mobile phones. Sloane closed his hand round the coins in his pocket and opened it again beneath the street light: he had one pound, seventy-nine pence to his name.

4

SLOANE LAY DOWN WARILY, anticipating uneasy dreams, yet when he awoke more than eight hours later he felt rested and refreshed, his mind untroubled. Cold water on his face. Dumar put the price of breakfast on his slate. No sense in arriving earlier than eleven, he read the paper pretty much from cover to cover, had a second cup of tea and then a third. A short stroll through the back doubles and he came out on to Malden Road. In earlier times there'd been a cinema here, tatty and cheap, and afternoons Sloane had bunked off school and spent his dinner money on third-rate double bills: 'Wild Bill' Elliott in *The Last Bandit*, Dan Duryea and Lizabeth Scott in *Too Late for Tears*. Between shows the usherettes would walk slowly down the aisles, spraying pesticide. When the 24 bus came, Sloane climbed on and bought a ticket to Trafalgar Square. Another brief walk, past the students already massing outside the National Gallery, took him south of Piccadilly Circus and into Cork Street. First right and he was there.

One of Parsons's chinless assistants was maneuvering a large canvas inch by inch towards the center of the window. An elderly couple, gray-haired, stood holding hands and staring at an oil painting of somewhere like Deauville, admiring the bleached boardwalk and sandy beach, and speculating on the price. Parsons was sitting behind his highly polished desk, flanked on one side by a pale green vase of flowers, on the other by a Giacometti bronze— a girl with outstretched arms.

Sloane took up a position at an angle to the desk and waited. It was less than a minute before Parsons realized he was there and when he did he scarcely missed a beat. A quick smile of recognition across the top of his spectacles and he blotted what he'd been writing, screwed the cap back on his Mont Blanc pen. 'Dear fellow,' Parsons said, holding out his hand. 'Welcome. Welcome back to the land of the free. But you should have called ahead, some advance warning. A celebration. Champagne, at least.'

Sloane shook his head. 'The money will do fine.'

Behind his glasses Parsons blinked. 'Of course, of course, but all in good time.'

'Now,' Sloane said, stepping closer. 'Now's a good time.'

'I know, but lunch . . . Let me buy you a decent lunch and then . . .'

Sloane reached down and his hand covered Parsons's as it touched the telephone. 'You do remember?'

'I think so.'

'Remember what was said.'

'Yes.'

'Then, Robert, I don't understand the fucking problem.'

The elderly couple turned their heads, alarmed. The assistant hovered closer and Parsons waved him away. What Parsons had said, the very last thing he had said, after 'I'll make it up to you', was, 'If you can keep me out of this, totally out of it, there's twenty thousand waiting for you when you're released.'

With a small sigh, Parsons sat down and opened a drawer, took out a chequebook, uncapped his pen.

'Make it out to cash,' Sloane said.

Just the faint sound of nib on paper, the amount, then Parsons signing with a flourish. 'Here.'

Sloane took the cheque, read it twice in case he was the one who'd made the mistake. 'What's this?'

'Five thousand. On account.'

'On account of what?'

Parsons glanced past Sloane, lowered his voice. 'There's a proposition, in the pipeline, I know you'll be interested. Just your kind of thing. No risk. None at all. I should have the details in a matter of days, a week at the outside. Once we've discussed them, when you're signed up, fully on board, I'll give you another five. The rest will come along with your fee.'

Sloane picked up the Giacometti sculpture and struck Parsons full in the face, breaking his nose.

Parsons screamed and stumbled backwards, hands raised. The couple scuttled through the door. Moving towards the alarm, the assistant was stopped by Sloane's stare. Blood ran between Parsons's fingers. One of the bronze's slender arms lay on the floor.

'The safe,' Sloane said. 'I know there's a safe. I need as much cash as you've got. Make a cheque out for the rest. All of it. Do it now.'

The front of Parsons's shirt and the surface of his desk were speckled red. 'You bastard,' he said, but the words came out in a spluttered blur. 'You lousy bastard.'

'Just be careful,' Sloane said, 'you don't get blood all over that cheque.'

At the door he stopped and turned. Parsons was dabbing at himself with a handkerchief, wincing at the anticipated pain. 'You know,' Sloane said, 'I'd never have shopped you to the police, no matter what.'

5

DELANEY WAITED. THE LEATHER upholstery of the Lexus GS was smooth and cool along the armrest where his fingers drummed a tight little figure—di-dat, di-dat, di-dat—over and over. Manicured fingers. Delaney wearing his second-best blue suit, a shade off navy, pale blue shirt, pearl tie, gold links at the cuffs—a little old-fashioned, he knew, the links and maybe even the tie, but hey! Delaney glancing at himself in the mirror, fifty-three last birthday and not a gray hair on his head, not a line on his face, laugh lines round his eyes aside. Vincent Anthony Delaney.

The alley ran the length of the entire block, opening out on to a parking lot which served the Irish bar and the Tex-Mex diner as well as the Manhattan Lounge. Which was where Diane was singing, two sets nightly, Mondays excluded, eleven and one. Standards, mostly—Gershwin, Jerome Kern—her voice wispy enough to get mistaken for Peggy Lee, she'd feature 'Fever', 'Black Coffee'—a couple in celebrating their silver wedding, 'The Folks Who Live on the Hill'. Diane working with a nice little three-piece band: keyboard, bass, electric guitar. Forget the drums.

Delaney was parked a few car lengths from the rear of the building, in against the shadow of a six-storey warehouse. Window lowered a crack to let out the smoke from his cigarette, he could hear music seeping through the club's heating ducts, the air vents, the heavy-duty door to the kitchen wedged open by metal trash containers overflowing with vegetable peelings, chicken bones, fish heads and crab shells, the soft, sweet mush of mango left too long. His watch read 1:49. On stage, Diane would be running through her ritual thank yous to the musicians in the band, reminding the audience of her own name with just the right degree of self-deprecation—Diane Stewart, ladies and gentlemen, of the Winchendon, Mass. Stewarts—before launching into 'Lady Is a Tramp', her final number. Anniversaries and birthdays aside, Diane wasn't bothered by encores overmuch.

Delaney leaned back and for a moment, several moments, closed his eyes. Diane in the toilet that passed for a dressing room, peering into the mirror as she peeled off her eyelashes, wiping a Kleenex back and forth across her mouth. Reaching round now to release the hook at the top of her dress, slide down the zip. The second car eased into the alley, a Lincoln, gray, pulling wide just enough before slowing to a halt close by the club's rear exit, the fire door to the kitchen's right. The driver, a black man with a chauffeur's hat tipped back on his head, glancing at Delaney as he passed. Now he cut his lights and left the engine running, knowing Delaney was there but not caring. A skein of pale smoke curling from the Lincoln's exhaust.

Less than five minutes later Diane pushed the fire door open, coat that Delaney had bought her round her shoulders, soft leather two-tone case in one hand. Looking neither left nor right, she opened the rear door of the Lincoln and climbed in.

Delaney waited until they were almost at the far end of the alley before turning the key in the ignition.

It was somehow typical of Kenneth that he would send a car to collect her and take her to the hotel, rather than meeting her himself. She wasn't sure what she thought of that. Maybe not much. He had wanted to keep the Lincoln sitting around picking up waiting time, then take her back home, the home she shared with Delaney, but Diane had said no. 'Hell, let him go. I'll find ways of spending your money soon enough, wait and see.'

Kenneth had reached for her then, Diane turning her head sideways so that the kiss only smudged the corner of her mouth. His hand moving for her breast. It wasn't that she'd have minded giving it another twirl, he was good enough in that department, heaven knows, not as selfish as most, but she had an appointment that meant she couldn't sleep past midday and besides, Kenneth was booked on to a 6 a.m. flight from JFK.

'Save it up.' She'd grinned, brushing the back of her hand against his crotch. 'Next time.'

'Phoenix.'

'Hmm?'

'Next time. Phoenix.'

Diane's expression tightened, alarmed by the eagerness eating into his tone. Kenneth Baldry: pale blue contacts, close-cropped hair, shirt still undone. In the list of Arizona's fifty richest men under fifty he was number thirty-one. Smart enough to get his software company swallowed up by Microsoft and living now off Bill Gates's largesse. That was the way he had put it himself, the time he'd come back to the Glass Box alone, leaving the rest of the computer geeks to their own devices. Kenneth in the city for a conference and staying at one of those corporate midtown hotels—not like tonight, Fifth Avenue across from Central Park. He hoped he wasn't being out of line or anything, but he wondered if she'd care to join him at his table, allow him to buy her a drink? Diane had remembered him from the previous evening, practically the only one who'd been listening, really listening, in the midst of all the buddy-buddy drinking and laughter, a bunch of mostly married men out on the sly. Sure, she'd told him, come and sit with me at the bar and you can buy me two.

'Diane, you promised,' Baldry said now.

'I don't think so.'

'Phoenix, you said you'd come out.'

'I said I'd think about it. I said I'd see.'

Baldry sighed and turned away, hangdog, forty-four going on fifteen; a grown man in love for the very first time. 'Oh, Kenneth . . .' She nuzzled her face against the middle of his back; kissed, quickly, the nape of his neck.

'I'm sorry,' he said, catching her hand. 'It's just I get so impatient and. . .'

'I know, I know. But patient's what you've got to be.'

'That's easy for you to say.'

Smiling despite herself, she'd pressed a fingertip to his lips. 'There's no need to rush, okay? It's not as if we don't both know what we want.' There'd been times this past month or so she'd come close to believing that might actually be true. Diane, pushing thirty-five and silicone-free, and not above wondering how many more chances she was going to get.

'You will talk to him? Tell him.'

'When I can. When it's right.'

'But soon?'

'Yes, soon.' Knowing, even as she said it, that the only conversation she could ever have with Vincent about her leaving would be once she had already gone, a good few hundred miles safely between them.

Through buttoning his shirt, Kenneth was looking round for his coat. 'I'll come with you now, in the cab. Walk back. It'll do me good.'

Diane had shaken her head, picked up her bag. 'What'll do you good is an hour's sleep.' She gave him a deft kiss on the cheek. 'Safe flight. Call me tomorrow. At the club.' Without looking round she let herself out of the suite and walked along the corridor towards the elevator, surprised when she swayed a little and needed to steady herself with one hand against the wall; Diane, suddenly aware she might have drunk a tad more than she'd thought.

Alighting at the corner of Second and 71st, she gave the cab driver a three-dollar tip on a four fifty fare and waited for him to smile; what he did was stuff the bills into a beat-up metal box he kept under his seat and flick on the light that said he was for hire. And a good night to you, Diane thought.

As she approached the gilt and glass door of the apartment building, the doorman stepped round from behind his desk and held it open wide. 'Good evening, Miss Stewart.'

'Good morning, George.'

The first weeks after she'd moved in he hadn't bothered with her name at all; just another of Mr Delaney's quick fixes, his instant flings. But now—what was it?—eight months? Almost nine? As far as George was concerned, Vincent and herself, they were good as married. And sometimes, from what she could remember, that was exactly how it felt.

The heel of Diane's right shoe was rubbing uncomfortably and she eased them both off, soft-footing across the marble floor. On her way up to fourteen she leaned her head forward till it was resting on the cool metal of the elevator door. Two Tom Collins followed by champagne, followed by whatever French wine Kenneth had ordered from room service, what did she expect?

For longer than usual the keys played cat and mouse with her hand. Faint sounds of music from under the door; thank God Vincent wasn't around to nag at her for going out without switching off the TV. When she stepped inside there he was, lounging back in his favorite chair, whiskey glass in hand, watching a rerun of *Shannon's Deal*.

'Hey, Diane. Sweetheart.'

She stood there too long, mouth open, shoes in one hand, Delaney smiling his slow smile, sliding his gaze up her body, up and down, before turning back to the screen.

'They killed this show after—I don't know—one season, maybe two. You believe that? The shit that goes on getting made. Time after time.' Delaney shook his head. 'Guy behind it, he did that movie, the White Sox, the time practically the whole damned team threw the game. The series, the world fucking series. Shoeless Joe along with the rest of them. You ever catch that? Say it ain't so, Joe. Say it ain't so. One terrific movie. You missed that, you missed something. I bet it's around, though, video. We could check it out some time, watch it here together, the two of us, one night you're not working. *Eight Men Out.*'

Diane still on the same spot, case by her side, willing her head to clear. Sports, movies, what the hell was going on? 'I thought you were in Cincinnati,' she said.

'Right. Guy I went to see, sax player, Ohio's answer to Kenny G. Turns out he got into a fight, split his lip, can't play for a month. I'm supposed to stick around Cincinnati? Caught the first flight I could.' Delaney gestured towards her with one hand. 'You going to stand there all night? Look like you've taken root.'

'No, of course not. I was just—you know—surprised.'

'To see me.'

'Yes.'

'But pleased.'

'Of course.'

He smiled and turned his attention back to the set. Diane went into the bedroom and hung her coat in the closet, lifted her case up on to the bed; in the bathroom she brushed her teeth, washed a couple of aspirin down with water, stared into the mirror for tell-tale signs.

Delaney was still watching the show. She walked past him into the galley kitchen and opened the refrigerator. 'You want anything?' she called. 'A snack?'

'Thanks, I'm fine.'

She lifted out a container of blueberry yogurt and put it back. What she really wanted was a cigarette. Vincent's Chesterfields were where he always left them, on the table near the stereo, alongside his keys.

'You mind?' she said, holding up the pack.

'I thought you gave it up.'

'I did.'

He shrugged. 'Go ahead.'

Not seeing his lighter, she went back into the kitchen for a match.

'You did a couple of extra sets,' he called after her. 'Someone was throwing a party, what?'

'Yes. I mean, no. Not exactly.'

'Not exactly. Well, exactly what? Four in the fucking morning.'

Looking at him, Diane drew smoke down deep into her lungs. On the television one of the actors was laughing loudly; a phone rang, a door slammed. Delaney aimed the remote and the image fizzled to nothing.

'Terri, you know, she works the bar sometimes, dark hair, in a bob, pretty, it was her birthday.' Diane was conscious of the way her words were stumbling against each other, willing everything to slow down. 'A bunch of us, we hung around, had a few drinks, sort of, you know, celebration.'

'At the club? This was at the club?' Vincent sitting forward now, paying attention.

'Yes.'

'I went by there,' Vincent said.

'You did?'

'Couldn't have been more than an hour ago. You weren't back, I got to wondering, drove by. Whole place was locked up, dark as a fucking tomb.'

The drinks trolley was over by the window, near the balcony door. If she could get across to it without losing her footing, pour herself another shot, maybe that would give her time enough to think. Delaney watched her go.

'You want a refill?' she asked, holding up the J&B.

'Uh-huh.' He shook his head.

Diane poured herself a shot and drank half of it down straight. Below, on Second Avenue, a yellow cab cruised hopefully downtown. Outside the twenty-four-hour Korean grocer's a young man in a bright yellow coat, hood up, sat trimming the outer leaves from crates of cabbage.

'So? You weren't at the club, where were you?' Delaney sounding more relaxed now, almost laid-back.

'Terri, she didn't want to call it a night. We went out for Chinese. I don't know where, Chinatown somewhere. Just a few of us. Terri, me, Charlene, Paul.'

'Paul? He was there?'

'Sure.' Paul, who supervised the waiting staff and acted as maître d', was camp as Christmas in July. 'Paul's okay, he's a laugh.'

'All girls together.'

'That's right.'

'Maybe I'll have another Scotch after all,' Delaney said. 'Nightcap.'

Diane smiled. 'Why not?' It was going to be okay. She could tell. Leaning, she tilted the bottle towards Vincent's empty glass.

'Chinese, though. That's what you said. Chinatown.'

'Yes.'

'Last time I saw the Pierre, it was on Fifth Avenue.'

Whiskey splashed on to the inside of Delaney's leg. 'The Pierre, Diane. Remember? Or are you so smashed you forgot which fancy hotel you were whoring in tonight?'

'I don't know what you're . . .'

She saw the fist coming, but didn't have time to duck. By the time the fifth or sixth blow had been struck, mercifully, she had lost all sense of feeling.

Delaney repeating over and over to himself, 'Say it ain't so, Diane. Say it ain't so.'

6

PISA AEROPORTO INTERNAZIONALE. SLOANE was sitting on the wrong side of the plane to catch more than a glimpse of the famous leaning tower. During the journey he had riffled idly through the in-flight magazine, snacked on peanuts, tried to concentrate on the significant section of the travel guide he'd picked up at the airport. As far as he could tell the village where Jane had sequestered herself was high into the north of Tuscany, well off the normal tourist track amidst the hills and valleys of the Garfagnana. On the map Sloane saw a road that snaked between two mountain ranges, following the curve of the sea. The Riviera della Versilia. His mother had once gone on holiday to Viareggio, herself and two girlfriends. He could remember the photographs she had sent him, the three of them on the promenade, laughing, an avenue of stately palm trees behind them; his mother, alone at a café table, smiling out from behind white-framed sunglasses. He could remember the way his father had pushed them to one side dismissively, unworthy of even a second look. Moments that snag and hold for no clear reason, like burrs buried close along the skin. Jane's face turning from his before boarding ship. . . *Paris soon yourself. You'll come and look me up.* By the time—twenty-five and studying at the Slade in

London—he had crossed the Channel to Paris she had already moved on.

When the flight attendant first asked him what he would like to drink he had waved his hand and gestured nothing; after that he had changed his mind perhaps too often. Two half-bottles of purplish Cabernet and two miniatures of gin. When he had telephoned Valentina from London to confirm the arrangements he had asked her for the exact details of Jane's illness. *Chronic myeloid leukemia.* Her strongly accented voice sounding the words like stone on stone. Leukemia. Bone marrow cancer. Sloane imagined intravenous drips, hair loss, nausea, helplessness: a woman he was frightened he would no longer recognize, pinned to her bed to die. He wanted another drink, but it was too late, they were moments from landing. A bump and then the roar of deceleration, passengers around him starting to fidget, willing the seat belt sign to flick off.

The terminal building was surprisingly small, unfussy: Valentina Ceroni was standing to one side of the arrivals area, a book of Jane Graham's paintings held clumsily across her chest by way of identification. She was shorter than Sloane had pictured, no more than medium height, strongly built; her stockiness accentuated by the padded car coat she wore unfastened, sleeves turned back. A rust-colored sweater, dark green cords. Sloane was wearing jeans, a faded blue shirt, a scuffed leather jacket with paint marks faint along one sleeve.

He held out a hand and her grip was strong, fingers blunt and broad. Beneath a fall of dark hair flecked with gray, the eyes that studied him were greenish-brown. The lines of a perpetual smoker etched deep around her mouth and eyes. He had looked her up in a reference book before leaving: Valentina Ceroni, sculptor. Born, Bagni di Lucca, Italy, 1953.

'This is all you have?' she asked, nodding towards the duffel bag slung over Sloane's left shoulder. 'No more baggage?'

'No, this is it.'

'Okay, so let's go.' She led him through a set of double doors and out into a parking area, stopping by a gray Fiat van. Inside, a brown and white dog of indeterminate pedigree lay sprawled across the front seats. Sloane looked up into the darkening sky: once they were clear of the city, night would settle in fast.

'The journey,' he said, 'how long's it going to take?'

Valentina shrugged. 'Not so long. An hour, maybe two.' When she unlocked the door the dog clambered, unwillingly, into the back of the van.

The interior smelled of cigarettes and damp fur. Valentina turned the key in the ignition and the engine coughed asthmatically to life. Two then, Sloane thought, rather than one.

'How's Jane?' he asked.

'You know she is dying.'

'Yes, but . . .'

'When I left she was sleeping. The doctor had given her more morphine for the pain. If she is still sleeping when I get home I shall say a prayer she will not wake again.'

'I don't understand.'

'No. No, you don't.'

Before he could say anything else Valentina switched on the radio and several voices began to argue in Italian simultaneously. The van eased out on to the exit road and Sloane leaned back and slotted the metal clip of his seat belt into place.

The first part of the journey was on a fast motorway, Valentina hugging the inside lane, snorting occasional disapproval at other drivers or some remark from the radio Sloane had failed to understand. All too soon they turned off on to the narrow road, one carriageway in either direction, which would take them, almost, to their destination. Valentina lit the first of many cigarettes and Sloane lowered his window several centimeters; impatiently, Valentina switched the radio from channel to channel before snapping it off in exasperation, leaving only the silence, heavy between them.

Diécimo.

Borgo a Mozzano.

Fornaci de Barga.

The road climbed with caution, crossing from one side of the river to the other without apparent reason. Garish wayside signs advertised hotels and pizzerias but the towns themselves were already quiet, closed off for the night; the only life briefly sputtering from small bars where men in work clothes sat and drank, illuminated in a spool of yellowing light. Behind Sloane the dog licked and snuffled in the dark, and all further attempts at conversation were met by Valentina with feigned or real incomprehension.

At Castelnuovo di Garfagnana she relented, following a cobbled street until it opened out into a broad square with cafés on three sides, chairs and tables set outside. Valentina chose the quietest of the three and soon had the young waiter scurrying to and fro with bottles of San Pelegrino, bread, one plate of olives, tomatoes and grilled peppers, another with several different salamis, cheese and wafer-thin ham.

Sloane quickly understood that most of the food was for him; Valentina drank water, nibbled at a crust of bread, tasted one black olive and smoked. She fed sausage to the dog.

'You don't approve,' Sloane said. 'Jane contacting me. You don't think . . .'

'It is not of my business.'

'Surely it is.'

Tilting her head backwards, she released a plume of smoke. 'This thing, whatever it is, between you. It is the past.'

'Yes, but I'm here now.'

'Yes.'

Sloane looked across the square as first one scooter, then another noisily circled round before coming to a halt by a group of youths sitting outside one of the other cafés. Shouting and laughter.

'You have to understand,' Valentina said, 'her mind . . . she is sick, she does not always know where she is. When she wrote to you her mind was clear. It was a long time ago.'

'She may not know who I am. Is that what you mean?'

Valentina shrugged and stubbed out her cigarette, almost

immediately lighting another. Beckoning the waiter, she ordered coffee. 'Sometimes she does not even know me.'

'How long have you been together?' Sloane asked after an interval.

For the first time since he had met her Valentina smiled. 'She was visiting Montpellier with friends, from Paris. One day they came out to Frontignan, it is near. I had a studio there. That was twenty-one years ago. We came here to Italy, to Verrucole, twelve years ago this May. Almost thirteen.' She finished her espresso in a single swallow and rose to her feet. 'Come. We must go.'

Several villages on they were entering the main street of Camporgiano, at the far end of which they turned right down a steep, winding road. A quarter of a mile along Valentina steered off between wrought-iron gates and past the edge of a small vineyard, coming to a halt outside a single-storey building with a large barn to one side, louvred shutters across windows and door.

When Valentina got out the dog stayed in the van. 'This is where you will sleep tonight.'

Sloane shook his head. 'I don't understand. I thought we were nearly there.'

Valentina took a pace back and pointed towards a small scattering of lights faint in the darkened hills. 'Up there is Verrucole. In the morning you can see Jane. It is her best time.'

'And this place?'

'It belongs to a friend of mine. In the summer it is for visitors. Now it is for you.' Unfastening the shutters, she pulled them back and unlocked the door. 'There is a bed made up. Coffee in the kitchen. A few other things. Sleep well. I will collect you tomorrow.'

Sloane stood on the broad circle of grass, listening to the sound of the van's engine until it had faded to nothing and all he could hear were the echoing call of an owl and the wind shuffling stiffly along the branches of the trees.

7

SLOANE WOKE A LITTLE before six, close to the furthest edge of the bed. Most of the covers had slipped or been kicked to the floor. He sat up slowly, his head thick and heavy. Opening the window, he unfastened the shutters and pushed them back: breathed in cool air. Birdsong. Hills hazed in violet mist. Pale blue of the sky. His hair, his skin seemed to smell of cigarette smoke; last night's journey less than real. His body ached.

The water in the shower was tepid at best, the towel rough. In the kitchen he found a small espresso pot by the stove, ready-ground coffee in a paper bag, milk in the fridge. Half a crusted white loaf, butter, cherry jam. He heated water in a pan, filled the coffee pot and set it on a low gas while he shaved. When the coffee was ready he poured it into a bowl, steaming and black, added warmed milk, then carried it outside.

The front of the house was pink with terracotta tiles, the shutters recently painted dark brown. Immediately in front of the door, where Sloane now stood, was a narrow paved area which led to a small well and beyond that a broad expanse of grass with a vineyard to its right and, front and left, two lines of fruit trees coming into blossom. Apple, Sloane wondered? Plum? He thought the corner tree with darker leaves might be quince.

What was certain, now that the light had brightened, the mist all but dispersed, was the beauty of the surrounding hills, folding back one upon another in undulating circles, the varying shades of green and brown broken by sudden outcrops of volcanic rock and, here and there, small clusters of houses, white-walled and red-roofed, each village, however small, with its own church tower.

Only days ago his horizons had been foreshortened by prison guards, prison walls; now they were boundless, the rest of his life a clean slate, a fresh canvas, ready primed.

Except the reason for his coming, the fact that in the midst of all this beauty Jane Graham lay dying.

◆

He was drinking a second cup of coffee, finishing his breakfast of bread and jam, when he heard the van approach. The dog bounded out, showing an energy that took Sloane by surprise, and sniffed good-naturedly at his legs before trotting off in the direction of the vines.

'You sleep okay?' Valentina asked.

'Fine.' He wondered if she were wearing dark glasses against the brightness of the light, or to disguise the tired puffiness around her eyes.

'How's Jane?' he asked.

'Rested a little, I think. But come, you will see.'

'She knows I'm here.'

'Of course. She is expecting you.'

Valentina whistled for the dog, which came at second bidding. Sloane fetched his jacket from inside the house, locked the door and, after a moment's hesitation, pocketed the key. Valentina reversed into a parking bay beyond the barn, then paused at the gates as a tractor went slowly past.

'There is a shop, a small supermarket, just back into Camporgiano, at the top of the hill. Later you can get what you need.'

Sloane thanked her and hung on as she accelerated sharply into the road and sped down the hill, as if suddenly aware they were wasting precious time. At the bottom of the valley the road levelled out, bridging a broad, slow-moving river before climbing steeply through a series of tighter and tighter bends. Between the trees—stands of dark fir mixed with beech and sweet chestnut—Sloane saw the ground was enmeshed with patches of brightly colored spring flowers, yellow, blue and vivid orange, none of which he could name.

At San Romano the road angled to the right, before rising again towards what Sloane could clearly see were the ruins of a substantial fortress, open to the sky.

'The Fortress delle Verrucole,' Valentina said, pre-empting his question. 'Built by the Estensi in the fifteenth century.' She glanced across at him. 'You know history? The history of my country?'

Sloane shook his head. A few staples aside, like Harold and the arrow and the princes in the Tower, outside of the twentieth century Sloane was pretty shaky on his own.

Valentina accelerated again, drawing a protesting whine from the engine: one more incline and, when the road they were following veered off sharply to the right, Valentina swung the van left and they had arrived.

Dwarfed by the fortress, the tiny village of Verrucole lay clustered in its shadow. To one side of the road was a skimpy general store and bar; on the other the scarred stone of a medieval bell tower and a small more recent church alongside.

'Here,' Valentina said, pointing towards a square building, separated by a flagged path and low stone wall from the church, which it faced.

From the outside the house was large and, Sloane thought, ugly; the green-shuttered windows on both floors the sole relief from flat plastered walls painted a paler, fading green. Left and right of the steps leading to the main door, a pair of semi-abstract figures faced one another across a gravelled courtyard, thick-limbed, life-sized, stone arms outstretched in combat or reconciliation.

'Remember, she is very sick.' Dog swerving between her legs, Valentina went swiftly into the house, leaving Sloane to follow.

◆

Jane Graham lay on a white bed at the center of a white room, dwarfed by everything around her. White sheets, white pillows, slack and sallow skin: sepulchres, Sloane thought, shrouds. An oxygen mask, cylinder close by. Coiled tubing. Water jug and glass. A needle taped inside her arm. One of her own paintings, purple and mauve, hung from the facing wall. On a pedestal between the bed and the far corner of the room, almost mockingly, stood a bronze of the dying woman in her prime, the work of Valentina's hands. The smell of sickness hung sweet and heady in the air.

As if aware of their presence, Jane's breathing changed and slowly she raised her head and opened her eyes. Her voice when she spoke Sloane's name was barely above a whisper, faint and harsh.

Valentina lifted her gently, easily, rearranged her pillows, settled her back down and stepped away.

Leaning forward, Sloane rested his lips, lightly, upon Jane's forehead and then her cheek. Her skin was damp and coarse, and patched with sweat. Most of the hair had gone from her head. The backs of her hands and wrists were spotted with dark ruptures of blood.

'You came.'

Sloane opened his mouth but the words stalled on his tongue.

She smiled, the vestige of a smile, and there were tears in her eyes. She patted the sheet, summoning him to sit, and when he did so seized his fingers with her own. 'I may not be able to talk for long, so you must listen. Please. Let me say what I have to say.'

Sloane nodded. 'I understand.'

'When I first came to Europe, all those years ago . . .' She turned her head aside to cough and Sloane realized that Valentina had slipped from the room, leaving them alone.

'When I left for France, left you, left New York and all my friends, I was pregnant with your child.'

Low inside Sloane's stomach something kicked and turned. The backs of his legs like sudden ice.

'I was going to have an abortion, in Paris, that was what I thought. It just . . . when it came to it . . .' She broke off as the coughing resumed, harsher than before. Sloane poured water from the jug and held the glass as she sipped. Her breathing steadied and she reached for him again, her fingers like twigs against the back of his hand. 'Connie was born in April. April the third. Forty-two years ago.'

Now it was Sloane who was finding it difficult to breathe. Pushing himself from the bed, he took three paces towards the door and stopped; strode towards the wall and stared at the face reflected back at him from shuttered glass.

'Please, don't be angry. Please.'

'Then what? I mean, what the fuck . . . ? Why're you . . . I mean, does she know me? Does she even know who I am?'

'No, she doesn't know . . .'

Sloane slammed his fist against the wall.

'She doesn't know who you are.'

'Then why now? Why tell me fucking now?'

'Because this bloody disease . . . Because I'm going to fucking die.' She cramped forward, creased by a sudden blade of pain.

Sloane had scarcely noticed Valentina coming back into the room. Now he stood and watched as she eased Jane back into a comfortable position and fitted the mask over her face, adjusting the flow of the oxygen. 'Go for a walk,' she ordered Sloane. 'Clear your head and then come back.'

Sloane crossed the dusty street towards a statue of the Virgin Mary and gazed down into the other side of the valley. Jane's words raced headlong round his brain. Forty-two. A child. *Perhaps you'll be in Paris soon yourself. You'll look me up.* Another world. Another life. Another life other than his own. Connie, was that what she'd said?

At the bar he ordered a brandy and stood out on the terrace while he drank it, unable to sit down. What was he supposed to believe? What the hell was he supposed to feel? He drained his glass and set off back towards the house. Fresh flowers had recently been placed on either side of a marble slab attached to the tower wall. *Verrucole Ai Suoi Caduti In Guerra. 1915–1918. 1940–1945.* Eight names remembered, eight dead. When he looked up towards the fortress and the hills beyond the exhilaration of their beauty had faded, his freedom no longer untrammelled, but laid siege to by his past.

Valentina had lifted the mask away, readjusted the pillows, wiped Jane's mouth and dried her eyes. When Sloane reappeared in the doorway she spoke reassuringly into her ear, kissed her on the mouth.

'Listen,' she said to Sloane. 'This is not all about you.' A long, warning look and she withdrew.

Sloane hesitated, uncertain what to say or do.

'Please.' Jane's fingers tapped the sheet. 'Come back and sit down.'

This time he took her hand, cautious lest he press too hard.

'I always wondered,' she said, 'if I should have told you at the time.' Her voice so quiet he had to lean forward to hear. 'But you were just a boy—no, it's true, you were—just starting out, you didn't want that sort of responsibility . . .'

Sloane shook his head. 'How can you say that? How could you know?'

'Maybe I couldn't, you're right. But I thought I did. And later, telling Connie, when she was old enough to ask, it didn't seem to make sense.'

'You brought her up alone?'

'Yes, more or less.'

He glanced towards the door. 'Then Valentina . . . ?'

'We didn't meet until later. Connie was well into her teens.' She smiled with her eyes, remembering, then frowned. 'It made for a rocky patch, I can tell you that. Ended with Connie going to New York. To sing. That's what she does. Or did, at least. There was this big row, ten years ago. I haven't seen her since.'

'Or heard?'

'A few letters, asking for money. The last was, oh, a long time back.'

'I'm sorry.'

Jane's fingers made a fist inside his hand. 'I want you to find her. Talk to her. Make peace between us. All of us.'

Sloane's head was starting to throb.

'Say you'll do it, please. Promise me.'

'I don't know.' He could no longer look her in the eye.

'She's your daughter, for God's sake.'

He stared at her then, not knowing what to say, what he wanted to believe.

'Please.'

Again he looked away. 'Okay. All right. If I can.'

'You promise?'

'I promise.'

'Thank you.' He could barely hear the words. A smile brushed her face and again her fingers stirred inside his hand. Turning her head into the pillow, she closed her eyes. Within moments, exhausted, she was fast asleep.

8

FOR THE REMAINDER OF the day Jane drifted in and out of con-
sciousness, and Valentina, more relaxed in her own surroundings,
offered to show Sloane around. Her own studio, to the rear, was a
jumble of tools and sketches, pieces of unworked stone; Polaroids
of finished projects were tacked haphazardly to the walls, a slab of
pink-hued marble, newly worked, dominating the center of the
room. A film of opaque dust lay over everything.

Jane's studio, on the first floor, was not so different from
Sloane's own. The same bottles filled and refilled with white spirit,
similar cans stuffed with brushes of all sizes, tubes of paint and sticks
of charcoal, sketch pads and pencils, curled sheets of paper, globs of
color crusted on to table top and floor. The wall behind her desk
had been filled with postcards of other painters' work, pages torn
from newspapers and magazines, photographs of herself and
Valentina in Venice, others taken in a city which might have been
Rome; one, alone, of Jane as Sloane had first known her—a young
woman standing on a New York street, white blouse, dark skirt,
feet set firm upon the sidewalk, one arm raised pointing at the
camera, mouth open in a smile.

Sketches and preparatory studies, often little more than

overlapping bands of color, were pinned, one above the other, along the remaining walls. Stretched in a position where it got most light, recently started, a large canvas had been covered evenly in silver gray, a single slash of vermilion like a cut above the mid-point, quick and clean.

Elsewhere in the house—living room, dining room, hall and stairs—other paintings and sculptures sat easily among the high-backed chairs, the oak tables, the low settees.

When the tour was over and Valentina left him to check on Jane, Sloane went back to the trio of abstracts hanging opposite the marble fireplace in the dining room, each canvas no more than 60 centimeters by 45. Abstract, yes, but now that he had seen where Jane had lived the last years of her life, Sloane could see in them not just the colors, but the shapes of the mountains, the surrounding hills. He was still standing there when Valentina returned.

'You like these?'

'Very much.'

'The work she did here, these last years . . . She was content, more calm.'

Sloane thought about the unfinished painting in Jane's studio, that brilliant tear of angry red. Something that beat inside her still, unquenched.

They had lunch in the walled garden at the back of the house: pasta e fagioli, all the better for being made the day before; roast aubergines and peppers steeped in olive oil, bruschetta and blue cheese. Red wine.

'You meant what you said?' Valentina asked. 'To Jane. Before. Connie, you will go and look for her?'

Sloane studied her for a moment across the table. 'It's what I said.'

'Promised.'

'Yes.'

Valentina tore off a piece of bread. 'It would have been easy to say the words. Let her hear what she wanted to hear.'

'Not for me.'

'And you have time to do this?'

'All the time in the world.'

'And money?'

'Enough.'

'Because if you do not . . .'

'It's fine.'

For several minutes they ate without speaking, the silence broken only by the scraping of a chair, a child's laughter rising up from the valley. Valentina looked back towards the house. 'I don't think it will be long now. I think she waited for you to come.'

Sloane drank more wine. 'It must make you really angry.'

'I don't understand.'

'Jane and I. The way she's dredging it all up now.'

Valentina smiled. 'When you are dying, you see things in a different light.'

'Even so.'

'Okay, I was angry when she said she would write to you. Ask you to come here. But then . . .' Still smiling, she poured more wine into his glass. '. . . I have had more than twenty years, and you. . . What was it? One?'

Sloane nodded. 'More or less.'

'Then perhaps I should not—what is the word?'

'Begrudge?'

'Maybe I should not begrudge you this. These hours with her. Your quest.'

Lunch over, they went back into Jane's room where she was still sleeping, head to one side, one skinny arm thrust out across the sheets.

'She looks better,' Sloane said. 'More peaceful.'

Valentina shook her head. 'It's the morphine. I increased her dose.' Reaching down, she touched the tips of her fingers to Jane's cheek. 'There has been no better for a long time.'

'Was there never any chance?'

'If it had been caught earlier, perhaps. Even then, I'm not so sure. But for a long time she felt unwell, nothing special. Sweating at night. Sore throats, one after another. The doctor, he gave her medicine and always they came back. When finally she had a blood test the leukemia was advanced. They treated it with busulphan and talked of bone marrow transplant. By the time a match was found that was too late also.'

As if at some level she had been listening, Jane stirred and her eyelids fluttered without opening.

'We're disturbing her,' Valentina said. 'Let's go outside. There's one more thing I have to show you.'

When she led him back up the stairs and into the studio, Sloane thought there was another of Jane's paintings Valentina wanted him to see, but instead she crossed the room and pressed both hands, outstretched, against the wall and when she did so it swung slowly backwards to reveal another room.

'Here. Come through.'

Several paces in, Sloane stopped and turned and stared. Valentina adjusted the level of the light. Displayed around the room were a dozen canvases—Sloane thought a dozen, he was too stunned to count properly—by the giants of American abstract art. De Kooning, Larry Rivers, Pollock—not one Pollock, for Christ's sake, but two—Franz Kline. All those he knew as effortlessly as breathing. And that was a Joan Mitchell, facing. Helen Frankenthaler. What could be Robert Motherwell. Sam Francis. Lee Krasner? The view across the city through a window, Jane Freilicher, he was sure.

'Some of them,' Valentina explained, 'Jane bought when they were inexpensive, but mostly they were gifts, pictures taken in exchange. Her friends.'

Glorious, Sloane thought. Magnificent. All his masters, most of them, gathered in the same room.

'One of the Pollocks,' Valentina said, 'the tall, narrow one, it's going to MoMA in New York. The Rivers is a gift to the Phillips in Washington. The rest, as soon as arrangements can be made, they will be sold.'

'Jesus!' Sloane breathed softly. The de Kooning alone would fetch millions of dollars.

'The money will be used to set up a foundation in Jane's name. There will be grants for students who will come and work here, study. Her studio will remain as it is today. We hope also to set up a permanent collection of Jane's painting somewhere else, possibly in America, maybe here in Italy.'

'And that's it?' Sloane asked. 'That accounts for everything?'

Valentina shook her head. 'Within the terms of the will, once the foundation is established, a sum will be set aside for Connie and myself.'

'How big a sum?'

'That will depend on the trustees. And how much is left. But enough for me to live on here in Tuscany, I would hope.'

Slowly, Sloane walked from canvas to canvas, pausing at each. Most of his life had been spent striving to achieve something comparable to this.

For more than an hour that afternoon he sat with Jane, listening to the rhythm of her breathing catch and change. He was sitting opposite her in Jim Atkin's diner on Sheridan Square, watching her wolf down a second helping of hash and scrambled eggs; listening to Bird on a record player in some poet's apartment, while Jane argued, laughed and danced. Beyond happiness, the pair of them. Or so it had seemed. Shifting position, she moaned and said what might have been his name. Her fingers sought and found his hand.

'I've been looking at your paintings,' Sloane said. 'The three by the fireplace, landscapes I almost want to call them . . .'

A small, nodding movement of Jane's head.

'They're beautiful.'

'Have them.'

At first he thought he hadn't heard.

'Have them, please. Please.' Like feathers, her fingers fluttered against his.

'Thank you,' Sloane said and bent to kiss her face.

Valentina drove him just beyond San Romano and he said he would walk from there. He could smell the flowers now as well as see them; see the hills with Jane's eyes as well as his own. When he had told Valentina that Jane wanted him to have the paintings, she did little more than grunt and nod. In the town he bought milk, more bread, bacon and eggs. He had borrowed a catalogue of Jane's paintings from a show at Walker Art Center in Minneapolis and, sitting near the quince tree in the garden, he turned slowly through the pages, drinking coffee, committing the reproductions, almost, to memory. Later he walked back up the hill and bought a bottle of local wine. Later still he cooked eggs and bacon, turning the eggs carefully as the bacon fat sizzled in the pan. When the wine was all but gone, he lay down in his clothes and fell asleep. He was awake, it seemed, before the telephone had finished its first ring, stumbling towards it from the bedroom, knowing what he would hear.

As he looked down at her face, first light was slanting through the room. He would have said she was at peace, except that there was no one there. A skull. Some skin.

9

THE 10TH PRECINCT OF the New York Police Department was situated in midtown Manhattan, its headquarters a flat-fronted cement and stone building in an otherwise mainly residential street. A flagpole—flag currently wrapped tight about it by the east wind—angled out several storeys above the wooden door which, clearly but discreetly, bore the Precinct's name. To any casual observer, hurrying past, head down against the driving rain, only the blue and white patrol cars parked out front would have drawn attention to the building's purpose.

Dry and relatively warm inside, Catherine Vargas caught herself looking at her watch for the third time in as many minutes. The squad room was empty save for herself and a fellow detective sitting by the far wall, hunched over a stack of case files, humming to himself and tapping the end of his ballpoint erratically against the desk. At least a dozen phones in the room and all of them silent. To Vargas, the second night of duty since her transfer, it didn't seem real. Back in the Bronx there'd scarcely been time to go to the bathroom.

She knew it couldn't go on like this, some kind of phoney peace, but for as long as it did she felt all wrong. Vargas in Wonderland. Any minute now the guy across the room would kick into the lobster quadrille and Grace Slick would come loud and strong through the air-con, that song she did with the Airplane, the first time psychedelia hit big. One pill makes you larger and one pill makes you small. 'White Rabbit'. What her grandfather had called her when she was just starting to walk, when he was still alive: rabbit, little rabbit. Because she loved her greens.

When her late colleagues had heard about her transfer to Manhattan, they'd laughed and accused her of chickening out, said it was a sure sign she was getting old.

Vargas didn't think so. She was on the tall side for a woman, five seven, square-shouldered and square-jawed, brown eyes and thick, arching eyebrows, dark hair usually pulled back from her face and held in place with a barrette: she was thirty-seven years of age and worked out at the gym four times a week. One thing she didn't feel was old. Catherine Vargas, Detective First Class, wearing Gap chinos and a maroon tank top over a cream shirt, her maternal grandmother's gold ring on the third finger of her left hand, the only place it fitted perfectly. Let people think what they liked.

She stared at the phone on her desk and willed it to ring. Thirty seconds and if nothing happened she'd pour some more quarters into the drinks dispenser in the hall.

She was on her way back across the room, polystyrene cup filled almost to the brim, when a phone suddenly burst to life behind her and she jumped, spilling hot coffee over her wrist and the back of her hand.

'Shit!'

The other detective casually turned his head before resuming humming and tapping as before.

Vargas set down the cup and lifted the receiver, identifying herself as she wiped her hand down the outside of her chinos. A woman's body had been found off the West Side Highway, between 42nd and 43rd.

It was raining just enough for Vargas to keep her wipers working as she drove west and north from the precinct house on West 20th, finally parking behind two patrol cars; cold enough at nearly four in the morning for her to grab her well-worn thrift shop leather jacket from the rear seat.

Traffic swished along the highway, ever present, slowing for the emergency repairs that were taking up the best part of two lanes and would cause havoc come rush hour if they were still unfinished. Contractors' floodlights illuminated an area on the far side, a jumble of upturned concrete and excavated hardcore, bags of sand or cement and temporarily abandoned machinery. She waited for a gap between vehicles and ran across, lifting the yellow police tape lettered DO NOT CROSS and ducking beneath.

Not recognizing her, the nearest of several uniformed officers moved quickly across to intercept, one arm raised and fingers spread. When Vargas showed him her ID he took a pace back and gave her a look.

'Something wrong?'

'I guess not.' He was pushing forty, Vargas thought, maybe forty-five; sliding towards his pension like a sack of flour on a slow conveyor. All he wanted right now was to be out of the rain and home in bed.

'You've got a problem?'

'No, ma'am.'

Off to one side, two of his colleagues were talking earnestly to a small group of workmen; they could have been gathering evidence, but from their demeanor Vargas thought they could equally well have been discussing sports.

'How about a body?' Vargas said.

'Over there.'

She followed the line of his pointing finger and saw something protruding over the edge of a pile of rubble, some twenty meters back from the highway. Closer, she saw a woman's leg partly clothed in shredded pantyhose, a low-heeled shoe on the ground nearby. The uniforms would have secured the scene and carried out a preliminary search, leaving any evidence undisturbed. The body would not be moved until the arrival of the medical examiner and whichever detective caught the call.

Vargas hunkered down and, slipping her Maglite from her pocket, snapped it to life. The woman's other leg seemed to have folded awkwardly beneath her, the now sodden fabric of her dress covering hips and waist. The head and upper part of the torso were tilted backwards and partially obscured from view, though Vargas could see what looked like dried blood, contusions, swollen skin.

'Who found her?' she asked, straightening. The rain was falling harder now, the wind off the Hudson slanting it into her face. Fine lines shining silver in the floodlights, the roadway slick and dark.

The officer indicated one of the workmen, a stocky, slope-shouldered man standing a short way off from the others, faint red glow from the cigarette cupped at his side.

Vargas nodded; she would take a statement from him later. She was wondering how long the body could have lain where it was undiscovered. Maybe days.

Paying too little attention to the warning signs, a truck approached too fast and was forced to brake, rear wheels losing their grip momentarily on the wet surface.

'Hit and run?' Vargas asked, speculating aloud.

The officer shrugged and tugged at his collar.

'How about her purse? Personal effects? Anyone come up with a bag of any kind?'

'Not as far as I know.'

'But you looked?'

'Of course.'

'Then I suggest you look again. Instead of standing around with your thumb up your ass. And find something to cover her with. Now.'

'The ME'll be here any time.'

'Right. And until he is, let's get her under cover.' Vargas waited, looking him full in the eye, until, grudgingly, he moved off to do her bidding.

◆

The medical examiner wore three-piece suits in Harris tweed, the vest normally undone, all the better to display a natty line in striped silk ties—when he wasn't in scrubs, that is. No matter how many small, bullet-shaped mints he sucked, how much L'Occitane Pour Homme eau de toilette he sprayed, nothing would rid him of that faint yet persistent smell of chemicals, that sense of recently rendered flesh.

Vargas, doing her best to ignore what lay on gurneys to either side, opened her notebook and uncapped her pen.

The dead woman was between thirty-five and forty, five five, one hundred and forty pounds. Hazel eyes, the original color of her hair mid-brown. A pregnancy which had not gone to term. A small tumor, the size of a finger end, lay, most likely undetected, in the subcutaneous tissue of her left breast. There was evidence of numerous injuries to the body, all of them recent. Three cervical vertebrae and four lumbar vertebrae cracked, with adjacent signs of internal hemorrhaging; the right patella shattered; the right wrist and all the fingers of the right hand broken. Significant signs of bruising and trauma around the area of the pelvis, in addition to a fracture of the skull and concomitant damage to the brain. Coffee, alcohol, aspirin. Semen. Nothing to suggest that any sexual activity was other than consensual.

'Questions?' The ME popped another mint.

'I suppose what killed her's too straightforward?'

'Not necessarily. Any serious head injury of this nature causes the brain to swell and compress its base against the skull; enough pressure there and breathing becomes difficult, the flow of blood to and from the heart stops. That's where my money would be.'

'The blows to the head,' Vargas said. 'There's no way of knowing how they were caused?'

'A collision with something hard and solid . . .'

'So she could have been struck by a passing vehicle, knocked off the roadway and rolled?'

'It's possible.'

'And could that account for the rest of her injuries?'

The ME gave it due consideration. 'The shattered kneecap certainly, possibly the hand . . .'

'But not all?'

'I think not.'

She could have been beaten up, Vargas thought, then dumped; thrown from a moving car. In which case was she already dead when that happened? She wondered if there was any way of proving that for certain. Hard and solid. She wondered why, unbidden, the same image kept forming in her mind, a woman being swung, full-force, against a wall.

There was nothing on the body that afforded identification; what clothes the dead woman had been wearing were so common as to be untraceable. Vargas ran the description through the computer, contacted the various agencies and failed to come up with a significant match. Or, rather, she came up with too many. White, medium height and build, on the cusp of middle age: Jane Doe. Vargas chased down all the missing persons reports she could without results. And by then her wish had come true and the phoney peace was over: no more sitting at her desk, waiting for the phone to ring. Now she glared at it and swore at it to stop. The woman from West Side Highway was one unsolved case among too many.

10

DUMAR'S CAFÉ WAS BUSY today, busier than it had been before. The usual working men eating lunch and swapping stories, drinking tea; a young woman in velvet and faded denim, rings and studs on her face and hands, smoking roll-ups as she read about inner health and calm.

Sloane had dropped off his duffel bag at home, changed his shoes, splashed water on his face and cleaned his teeth. Ten minutes later he was on his way round the corner to the café, seeking company. Much of his adult life he had lived alone and happy that way, sought solitude. Now he was getting jumpy at the sight of four walls and the sound of his own breathing. Maybe it was one of the things prison did to a man. Maybe it was something else.

Breaking a piece of bread in two, he wiped first one, then the other around the inside of his bowl, Dumar's soup too good to waste. Yellow and thick with yam and sweet potato, spices and split peas.

'You like?' Dumar asked. He was standing by the table, blue and white striped apron tied at his waist, sleeves rolled back. His dark hair was beginning to gray at the temples. Sloane had not noticed before the length of his fingers, the breadth of his hands.

'Great,' Sloane said.

Dumar grinned with pleasure. 'You want something else?'

Sloane shook his head.

'Your friend, how is she?'

'She died,' Sloane said.

'I am sorry,' Dumar said solemnly, before turning away.

Sloane picked up a newspaper from one of the other tables and scanned the front page. ESCAPE FROM HELL read the headline. 'Paras go in. Airlift of trapped Britons begins.' In the central photograph an African youth, no more than fourteen or fifteen, lay on his side, eyes open, blood spilling from beneath his Nike shirt like paint spread too thick across pink and arid ground.

Sloane realized he didn't know from which country in Africa Dumar came.

◆

The dress shop on Kentish Town Road where Sloane's mother had worked had long since been bulldozed aside to make room for offices, shoddy now in their seventies concrete and glass. Higher up the street the bookshop where he had spent his birthday money on the adventures of Biggles and his mother had bought him the Cadet edition of *The Cruel Sea* had been replaced. The Palace cinema was home now to the Community Health Council, the Gaisford a block of flats. Real Irishmen and women drank in fake Irish pubs. Posted everywhere, police flyers asked for information about a fatal shooting near the railway bridge, for witnesses to a skirmish in the local McDonald's, two youths stabbed in the middle of an otherwise quiet Saturday afternoon. Woolworths was still where Sloane remembered it, but now there were uniformed guards on duty just inside the doors.

Immediately past the Tube station he turned right, then left, skirting the Brecknock to pass the basement flat he and his mother had moved into the year he started secondary school. Two rooms and a kitchen in which the radio always seemed to have been playing: Billy Ternant, Joe Loss, Ken Macintosh. His mother singing along, knowing all the words. His mother's dressmaking dummy stood in the living room close by her sewing machine. Lengths of material, carefully pinned, lay draped across the Put-U-Up that folded out to become his bed. Letters from his father in America that she would read to him again and again.

Summer evenings when clients called round for a fitting, he would be let out to run the streets, cadging cigarettes from his mates and passing round copies of Hank Jansen and Peter Cheyney, soiled and thumbed; calling after the girls from the council flats on the corner, daring them to play strip poker, lift their skirts.

Now Sloane walked the length of the street where, in winter months, he had played soccer till light faded and his mother called him home. He crossed into a small children's playground, deserted save for an au pair listening to her Walkman as she leafed through the pages of *Hello!*, and a fair-haired two-year-old jumping, again and again, from the bottom of the metal slide into the sandpit.

Sloane sat on the furthest of three wooden benches and slipped the brown envelope from his pocket: photographs of a girl who might be his daughter spilled into his hands.

Connie at twelve or thirteen, lower lip jutting out as she glared at the camera with teenage disdain; older and happier, dark-haired and smiling, she and Jane together by the sea, more like sisters than mother and daughter—*Rimini 77*, written on the back in Jane's steeply angled hand. Images of Connie as a toddler, the same age, more or less, as the child who had now tired of the sandpit and was calling to be pushed on the swing: in some of these she is laughing, Connie, carefree; in others the pout is already in place, the fierce stare.

Only one picture showed her as a young woman, mid-twenties, caught mid-stride crossing a slatted bridge in what is clearly Venice, the oval of her face pale against the blue and terracotta buildings behind.

And one last, small and creased, a damp-haired baby, just born, slippery in her mother's arms.

Sloane spread the photographs out, chronologically, along the bench. Searching for what? Some semblance of himself? What he saw was a child growing into a woman: someone who, though capable of happiness, was angry, unhappy, straining to be away.

◆

'She was no good,' Valentina had said, their last conversation before he had left Italy. 'Connie. By the time she left to go to America she was already no good. Every week Jane would write, begging her to reply, tell her how she was. And when she did reply all she did, every time, ask for money. Money, money, money. When she came to stay it was the same. Worse. The last time she was here they have this big fight.'

'What about?'

'Stealing. Connie stealing money from the house, from her purse. From me, also. Oh, she had done that, I think, every time, but this was worse. Connie went mad and started hitting out and I try to—what is the word?—intervene. That is when she hit me across the face, call me bitch. Bitch and whore.'

'You hit her back?'

Valentina shook her head. 'I wish I had.'

'And Jane?'

'Jane told her to apologize or leave. Connie said she would sooner die. Call us both terrible names. After that, Jane wrote and told her it is best she not come again. She did not write back. Silence. For years. Then when Jane became ill, she wrote to her again, try to heal things over. The letters came back marked "Moved Away, No Longer at this Address".'

'How did she take that?'

'Bad, of course. Terrible. Many tears.'

'And you?'

Valentina looked at him for several moments before answering. 'For myself, I was glad. But for Jane, no, I am sad. She is her daughter; she want to see her again before she dies. Not leave all of this bad feeling between them. Bad blood.' Valentina pushed the envelope containing photographs and the details of Connie's last known address into his hand. 'Now it is for you to honor your promise, make things right.'

Sloane held her gaze. 'Just like the promises you'll make sure are kept.'

'I'm not sure I understand.'

Rising, Sloane shook his head. 'I think you do, Valentina. I think you do.'

◆

The temperature had dropped enough for Sloane to fasten the buttons on his coat. A pair of magpies aside, he now had the playground to himself. Slowly he spread the photographs once more along the bench. All those years in which he had become resigned to living, to being alone, no ties, and now . . . He slipped the photographs from sight, not knowing what he wanted to believe. Through the hum of traffic, the radio playing from an open window, he could almost hear his mother's voice, calling him home.

◆

Dumar was waiting for him near the entrance to his street, a bottle of whiskey inside his coat. 'I thought we would drink a toast,' he said as Sloane ushered him inside, 'to the memory of your friend who died.'

Sloane switched on a light, rinsed glasses and held them while Dumar poured. 'Your friend . . .' Dumar began.

'Jane.'

'She lived a good life?'

'I think so, yes.'

'Good. To Jane.'

They drank and refilled their glasses.

'You will stay here now?' Dumar asked.

Sloane shook his head and explained briefly the reasons why.

'This girl,' Dumar said, 'this woman, Connie—you don't know whether to believe she is your daughter or not?'

'No.'

'When you find her, then you will know.'

'How? How will I be sure?'

Dumar smiled. 'Because of what you will feel. When you see her. Feel in the blood.'

For a while, neither man spoke; the whiskey bottle passed back and forth.

'You have children, don't you?' Sloane asked eventually. 'In Africa. I think that's what you said.'

'Two. Two boys. My daughter is studying here now, England. Manchester. I will bring my sons too. When I can.'

'But they're okay?'

'Oh, yes.'

'I saw that picture in the paper, the fighting . . .'

'Sierra Leone. My family are from Mali, many, many miles away.'

'And safe.'

'Yes, safe. For now.' Dumar drained his glass. Hesitated. 'Eight years ago there was a revolution in my country. Many died. My older sons were fighting, a hundred miles to the north. My daughter and I were already here. One day my wife and our two youngest children went to the nearest town for supplies. She travelled with three or four other families in convoy. For safety. They were ambushed on their way back. My wife was killed outright.'

'And the children?'

'A few scratches, nothing more.'

'Thank God for that at least.'

'Thank God.' Dumar's voice so quiet now it seemed to float on the stillness of the air. 'Less than a month later they caught a fever, first one and then the other. They were seven and nine. They died and there was no one to bury them. No mother. No father.'

For several moments Sloane didn't seem able to breathe. Didn't know what to say. 'Dumar, I'm so sorry,' the only paltry words he could finally manage.

'You know,' Dumar said, rising, 'those people who tried to break in here, they were not the only ones to hang round while you were away.'

'How d'you mean?'

'There were two men, asking questions. I think they were police.'

'You're not sure. I mean, they didn't say?'

Dumar shook his head. 'Everywhere they are the same, your country, mine. You learn to know them.' He rested a large hand on Sloane's shoulder and squeezed. 'My friend, take care.'

◆

Sloane bought all the broadsheet newspapers, an orange, two apples and a bottle of water, and headed back along Prince of Wales Road. The car was parked at the corner of the street, windows wound part-way down. The man on the passenger side got out first, dropping his half-smoked cigarette on to the road and stubbing it out. The driver glanced at Sloane across the roof of the car before turning the key in the lock. Careful, soberly suited men, hair cut fashionably short. Dumar had been right, you could recognize them anywhere. And this pair Sloane had met before. Dutton, that's what the tall one was called, he remembered now. Dutton and his cohort with the Welsh accent decently suppressed was Boyd. Detective sergeant and detective constable respectively.

'We should have been here a good few days ago,' Dutton said. 'Would have been, pressing business aside. Welcome you home.'

'One of the few ways in which our present prison system falls down,' Boyd said, 'preparation for the outside world. Acclimatization, I believe that's the word.'

'When we did call by,' Dutton said, disapproving, 'it was only to find you'd gone away.'

'Left town.'

'And country.'

'Compassionate, we believe. The reason for your travel. Your friend from the café explained. Just the barest details, of course.'

A van turned the corner, heading for the entrance to the Imperial Works, and the three of them were forced to take to the pavement, abandoning the road.

'The thing is,' Dutton said, reaching into his pocket for another cigarette, 'since we were the ones made the initial arrest, worked up the case, well, we feel responsible. I don't think that's putting it too strong.'

'What do you want?' Sloane asked.

'Parsons,' Dutton said. 'You went to see him almost as soon as you came out.'

Sloane shook his head and sighed. The fact that he'd done his time, how much was that ever going to count for with them? It had been Parsons the Squad had really been after and in their eyes they'd failed. That they didn't like. Not one little bit.

'Rumor has it,' Dutton said, 'Parsons and yourself, you had something of a falling out. Harsh words, blows. Not to say damage to a rare work of art.'

'As well it wasn't anything more substantial than a Giacometti,' Boyd said. 'That's substantial in a purely physical sense, of course, nothing in the way of an artistic judgment intended.'

Christ, Sloane thought, all this bollocks and I've got a plane to catch.

'What it is,' Dutton said, 'with things between Parsons and yourself no longer seemingly so hunky-dory, well, we wondered if you were any closer to going on record about that business with the Vuillard. Parsons's involvement, that is.'

'Was he involved?' Sloane asked.

'A pity', Dutton said, 'that you should take that attitude. Short-sighted, in fact.' He angled his face aside and released a coil of smoke.

Sloane checked his watch. 'I've an appointment, in town. Sorry you've been wasting your time.'

'Is that what we've been doing?'

'I think so.'

'You're not planning any more trips?' Dutton asked. 'Not leaving the country again, for instance?'

'Unlikely.'

'Good. Because we really should keep in touch.'

Sloane nodded slightly and left the pair of them where they sat. Within an hour he would be on the Airport Express from Paddington to Heathrow, bound from there for New York.

11

SLOANE SWAPPED SEATS WITH a disgruntled Swede whose legs needed the aisle even more than he. Settled in against the window, he gazed past the tip of the wing and looked down on a brief hatchwork of runways, toy trees, the neat clutter of sub-urban homes; before the plane banked again he glimpsed the upper reaches of the Thames curving steeply through flat fields and then they were in cloud. Blistery gray becoming soft, impossible nursery white.

When you find her, then you will know.

Taking his wallet from his pocket, he slid the smallest of the photographs into his palm. The way the dark hair wedged to a point above the center of her forehead, fingers of one hand reaching for her mouth; the hint of worry in her already blue eyes. Connie. Sloane pushed the picture from sight. Head sideways, he closed his eyes and feigned sleep.

Only when the plane lurched Sloane awake did he realize he had truly slept. Turbulence over, the cabin crew made their way along the aisles with offers of refreshment, bottles of red wine just above ice cold, free booze; he lowered his tray table to accommodate a miniature meal nestling in foil and plastic, each item signally failing to live up to its lavish description on the printed menu.

Once this had been cleared away he stretched his legs past the Swede and pulled his duffel bag down from the overhead locker. Of the four newspapers he had bought, two had no mention of Jane Graham's death and one carried a short news item together with a color reproduction of a tall, slim painting that hung in the Musée National d'Art Moderne in Paris. Sloane wondered if the picture editor had chosen it because he could fit it into a single column's width.

The *Independent* alone carried a full obituary, illustrated by a photograph of Jane in what he guessed were her forties, head and shoulders, smiling, and another of an early painting which, in black and white, looked like a morass of blotches and squiggles, little more. He had already read the text so many times, parts of it were committed to memory. Draining the glass of his second whiskey, he read it again.

Jane Graham, who has died of leukemia at the age of seventy-three, was one of the foremost painters of the New York School. Identified with the Second Generation of Abstract Expressionists, a diverse group over which the brooding presence of Jackson Pollock cast a huge shadow, and which included disciples of Mark Rothko on the one hand and de Kooning and Kline on the other, Graham's style leaned toward the more painterly approach of the latter.

From the mid-fifties her canvases, which had previously echoed the busy surfaces of Pollock, one of her strongest early influences, took on a degree of spareness and calm and displayed an increasing interest in the effects on color of natural light.

'Pollock,' he remembered Jane saying, 'that great oaf. That ox in plaid shirts and cowboy boots. The first time I saw him, one of the bars down on Tenth Street, he pushed his hand up my skirt, feeling for my crotch. He was drunk, of course, looking to get laid, looking for a fight. Either way, there was usually someone ready to oblige.'

Pollock had died the year before Sloane had arrived in New York, having driven the Oldsmobile containing himself, his mistress and her best friend off the road and into a tree. All Sloane knew were the stories: the paintings and the stories. The paintings, the best of them, he loved. They were why he had wanted to come to New York.

'I was at the opening of his wife's show at the Stable Gallery,' Jane had told him. 'Lee Krasner, you know. She was nervous as hell about how he'd be, whether he'd even show. Half hoping, I think, he'd get drunk somewhere, stay away. Anyway, in he comes, wearing a suit and tie, stone cold sober, charming, couldn't be nicer. Half an hour later he's got me pinned up against the wall in a corner, asking me if I'd go out back with him and fuck. Tried to persuade me that somehow I'd be a better painter if I did. The asshole.'

She'd told him this story the third occasion they'd met and Sloane remembered thinking he'd never heard a woman say fuck before; not in the course of normal conversation.

Born in St Paul, Minnesota, Graham studied painting at the Pratt Institute in Brooklyn and with Hans Hofmann, taking up residency in Greenwich Village in the early nineteen fifties. Here, she quickly immersed herself in the then thriving bohemian lifestyle, which brought together artists and poets, playwrights, musicians and experimental film makers in a heady, often volatile brew centering on the Cedar Tavern on 8th Street and University Place.

When Sloane had first arrived in New York, pitchforked into the middle of that turbulent world, he was cocky, uncertain, garrulous, almost obsessively silent, ricocheting between the arrogance of eighteen-year-old self-confidence and crippling self-doubt.

Stuart Hazel, a painter Sloane had known in Chicago, offered him floor space in a cold-water loft below Houston, a former garment factory between East Broadway and Delancey. Whitewashed walls, bare boards, a partitioned-off kitchen the roaches roamed at will. 'Six months, okay? Whatever you can let me have toward the rent, that's okay. But after that, you're on your own.'

Hazel, who chain smoked and listened to the classical music station while he worked, had already exhibited in a co-op gallery on West 4th Street and been well reviewed in *ARTnews*. There were rumors, mostly spread by Hazel himself, of a solo show on 10th Street, the Tanager or the Hansa. He was certain he had it made.

When Sloane ran across him, years later, loud in the bar of some midtown hotel, he was wearing three-button suits and big in margarine.

Graham was fortunate that the more misogynistic attitudes which had been prevalent a decade earlier, and had impeded the progress of women artists such as Louise Bourgeois, Elaine de Kooning and Lee Krasner, Pollock's wife, were no longer as widespread. So she was able to find acceptance, and flourish, within a community which included, among others, such notable artists as Grace Hartigan, Helen Frankenthaler, Jane Freilicher and Joan Mitchell.

Featured in Time magazine as one of half a dozen exceptional young talents, Graham had her first solo show at the Tibor de Nagy Gallery, where, although attacked as over-referential by the formalist critic, Clement Greenberg, her paintings were strongly praised, notably by poet-critics James Schuyler and Frank O'Hara in the pages of ARTnews and Evergreen Review. O'Hara, who was Associate Curator of Painting and Sculpture at the Museum of Modern Art, remained a powerful advocate of Graham's work.

He had been with Jane once at a party at Joan Mitchell's and O'Hara had read a poem he'd written for the occasion. All Sloane could remember clearly was the way people had laughed during the reading and cheered and clapped like crazy at the end, and that O'Hara, who had been getting progressively drunker as the evening wore on, finally fell asleep stretched out on Mitchell's sofa, his head in the lap of a pretty young man in pale blue jeans.

In common with a number of other artists—Ellsworth Kelly, Sam

Francis and Joan Mitchell among them—Graham felt the pull of Paris as an alternative art center to New York and moved to that city in 1958. Brief visits aside, often made in conjunction with exhibitions of her work, she was never to return to the United States. In the seventies Graham moved to a studio near Montpellier, in the south of France, and although she continued to paint with the same clarity and vigor, her moment had passed. In 1988 she moved again, this time to the small village of Verrucole in northern Tuscany, where she lived and worked alongside her long-time companion, the Italian sculptor, Valentina Ceroni.

The canvases she produced during the last dozen or so years of her life, while still predominantly abstract, tend increasingly to reflect her natural surroundings, as if the term 'Abstract Impressionism', which had been applied, tongue-in-cheek, to her work near the beginning of her career, had finally become valid.

Jane Graham's paintings hang in most of the major collections of twentieth-century art, including the recently opened Tate Modern in London, and in 1982 a major retrospective of her work was held at the Walker Art Center in Minneapolis.

Sloane folded the newspaper closed. Through the window the sky was a perfect, untrammelled blue. In another four hours, slightly less, they would be touching down at JFK.

12

FROM THE STREET IT looks nothing special: the name, Lucille's, faded on its awning, the menu in its plastic cover in a wooden frame beside the door. Fine dining. Specialities of the day. Green plants slowly dying on a ledge inside the window. Neon signs for Bud and Miller Light. A handwritten notice, blue print careful on white card, 'Music Tonite'.

Once inside, it's clear this was once two separate buildings, opened up and none too artfully joined. A horseshoe bar dominates the center, more than half the stools taken by solitary drinkers, men—they are all men—who stopped off after work and have yet to make it home because there's little if anything to go home to. Spaced out along both sides of the bar are tables in double rows and most of these are occupied. A few families, one with a child who can be no more than two or three; couples in varying stages of relationships, the ones who talk too much, those who scarcely talk at all; a party of women, five in all, celebrating someone's birthday with Chardonnay and shrill laughter; single men, lighting up between courses, some making a show of reading the sports page of the paper; one with a novel propped open as he forks up his spaghetti, a paperback novel; another who flirts automatically with the waitress, a large-hipped, buxom woman of sixty whose grand-children are entering their teens and whose feet throb. And, yes, there are candles on the tables, candles jammed into the necks of bottles, white folds of solid wax cascading down.

In the right-hand room, furthest from the door, a dapper man with little hair but all of it neatly brushed in place, cuffs of his shirt rolled evenly back above his wrists, leafs through the selection of sheet music he carries with him in his case, pulling out a dozen or so tunes, the ones he thinks she'll sing, those for which he needs the notes, the key, the chords. A quarter past nine and already she's fifteen minutes late. Glancing over his shoulder, he catches the eye of the waitress, who shuffles to the bar and returns with a double measure of Scotch, Macallan, which she sets carefully atop the piano, a large glass of iced water alongside. The pianist nods his thanks, sips the Scotch, lights a small cigar.

It is another ten minutes before Connie, chivvied by the man-agement, emerges from the ladies' room alongside the kitchen where she has been assiduously working her way through a half-bottle of vodka; earlier she has changed from her street clothes into a red and silver dress, the silver a bright slash across from breast to hip, the red the red of drying blood. She wishes she had some cocaine, coke to get her up, but she is new in town and doesn't know where to score safely and, besides, hasn't she promised herself she'd call a halt, stop using, give it up? Without it she's unsure exactly how she's going to get through this: the next half-hour, first set of three. Lucille's in Albany, New York, a hundred and fifty miles north of Manhattan, the closest she's worked to the city in years.

She walks between the tables, one foot before the other, with exaggerated care. Walking on wire.

The pianist plays a chord in E.

Connie touches his shoulder briefly, hesitates as she reaches his side. Glancing up, he nods. The microphone is resting on a stool and she lifts it up, slides the switch down with her thumb and taps the head lightly, making sure it's on. There is no stage as such, only this, a space she has to fill.

She looks out into the interior, the tables, waits for a silence that doesn't come. Her hair has been pulled back from her face and her cheekbones show too clearly through her skin. At slow to medium tempo, the pianist feeds her the first eight bars of 'Just One of Those Things'. Perhaps she doesn't hear? Fails to recognize the tune? Eight bars more and then he's into the release, the bridge. Connie, microphone between both hands, is staring at the floor. With a skip and a hint of stride, he reaches the end of the sequence and as, irrevocably, another begins, Connie, still looking down, starts singing, her head slowly lifting with the words, those fabulous flights, the bells that now and then ring. After a chorus she relinquishes the song to the piano player for his solo, claiming it back with an emphatic note at the beginning of the middle eight, and by the time they arrive, dovetailed, at the end, some part of her has remembered the how if not the why.

The party of five laughs immoderately at some ribald, indiscreet remark; the child spills ice cream into its lap and cries; from among the scattering of single men, the couples, some of whom may have been drawn there specifically by the music, there is a smattering of applause.

'"Just Friends",' Connie says to the pianist, hand covering the microphone. 'Two flats.'

Her voice isn't strong, not the strongest in the world, but there's a quality to it, a depth in the lower register, a way of phrasing that's neither showy nor affected, yet claims these words, these lines often heard, some of them, for her own. In the main she sticks to standards, things she first heard on albums her mother would play after work, relaxing, Ella, Billie Holiday, Sarah Vaughan. When the lyric to 'The Very Thought of You' eludes her, she knows how to laugh, crack a joke at her own expense, begin again. Someone has sent up an anniversary request, scribbled on a napkin, anything by the Beatles. She finishes her set with 'In My Life', slow tempo, her voice wistful and charged with wonder. Applause stutters out of the almost silence and fills out, holds. Connie bows her head; the back of her neck is slick with sweat. The pianist raises his glass to her as she steps away.

She is almost at the back of the room, her refuge, the bottle, when a hand reaches out, fingers tight around her arm.

'Connie,' Delaney says in his smooth croon. 'Long time no see.'

13

THE HOTEL ON WEST 11th was cheap and clean, each room tailored to fit the basic accommodations, nothing more. Sloane showered and changed and put in a call to his friend, Jake Furman, letting him know he was in town. At the corner of the street he took a window table in the French Roast and thumbed through the listings section of *Village Voice*, looking for any mention of Connie Graham. Afternoon traffic on Sixth Avenue was light, the sky a mottled gray. His club sandwich, when it arrived, would have satisfied a family of three, but even so, little remained on his plate when the waiter whisked it away and set down his coffee and the check. Ten minutes later Sloane was in a cab heading uptown to the Museum of Modern Art.

The painting was not where Sloane expected and for a moment he was turned around, confused, until he realized everything had been moved from where it had been for so long, the entire collection refocused, rehung.

Calm now, he moved through the interconnecting spaces, pausing here and there, until he turned the shoulder of one white wall and there it was, facing him, Jane's painting, and the blood stopped somewhere between his heart and his brain.

A large canvas, exhilarating, clusters of orange, magenta and blue tumbling through white space, one over another, the edges indistinct, slippery, moving, the eye caught up, sent scuttling; each slab of color in harmony, in collision, filaments of paint that spring up, spray out, finally drip and dribble and trickle down between.

Trinkle Tinkle (for Monk). Jane Graham. 1957.

◆

Sloane, skinny in Levis and a plaid shirt, had stood on line at the Five Spot for the best part of an hour and missed most of the first set. Inside, the only seat he was able to find squashed him close to several others on a table right up against the stage. Monk soloing against the rhythm, fingers held stiff above the keyboard then jabbing down, the bright percussive sound chiming through the buzz of conversation, clink of glasses, the occasional shout of laughter from the back of the crowded room.

Monk wearing a pale jacket loose across the shoulders, pale green, silver and gray striped tie knotted snug against the collar of his white shirt, dark hair neatly, recently trimmed, no hat tonight, no hat, goatee beard and moustache, dark glasses shielding his eyes. Fingers rolling a little, feeling for a rhythm in the bottom hand, rocking back upon the piano stool and then thrusting forward, elbows angled out, playing with his whole body, and the drummer, seated at Monk's back, following each movement, listening to each new shift and shuffle, quick and careful as a hawk. Monk's foot, his right foot, skewed wide and stomping down, punctuating the broken line as, stationed in the piano's curve, the bassist, eyes closed, feels for the underlying pulse. And Coltrane, John Coltrane, horn hooked over his shoulder, head down, fingers fluttering from time to time over imaginary keys, stands mute, focused, waiting his time.

Stuart Hazel had brought Sloane here first, only the second or third night he'd been in New York. 'This cat you gotta dig. Monk. Thelonious Sphere Monk, can you believe that name?'

Sloane's early years laboring over piano exercises, learning music, listening to his father practise, had been enough for him to know most things Monk was doing were foolhardy, next to impossible, kicking out against the commonplace, the rules.

Sitting, that first evening, fascinated, filtering out Hazel's incessant conversation as his friend chattered, gossiped, pointed out each and every celebrity in the club. 'Hey, Kenneth! How's it goin'?'

After that he had returned alone. The same riffs, the same themes torn this way and that.

'Ruby, My Dear'.

'Round Midnight'.

'Blue Monk'.

And that evening, Sloane shifting in his seat, half rising awkwardly to let somebody squeeze past and hearing a shout from a table near the side wall—'Jane! Hey, Jane!'—turning his head in time to see a woman near the entrance, dark-haired and smiling at the sound of her name, a hand raised towards her friends in recognition, in greeting; time enough to see that she is beautiful, before Monk launches himself along the keyboard in a clattering arpeggio which calls to mind a man stumbling headlong down a flight of stairs, never quite losing his balance, not falling, saving himself, miraculously, with an upward swoop and final, ringing double-handed chord.

'I Mean You'.

September 1957: the first time Sloane laid eyes on Jane Graham.

14

JAKE FURMAN HAD SEEN the writing on the wall. In sixty-one, when rents in the Village had risen way beyond what most artists could afford and when even the Lower East Side was becoming inflated out of all proportion, he had used a small legacy from doting spinster aunts in Tennessee to purchase—not rent, but purchase—a semi-derelict, fire-damaged warehouse building overlooking the Hudson River. Since which time real estate prices all over the city had escalated steadily, and Chelsea, the area into which he had bought, had become the smart, hip area where lofts were luxury items and where all the big art dealers wanted to be. So Furman had gradually leased out the ground floor in separate units, two of which were gallery spaces capable of housing the largest installations, the third a café bar in which Furman himself had a ten per cent stake. The middle floor was given over to a video workshop and several small photographic galleries, and Furman had kept the entire top floor to himself, a vast studio-cum-living space with wooden floors, rough plaster walls and high arched windows on all four sides.

Financially, Furman had no need to work, supervising his building and collecting rent aside, but he continued most days as before, rising early and painting for several hours in the realist style he had clung to stubbornly when most artists his age were still in the throes of abstraction; and now, with an irony that only Furman and his close friends enjoyed, his flat, high-gloss, brightly colored canvases—mostly portraits or still lifes—were highly collectable and fetched prices that were, Furman at his most mellow would confess, way beyond their true worth.

'But what,' he would ask, grinning, 'can a poor guy do? I mean, I can't exactly give them away now, can I? Start doing that and the whole system'll collapse around our ears.'

Sloane had first met Jake Furman when he was twenty, twenty-one, the beginning of the sixties, Furman some five or six years older and, buoyed up by a small allowance, learning his way around the edges of the scene. Shorter than Sloane by a head, round-faced and barrel-chested, Jake, in those days, was a serious drinker, a devotee of marijuana, a party-goer of legendary stamina. He had friends and acquaintances who were artists, friends who were poets, musicians. You were as likely to find him hanging out with broke but hopeful avant-garde film makers on the Lower East Side as indulging in in-depth conversations about the nature of art with Franz Kline in the Cedar Tavern, or listening to some young white guitarist faking black blues at Gerde's Folk City or the Bitter End. Furman played a little guitar himself, some rudimentary piano; when, as much for a joke as anything else, he put down his hat and busked in Washington Square, he had earned insults and small change in equal measure.

The two men had kept in touch down the years and, most times when Sloane was in the city, they would meet in a bar and listen to music or eat in Little Italy, Furman soft-peddling the alcohol now, keeping himself in pretty good shape.

When Furman opened the door he enveloped Sloane in a bear-like hug, then stepped back to usher him inside. Bright, thick pile rugs on the floor, matching settees, Furman's own paintings on the walls, the neat clutter of his workspace away to one side, a sound system that was playing Al Cohn and Zoot Sims. Furman's hair, Sloane noticed, still thick and wiry, was now firmly gray.

'Al and Zoot,' Furman said. 'Some time, I don't know, late fifties. Stuff they cut for Coral. Here, listen there, Mose Allison on piano before anyone knew who the hell Mose Allison was.' Furman picked up the CD case and put it in Sloane's hand. 'This is pretty much the band we saw at the Vanguard, you remember that?'

'Maybe.' Sloane recalled seeing Cohn and Sims, but that had been in London, surely? Ronnie Scott's. He had been living in a squat in Wood Green, still nursing a crush on Jane.

'Take the weight off,' Furman said. 'Have a seat. I'll put on something a tad more conducive to talk.' He silenced the two tenor players as they chased through 'Just You, Just Me', and settled for Bill Evans's piano instead.

'You want a drink? Wine? Coffee? Beer?'

Sloane shook his head. 'I'm fine.'

'Okay. We'll go downstairs later. Catch a bite to eat.'

Sloane sat in the corner of one settee, Furman centered on the other, a low pale wood table between them. 'You look pretty good,' Furman said. 'Fit and lean.' He reached for a handful of cashews and popped one into his mouth and then a second. 'I heard about your spot of trouble. Spending time inside. I'm sorry.'

Sloane shrugged.

'The time you got caught, it wasn't the first?'

'Not exactly.'

'You were good at it then, what you did?'

'I was okay.'

Furman nodded towards the nearest of his own paintings, a couple in profile, woman and man, facing one another against a vibrant green background. 'I'd best take care, you'll be copying me.'

'I don't think so.'

'Why not? They fetch more'n you might think.'

'Let's say, money aside, I like more of a challenge.'

Furman's face tightened and he sat upright, fist clenched, until Sloane's face leaked a slow smile. 'You bastard!' Furman laughed.

'Hard to resist.'

'Anyway, it's not what you're here to talk about, right?'

Sloane nodded. 'Perhaps I'll have a beer after all.'

Furman crossed the room and returned with two bottles of Anchor Steam.

'You remember Jane?'

'Which one?'

Sloane stared at him, cold.

'No,' Furman said quickly. 'Of course I know which one. It's just there's were so many Janes back then, it seemed to be the only name. But, yes, Jane Graham. The two of you, you had quite a thing.'

'You know she died?'

'In Italy, I saw the obits. Yes, I'm sorry.'

'I went over to see her.'

'I had no idea you were still in touch.'

'We weren't. For years. She wrote to me not so long ago, when she knew . . .'

'Knew she was dying?'

'Uh-huh.'

'That must've been tough. I mean, seeing her like that. That way.'

Sloane tasted his beer. 'She told me she had a child, a daughter, living in New York. A singer.'

Furman rested his bottle on the table top. 'Wait, wait a minute. Connie Graham, that's Jane's daughter?'

'You know her?'

'Know of her, sure. Or did. I mean, not well. But yes, there was a time when she was around. The clubs, you know. She even made a couple of albums, but hell, that'd be way back. Eighties, something like that. I haven't heard of her in a good while. I guess she sort of disappeared from the scene.'

Sloane was looking at him intently, rolling the bottle between his fingers.

'Jane and Connie, they drifted out of touch?'

'Something like that,' Sloane said. 'She asked me to find her if I could.'

'Well, I wish I could help. I mean, I can ask around. But like I say, I haven't seen her name in, oh, must be four or five years. If it's important, though . . .'

'It might be.'

'Then I'll do what I can.'

◆

Earlier, Sloane had taken the A train uptown, checking out Connie's last known address, an apartment block between Columbus and Amsterdam, a few blocks south of Morningside Park. Connie had lived on the second floor, a one-bedroom at the rear, with views out across a narrow space to the pigeons roosting on the ledges of the building opposite. The present tenant was a student at Columbia, a spectacled twenty-year-old with effusive manners and posters of Angelina Jolie on the walls. The apartment had been empty when he'd moved in less than a year before and Connie's name meant nothing. When Sloane tracked down the superintendent in the basement he got a more positive response, without anything the man could tell him being of much use. Yes, she'd lived there. A couple of years, no more. Mostly alone, but for a spell there'd been this guy. Some white guy. Didn't know his name. Here and then he was gone. And Connie? A forwarding address? The super laughed. All she left was bills and greasy underwear.

He'd kept her mail for a while, not that there'd been a lot of that. Junk, for the most part. Kept it for six-months, on the off chance she might come back, then tossed it out with the trash.

Sorry not to have been more help. You have a good day.

◆

Down in the café bar Sloane picked at chicken wings and drank another beer, while Furman ate a burger, rare, with onion rings and fries. The talk was of this and that, mostly inconsequential. They were finishing up when Furman noticed a generously built red-headed woman entering with a small party of friends, all talking animatedly.

'Rachel! Rachel, hey!' Furman jumped up as she approached and they kissed, leaving a faint blur of lipstick on his cheek. 'I didn't know you were back,' Furman said.

'I didn't know I'd been away.'

'You're always off somewhere.'

'Not this time.'

'You look great anyway.'

'Well, thank you,' Rachel said. When she laughed it was a rich sound, starting low in her throat.

Furman half turned towards Sloane. 'You two know each other?'

Sloane shook his head.

'No,' Rachel said.

Jake introduced them and they shook hands. Rachel's eyes were green and they didn't blink away.

'Rachel has a gallery a block south of here. Great stuff, terrific. You should stop by.'

'What he means,' Rachel said, 'I show Jake's work. Once in a while.'

Furman grinned.

'My friends,' Rachel said, 'I should catch up with them.'

Jake kissed the air close to her face.

'Nice to have met you,' she said to Sloane, but already she was turning away.

When Sloane left the bar some fifteen minutes later, he headed not south towards the Zander Gallery, but west towards the river. He wanted to think, clear his head. Staring out across the water, he was no more than a few blocks away from the spot where Diane Stewart's still unidentified body had been found days before, near the edge of the West Side Highway.

15

FOR SEVERAL NIGHTS DELANEY sat in the crook of the curved bar and alternated J&B with Heineken, smoked, talked sports to the bartender, chatted amiably to the waitresses, asked solicitously about their families, their feet. At the beginning and end of each set he sent a large Macallan down to the piano player, who gave thanks with a trill of the right hand and a nod of the head. When Connie sang he sat perfectly still, silent, eyes sometimes closed but mostly open, listening as if she were Billie, as if she were Ella, as if she were Sarah Vaughan. In her dressing room there were flowers, there might be champagne; before each show a line of sweet cocaine.

Connie, unnerved at first, accepted, relaxed: all she had to do was turn up on time and sing, let Vincent take care of everything else. The way it used to be. And as she relaxed her voice gradually became more supple, regained its sense of swing.

Changed after the final number, more than polite applause, she and Delaney would eat supper somewhere quiet, expensive: steak, fish, roast sirloin of veal. Back at the hotel, when she stepped out of her clothes, tied up her hair and showered, he would watch her, ribs against wet skin—Charlotte Rampling in *The Night Porter*—all she lacked, the numbers, blue and faded, tattooed along her arm.

Sometimes they made love, sometimes it was enough for him to listen to her breathing, its soft and urgent fluttering.

Daytimes they rose late, ate breakfast in their room, Delaney swam in the hotel pool; most afternoons they would drive out to this or that mall and catch a movie, a little shopping perhaps, then back to the hotel, a nap before getting ready for the evening.

'Hey!' Delaney said suddenly. He was sitting across the room, reading a fat book about Kubrick he'd bought that day. Connie lay dozing beneath a sheet. 'Hey!' startling her awake.

Turning, she pulled the sheet automatically across her skimpy breasts.

'I was just thinking, you remember when we first hooked up together, how it was? How we'd spend most of the time together, just the two of us. You remember that?'

Connie remembered.

'This coupla days, it's reminded me, you know?'

'I know.'

'How good that felt. How much I liked that.'

Laying the book aside, he crossed the room and stood at the end of the bed. Connie's foot, slender, poked out beneath the edge of the sheet and, reaching down, he began to stroke it, his thumb rolling back and forth across the small and fragile bones, while his fingers massaged the soft circle of flesh beneath.

Yes, she remembered: she remembered how it was.

Back arched, her head leaned back against the pillow and she closed her eyes.

◆

Seattle. Seattle had been the first time and almost the worst: the first time she had met Delaney and where it had all begun. Connie pretty much at rock bottom—not the lowest she would get, the absolute depths, the dregs, that was still to come, days when her self-esteem would be measured in whether she could look into the mirror without flinching or throwing up, nights she could not say no to whichever low-life propositioned her, because she was afraid to sleep alone and, besides, what more did she deserve?

Now, a stag party aside where she had worn a garter belt and a child's pink party frock and sung 'The Good Ship Lollipop' out into a haze of cigar smoke, Connie had not worked as anything other than a waitress in ten months. Ten months and almost as many jobs. The most recent, and current, a seafood restaurant and oyster bar down near the waterfront, the kind of fake authenticity that appealed mainly to tourists: long, rough-hewn tables and red checkered tablecloths, sawdust on the floor. Connie worked eight-hour shifts, wore an apron and a push-up bra, what little cleavage she could muster adding to the size of her tips. Large black and white photos of Marlon Brando on the walls, cheap reproduction posters of Gregory Peck in *Moby Dick*, *Captains Courageous*, Alan Ladd in *Two Years Before the Mast*.

When Delaney came in he came in on his own, early forties he would have been back then, good suit and quiet tie, hair just so. Connie had taken his order for a dozen oysters, blue points, juicy as they come. A nod towards the name tag near her breast. 'Thanks, Connie.' Delaney, exercising his smile.

She'd smiled back automatically, returned to her Japanese and her Koreans, whole families of Germans, a smattering of Brits. When she picked up Delaney's check he'd left her close to forty per cent. Nice guy. Best part of an hour later, when she slipped out back on her break, there he was, chatting to one of the bus boys. By the time she'd tapped a cigarette from her pack he had his lighter in his hand.

'Thanks.' Connie leaned her head back against the wall and drew smoke deep into her lungs, holding it down.

When she looked he was still there, risking the soft leather of his shoes to the slop that ran, haphazard, between the stones of the alley floor.

'This isn't an accident,' she said, squinting at him through a veil of smoke.

'No.'

'So what do you want?'

'I have to want something?' Again the smile.

Connie shook her head and cracked a wry laugh. 'You're what? Late thirties? Forty? Not wearing a ring, but nowadays that don't mean a thing. Slumming it back here in a suit cost twice what I make in a week, more. Of course you want something. Question is what, I mean, exactly, and how much are you prepared to pay?'

The smile was still there, in his eyes. 'You don't exactly beat around no bush.'

Connie glanced at the watch on her wrist. 'You know how long I get for this break?'

'Prob'ly better than you.'

Connie raised an eyebrow questioningly.

'The restaurant business, it's what I do.'

'Then you know I've got time to finish this smoke, see to my face, take a pee. That's it.'

Delaney nodded. 'You're off when? Twelve?'

'Thirty.'

Delaney reached into the side pocket of his coat, slipped something into the palm of her hand. Connie's fingers closed around a square of clear plastic, not needing to look down, guessing what it contained.

'Help get you through the night,' Delaney said. 'You're not interested, let me have it back later. Either way, I'll be out front. Across the street. Okay?'

Delaney smiling as he walked away.

They went back to his hotel, high on the thirtieth floor with a picture view across the Sound, an expanse of darkness flecked with lights. They shared a joint, some wine, a shot of J&B, several lines of what Connie would have said was seriously good cocaine. The sex was fast and rough and then, when they woke again at three, half on the couch, half on the floor, spaced out and slow, and when she said, 'No, I don't do that,' he smacked her once across the face and, of course, she did it anyway. By morning there was very little pain.

He heard her singing in the shower.

'Hey, you can really carry a tune, you know that?'

There was a place he was buying into downtown, cash return on his investment aside, he got to book the acts that worked the lounge, all part of the deal. Within a week she'd thrown in her job waitressing and was rehearsing with a pianist, Delaney offering suggestions here and there, a few changes in her repertoire, something a little more modern to offset the Gershwin and the Kern: Art Garfunkel, Elton John, Burt Bacharach. He took her shopping, chose her clothes, Connie feeling like Michelle Pfeiffer in that movie. And the funny thing, by the time she was due to step out behind the microphone, that first night, she really believed in herself, her looks, her voice, what she could do.

Her body was her own and she gave it to Delaney, gratefully, each night to do with what he would. It would be nine months, almost a year, before he would snatch the rug out from underneath and send her hurtling down.

Now Delaney lay on the bed, watching her, always watching. 'You know,' he said, 'I have to go back to the city. Tomorrow.'

It was what she had been waiting for. 'Sure you do,' she said.

Delaney reached for her arm, circling it with his hand. 'End of the week, when you've finished up here. Come join me.'

'I can't.'

'Why not?'

'I just can't.'

'New York, it's where you should be.'

She wouldn't look at him. 'Not any more.'

Delaney's hand slid across her body to her breast. 'There's a spot opening up at the Mint.'

'What? Waiting tables? Checking coats?'

'Don't do that.' Anger, sharp and sudden in his voice.

'Do what?'

'Put yourself down.'

'Oh, Vincent.' Slowly, she lowered her face against his chest.

'Say you'll come.' Delaney stroking the back of her neck, her hair.

'I don't know.'

'The apartment, it's getting out of hand. Needs a woman's touch.'

She levered herself away and looked into his eyes. 'What happened to Diane?'

'Who?'

'Diane, isn't that her name?'

Reaching forward, Delaney stroked Connie's hair away from her face. 'What do you know about any Diane?'

Connie arched her head back and his hand fell away. 'This guy I bumped into, a horn player . . . Ypsilanti, somewhere, I don't remember . . . he said you were living together, you and this singer.'

'Maybe.' Delaney shrugged and smiled and reached for her again.

'So what happened to her?' Connie asked. 'Diane?'

Delaney kissed her shoulder, letting his tongue work along the bone. 'Don't ask.'

'But . . .'

'Just don't, okay? You don't want to know.'

One hand hard against her spine, he kissed her mouth, holding her there until, his fingers sliding down, she kissed him back.

16

SLOANE WOKE LATE THAT morning, his head, for some reason, laboring under an ache that was slow to dissolve; showered and shaved, he lifted a fresh shirt, blue cotton, from its hanger and pulled on the same pair of faded jeans. At the French Roast he waited for a favored window seat, then sipped strong espresso while surveying the menu, eschewing finally the healthier options of granola with fruit and yogurt or McCann's Irish oatmeal for a tomato Gruyère omelette and a side order of sourdough toast. Around him a smattering of people, sitting alone, folded back the pages of the *Times* or leaned their heads towards a book, clearly settled in for the long haul, while others, the majority, bustled through their breakfasts amidst perky conversation and pushed back out again into the working day.

Jake Furman had furnished Sloane with several slender leads, numbers he might call, places where Connie might have worked in the past. Aside from that he was thrown back, pretty much, upon his own devices, the pleasure of being back in the city annulled to some degree by the uncertainty of what he was doing. Suppose he found her, Connie, this woman who might—or very well might not—be part his flesh and blood, a woman long grown into a life of her own, what then? Did he believe, as Dumar had suggested, in the jolt of recognition at first sight, in some intangible electricity of cells and genes that would catapult them into each other's arms? He did not.

And if what Valentina had told him about Connie—even half of it—were true, and her own mother's behavior towards her suggested that it was, was she someone with whom he wanted to become involved? But he had made a promise to Jane, a promise made as she lay dying, and he would honor it as best he could. Fulfill—what had Valentina called it?—his quest. Pass on to Connie her mother's love, the details of the will and walk away.

It seemed so easy, sitting there with his second espresso, replete, eyes caught every so often by the attractiveness, brisk and brittle, of some woman walking by, to decide that he would keep himself unto himself, apart, entire, separated from the world, if only by the thickness of plate glass.

Sloane asked for the check, placed money on the plate and left.

By early afternoon, two of Jake's suggestions had proved dead ends and the others were stalled in a tangle of message services and answering machines. Sloane bought a sandwich and coffee to go and took them into Washington Square, where the skateboarders were practicing their nifty moves on the steps around the central fountain.

When he got back to his hotel there was a message from Jake Furman to call him.

'Jake? Hi, it's me.'

'There's a pianist named Eddie MacGregor; he's got a trio at Zito's, just a block or so from where you're staying.'

'What about him?'

'He used to be married to Connie Graham.'

◆

Zito's was discreetly positioned midway along a largely residential stretch of West 22nd; easy to walk past if you didn't know you were looking. Even the poster advertising Live Jazz by the Eddie MacGregor Trio was restrained. Immediately inside, a long bar with well-stocked shelves and subdued lighting led towards an upscale Italian restaurant with linen tablecloths and the kind of prices that might be described as moderate by a man to whom money was little object. Piano, bass and drums were tucked in against the wall beyond the bar's final curve. Sloane gave the interior a quick once-over—one party of six, a few foursomes and half a dozen scattered couples—before taking a seat at the bar and ordering a Johnny Walker Black Label, straight up, with a water back. The trio were easing their way along 'On Green Dolphin Street', drums and bass reined in, the pianist giving it some attack with his right hand but not so much as to threaten anyone's appetite. Sloane took a small swallow from his Scotch and let it roll around his mouth. Dinner jazz, that's what it was.

A laugh rose up from one of the tables, a man's laughter, raucous and loud, fading quickly into the more moderate amusement of his companions. Almost without interruption, 'On Green Dolphin Street' segued into 'Autumn Leaves' and then 'My Heart Stood Still'. MacGregor was stockily built, ten years, perhaps, off Sloane's own age, with a full head of graying hair, which swayed side to side as he played; bassist and drummer, younger black musicians paying their dues, carried the rhythm with restraint and thought about the rent. More laughter. After a short, whispered conversation MacGregor slid into 'Waltz for Debby', the drummer sitting out; Bill Evans he wasn't, but he'd been drinking water from the same well long enough for it to show. Sloane signalled the bartender and eased his empty glass an inch or two forward. A ballad in three-four time: delicate and sweet.

This time the roar was part and parcel of an alcohol-fuelled tirade of humor and invective, which all but drowned out the filigree figures MacGregor was coaxing from the upper register.

Almost without knowing it Sloane was on his feet and striding back among the diners, one hand clamping down on the offending man's shoulder, the other reaching for the front of his suit jacket, hauling him to his feet with such force that his chair skidded out from underneath him and he stumbled forward, his face, startled and flushed with drink, finishing inches from Sloane's chest.

'Listen,' Sloane said.

The man raised a hand towards him and, contemptuously, Sloane knocked it aside.

'I'm just going to say this once. There are people here who want to listen to the music, who want it treated with respect. Nobody, nobody except perhaps your friends, wants to listen to you.' Sloane stood back, holding the man at arm's length. 'Shut up. Sober up. Or leave. Understood?'

Water dribbled from one side of the man's mouth as he nodded his head. When Sloane released him he lurched back on his heels, caught hold of the table edge, wobbled, then collapsed back into the chair one of his friends had providently retrieved and slid into place.

It was only in the instant before turning away that Sloane recognized the red hair and pale, now angry face of Rachel Zander, the dealer he had briefly met in the café bar in Jake Furman's building. A couple of waiters shepherded Sloane back to the bar from a safe distance. Without being asked, without speaking, the bartender freehanded more Scotch into his glass. The trio, who had fallen silent, launched into an up-tempo version of 'Hallelujah'.

When the party, six or seven of them, collected their coats some twenty minutes later, Rachel Zander peeled off from the group to confront Sloane at the bar. Sensing her approach, he swivelled round on his stool.

'Is that the way you normally behave?' Her voice was firm but clear.

'It depends.'

She reached past him and picked up his glass. 'On how much of this you've had?'

Sloane shook his head. 'It wasn't me who was out of control.'

'No?' Resisting the temptation to slam the glass down with a bang, she set it back carefully. 'Maybe you should think about that.'

She shot Sloane a final glance, turned on her heel and walked away.

The man behind the bar was cashing up; the youngest of the waiters, cigarette between his lips, was setting up for lunch. Sloane and Eddie MacGregor sat at one of the tables close to the piano: Sloane had secured a large espresso before the machine was switched off for the night; MacGregor was practically chain smoking Marlboros and nursing a club soda with ice and lemon, about all his liver would allow.

'I met her in Detroit,' MacGregor said, speaking of Connie, 'winter of eighty-four. Weather like to freeze your dick off. I was in the pit band for this touring production of *Pajama Game*. Mitzi Gaynor, can you imagine that? Cursing all the time in Hungarian and eyeing up the chorus boys. City to city, we'd pick up local musicians for the band, just the rhythm section stayed the same.' He paused for a drag on his cigarette. 'Anyway, there was this kid, played clarinet, tenor, you name it, talked a few of us into going along to this club after the show, regular jam session kind of thing.' He shook his head, remembering. 'I heard Connie's voice before I saw her. "Ghost of a Chance". You know, the old Billie Holiday tune. Voice sounded fresh, strong, maybe a little untrained. And to look at . . .' He waited till he was sure he had all of Sloane's attention; lit a new Marlboro from the butt of the last. 'Connie, in those days—she was what? Twenty-six? Twenty-seven?—she was a real looker. Flesh on her, not too much but where, you know, it counts. Sweet face. By the time she'd got to the end of the number I'd tipped the piano player the price of several drinks and slipped into his seat. Connie, she noticed right off, gave me this full-on, drop-dead smile. We got together pretty soon after that, made plans; I went out on the road with her, supper clubs, one-night stands. We got married, July of eighty-five. Philadelphia. Her mother, Jane, she came over for the wedding. Europe, that's where she lived, maybe still does.'

Sloane shook his head. 'She died. Not so long ago.'

'Sorry to hear that.' MacGregor sipped at his club soda. 'You knew her?'

'A little.'

'Then you know what a fine-looking woman she was. For her age. Any age. Her and Connie together, they could be sisters, give or take.' He shook his head again. 'Great-looking girls.'

A few more lights around them went out.

'The marriage,' Sloane said. 'It didn't last.'

'Six years, close on seven.'

'I'm sorry.'

'Yeah.'

'What happened?'

'The usual things. Boredom. Booze. Other women. Other guys.'

'Nothing else?'

'What more d'you want?'

Sloane looked at him and waited.

MacGregor reached over on to the table behind for a knife, edged his glass aside and brought the blade of the knife down in quick, short strokes on to the space in front of him. 'That sound, somebody once said it was the sound of the eighties. Connie was a cokehead before she could turn around.'

'You didn't approve?'

MacGregor gave a wan smile. 'At first I tried to keep up, you know, play along. But I realized pretty soon I didn't want to go where she was going. When she missed a date, third time in a row, I bailed out.'

'You keep in touch?'

'Not really. Used to run into her once in a while. This feller she was hanging with back then, Delaney. Looked out for her, managed her, I guess you'd say, he made it pretty clear he didn't want me butting in, talking about old times. I kept my distance after that.'

'You saying he threatened you?'

'Not in so many words.' MacGregor lifted the lemon slice with finger and thumb and set it between his teeth.

'And Connie, you really don't know where she is?'

MacGregor dropped the curve of lemon rind back inside his glass. 'The night after the divorce finally came through, she called me long-distance from Seattle. From all the background noise she was phoning from some kind of club; I don't know if she was working there or not. It doesn't matter. "You celebrating, Eddie?" she asked. "You celebrating, 'cause you should be. And you know what, Eddie, there's just one thing I want to say in honor of this occasion and that's fuck you. Fuck you, Eddie!" And that's the last conversation my ex-wife and I ever had.'

Sloane read the backwash of pain in Eddie MacGregor's eyes and wished he had never asked.

17

JOHN CHERRY, VESTIGES OF sugar round his mouth from the doughnut he'd just breakfasted on, ambled, loose-legged, towards Catherine Vargas's untenanted desk. A leather jacket, well worn, hung over the back of her chair. Her coffee cup was two-thirds full and faintly warm.

'Anyone know where Vargas is at?'

Of the half-dozen detectives present only one responded and that with a negative shake of the head.

'Vargas,' he tried again, giving it a little volume, 'she around?'

'Who knows?' called one.

'Who cares?' called another with a laugh.

'She's out back,' offered Brian Phelan, levering his chair on to its hind legs. 'The little girls' room. Anointing her tush.'

She was not. Catherine Vargas had stepped back into the room in time to hear Phelan's remark and now she stood well inside the door, fixing him with her stare. In the current climate she could have reported him for that remark, inappropriate language, seen Phelan relieved from duty pending disciplinary charges. And both of them knew it.

'Tell you what, Phelan,' she said, 'next time you can come with me, lend a helping hand.'

The laughter was general and on Vargas's side; Phelan, red-
dening, called her a name beneath his breath and tried for a smile.

'John,' she said, back at her desk, 'what can I do for you?' She
didn't know him well, John Cherry, not yet, but he seemed nice
enough. Quiet. He was younger than she, twenty-nine, thirty at
most, four or five inches taller. Brown hair neatly cut and a tendency
to wear loose-fitting suits in gray or blue. Today it was gray.

'You know the six-by-eights? The Jane Doe. West Side
Highway.'

'What about them?'

'I was taking a look.'

'And?'

'I think maybe I know who she is.'

Vargas's pulse quickened its pace. 'You just think or you're sure?'

'Pretty sure.'

Vargas had to stop herself taking a Kleenex from her pants
pocket, wiping the sugar from his lower lip.

It was a short drive down Seventh, hang a right on West 19th,
Vargas at the wheel. On the cross street they got stuck behind a
high-sided van with New Jersey plates unloading sheets of bevelled glass.

Cherry leaned to one side and liberated a pack of cigarettes from
his jacket pocket. 'You mind?'

Vargas shrugged. 'Your lungs, not mine.'

With a sigh he slipped the cigarettes back from sight and,
from his top pocket, drew a stick of gum. 'It's my last or I'd
offer you one.'

'Be my guest.'

Behind them horns blurted and rasped as the traffic backed up on
to the Avenue.

'How long ago d'you say it was you saw her? This Diane.'

Cherry nodded. 'Four or five months, could be more.'

'She was good?'

'She was okay. In a Peggy Lee sort of a way.'

94

Vargas resisted asking him what he was doing, a guy his age, relating to Peggy Lee. Unless it was one of those gay icon kinds of thing. Julie Andrews. Petula Clark. Long gloves and loud voices. Show tunes and chiffon. Liberace, for God's sake.

She looked across at Cherry as he peered out through the car window. Maybe he wasn't gay at all. Another rumor bent out of shape. Living with his mother out on Park Slope no more than a way of saving on rent. As the truck in front lurched forward and she released the brake, she gave him another glance. Just as well, she thought, he wasn't sporting a moustache.

The associate manager of the Manhattan Lounge was sitting at the bar in shirtsleeves, supervising morning cleaning from behind the pages of the *Daily News*. Disinfectant and last night's stale cigarette smoke hung in the air. The radio playing Bill Withers's greatest hit was a millimeter out of tune.

He looked at their shields without surprise, gave his name as Howard Pearl; half listened to Vargas's question and looked at Cherry when he replied. 'One night she's here, the next she's gone. A no-show. I'm stuck with a band, no singer. Like fries and onions, no fuckin' steak.'

'She didn't call?' Vargas asked. 'Give a reason?'

'Didn't I just say?' Pearl replied testily. 'Didn't I just say?' he asked Cherry over her head. 'Vince, he was pissed as hell.'

'Vince?'

'Delaney. Vincent. Vince Delaney. They were shacking up together, him and Diane.'

'And when she didn't turn up, you thought what?' Vargas persisted. 'That she was sick?'

'I'm her doctor?'

'It didn't occur to you something might have happened to her?'

'Happened? What d'you mean, happened?' He looked past her at Cherry. 'What's she mean, happened? Happened how?'

'An accident,' Vargas suggested. 'Maybe something worse.'

'Hey, you!' Pearl called over his shoulder. 'Yeah, you. Luis, whatever your name is. You think that's what I'm payin' you for? Push the dirt around, one side of the floor to the other. And somebody turn that radio off, s'gettin' on my fuckin' nerves.' Deliberately he folded the newspaper closed, then folded it again. 'You want to know what I think? I think she went off with this guy.'

'Which guy is this?'

'This guy been showin' up every once in a while, coupla months now. Out of town, had to be. Sends flowers. Front-row table. Champagne. Wife, doesn't, you know, understand him. Don't put out no more, either. You know the kind. Expects Diane to blow him while he shows her pictures of his kids.'

'He's got a name, this other guy?' Cherry asked. 'Flowers and champagne.'

'I can get it for you, sure. All the times he called.' Pearl climbed down off his stool and set off towards the office, shirt sticking in damp patches to his back.

'The manager,' Vargas called after him. 'Delaney? We'll need his address and phone number as well.'

'Luis,' Pearl shouted as he crossed the room, 'will you for Christ's sake stop waving that mop around like it's a fairy fuckin' wand and apply some fuckin' force.'

◆

Delaney was sprawled out on the couch in his apartment with the blinds half drawn, watching a movie on TCM. *Dark Corridor*. One of those cheap quickies, black and white, likely got turned around in ten, twelve days. Gail Russell reading the warning signs a little too late as usual, anyone with half a brain knowing the only reason Albert Dekker's in the movie is to scare all kinds of shit out of her, frighten her off to the funny farm where her straitjacket awaits.

Delaney thinking he'd make a fresh pot of coffee, watch the movie through to the end then take a shower, walk, maybe, over to the park, stretch his legs some. Time enough later to make a few calls.

He was in the galley when the doorman rang, letting him know there were two police detectives on their way up to see him. Delaney tipped more coffee into the filter, added water and turned up the heat.

Delaney held open the door and stood back to let them enter. Cherry at her shoulder, Vargas's eyes passed quickly over the apartment. There was a kitchen area to the right, dining table and chairs beyond it, close by the window that ran all the way along the far wall. A half-glassed door on to the balcony. Left, a hallway led to what she assumed were bedroom and bathroom. On the wall behind the couch hung a framed photograph of a singer she failed to recognize. A film was playing, soundlessly, on the TV.

'Coffee'll be just a few more minutes,' Delaney said.

She looked at him steadily: artfully tousled hair, dark pants tight across the hips, bare feet, pink shirt with the top three buttons undone. Enjoying her gaze.

'You're obviously busy,' Vargas said. 'We don't want to take too much of your time.'

Delaney smiled. 'Irony. I like that in a woman.'

Cherry crossed behind her and feigned interest in the apartment block across the street.

'Cream?' Delaney asked. 'Sugar?'

'Diane Stewart,' Vargas said.

'What about her?'

'How would you describe your relationship?'

Delaney grinned. 'In a period of change.'

'Meaning?'

'You ain't gonna find her toothbrush in the bathroom any more; I cleared the closet of her clothes. Haven't seen her in eight or nine days.'

'Which?'

'Eight.'

'And that was where?'

'Here. The apartment. Here.'

'What happened?'

'Happened?'

Delaney's eyes angled again towards Cherry, who was trying to read the titles on the bookshelf. *Why Sinatra Matters. The Sound of the Trumpet.* A biography of Dean Martin. A couple of encyclopedias of film.

'Doesn't say much, does he? Your friend. Leaves most of the questions to you. Seniority, I guess that'd be. Experience.'

'What happened?' Vargas asked again. 'Between you and Diane.'

Delaney gestured outwards with the both hands, palms up. 'We had a fight.'

'A fight?'

'She'd been seeing somebody else. I found out. Confronted her. After a lot of screaming and shouting, she storms out. Since when, *nada*. She didn't call, she didn't come by. The end.'

'You hit her,' Vargas said.

'No.'

'Of course you did. You hit her.'

'No.'

'You said, "We had a fight."'

'So?'

'A fight.'

'It's just an expression. A word.'

'Which means hit, which means slap.'

'Which means argue, which means disagree. Ask your pal. There's a dictionary, get him to look it up.'

'What did you fight about?' Vargas asked.

'I told you, she was seeing someone else. Screwing him in his hotel, then sneaking back here.' Delaney's eyes were diamond hard. 'I didn't hit her, but there's not a man'd blame me if I had.' He was looking at Cherry now, a look then away. 'The coffee,' he said, turning towards the galley. 'It'll be brewed to hell.'

'Black,' Vargas said. 'No sugar.'

'White,' Cherry said. 'Two sugars.'

Vargas waited until Delaney was on his way back. 'We found a body,' she said. 'It might be Diane.'

Delaney barely faltered as Cherry moved across and took the cups, passed one to Vargas and kept the other for himself.

'You said might,' Delaney said.

'Whoever this is,' Vargas said, 'she was pretty badly beaten. Injuries to the face as well as the body. Identification won't be easy.'

He stared at her a moment, letting it sink in. 'You want me to identify the body?'

'Yes.'

Delaney seemed to give it thought. 'Sure.' He tipped a measure of Scotch into his own cup and when he offered the bottle to the two detectives both shook their heads.

'One thing I'd like to ask,' John Cherry said. 'When she didn't come back, get in touch, why didn't your report her missing?'

Delaney rolled the doctored coffee round his tongue. 'I didn't think it was the thing to do, phoning the police because your woman left you for someone else. After all . . .' looking directly at Vargas now '. . . it's not a crime.'

18

IT WAS COLD. NOT cold enough to freeze out the sour-sweet smell of the recently dead, but enough for Vargas to zip her jacket up to the collar, push the collar up against her neck. Cherry stood beside her, hands in his pants pockets, chewing a fresh stick of gum he'd picked up on the way. Delaney had excused himself and changed into a dark suit, two-button, cream shirt, deep maroon tie. He was showing respect.

'Okay?' the attendant asked.

'Okay,' Vargas replied.

A shiver of metal on metal and, covered by an off-white sheet, the body slid into view. Vargas glanced at Delaney and his expression showed nothing at all.

The attendant gripped the sheet edge between forefinger and thumb. 'Okay?' he said again.

Vargas nodded and the sheet was snapped back.

Delaney blinked. Stepped forward. One pace, two and then a third. Whoever had worked up the body had sewn up the vertical incision with more than usual care; the face lay angled to one side, one eye closed, the features somehow misaligned.

'That's her,' Delaney said. 'Diane.' His voice was level, betraying no emotion.

'There's no room for doubt?' Vargas asked.

Slowly he turned to face her, hands down by his sides. 'Not a fucking one.'

Diane had family living up in Massachusetts; Delaney couldn't remember the name of the town, some pennyante little place, show him a state map and he'd pick it out. Parents, an aunt maybe; once in a while she said something about a brother living out on the coast. He didn't get the impression any of them were what you'd call close.

'And you?' Vargas asked.

'What about me?'

'Yourself and Diane, you'd say you were close?'

Delaney's shoulders rose and fell. 'You live with someone— what?—best part of a year. Hear 'em break wind, hear 'em snore, you pull their hairs out of the shower—yeh, I'd say we were close.'

'Only you don't seem . . .'

'What? Cut up? Depressed? You want me to throw some kind of a fit? Break down? Say I'm sorry, I should've kept my hands to myself. That what you want, huh?'

'Is that what happened?'

'Not keeping my hands to myself?'

'What you said.'

'I already told you.'

'Tell me again.'

'I never laid a hand on her, not a finger. Not then, not ever.' He leaned a little towards Vargas, arms resting on the table edge. 'Listen, one thing I know, one thing I've learned, this life. I know how to treat a woman, you know what I mean?'

'That's why she was leaving you?' Vargas asked.

Whatever was going on inside Delaney's head, he held her gaze, didn't let it show. 'You want to know why she was leaving me, what I think? I think she's met a guy, money creaming out his ass, figures she's had enough of workin' seven nights a week singing the folks who live on the fuckin' hill, she's gonna go off with this guy to some island, Hawaii, wherever, sit around drinking vodka martinis and getting fat.' Delaney spread his fingers wide across his thighs, looked at Vargas and Cherry both. 'I guess it didn't work out like that, huh?'

'Hawaii,' Cherry said, 'that's where he was from?'

'How the fuck would I know? I don't even know his fuckin' name.'

'Baldry.'

'What?'

'Kenneth Baldry.'

'That's his name?'

'Yes.'

'What kind of a fuckin' name is that?'

They were in a small room along the corridor from the lieutenant's office. Metal chairs with canvas seats and backs, a single table replete with the obligatory scuffs and scars. Two small windows that looked out on to industrial piping, wire mesh and more pigeon shit than you could spread across Yankee Stadium.

'When she left you, Diane, that evening,' Vargas said. 'That night. Where did you think she was going?'

Delaney shook his head. 'I don't know. I didn't care. I suppose now, thinkin' about it, thinkin' back, I guess I thought back to what's his name . . .'

'Baldry.'

'Yeh, Baldry. His suite in the fuckin' Pierre.'

'That's where he was staying?' Vargas asked. 'Or is that something like Hawaii, you just plucked out of the air.'

'I followed her, didn't I? That night at the club. This car he sends for her, like she's some high-class whore.'

'And if she didn't go there? Back to the hotel?' Cherry asked.

Delaney shrugged.

'How about friends? Girlfriends she might've stayed with?'

'I don't know. Yes. Maybe. Coupla girls from the club. Terri, I think that's what she was called. Worked the bar. Charlene.'

'You know where they live, this Terri? Charlene?'

'I don't have the least idea. Ask Howard Pearl.'

'You have the least idea,' Vargas put in, 'how Diane ended up off West Side Highway, the way she did? Beaten up the way she was? Dead.'

Delaney looked at her evenly. 'Not one.'

'And you don't care.'

'Look . . .' Delaney's arm moved fast, fast enough to make Vargas flinch. 'Look . . .' His finger pointing at the center of her face. '. . . when she lived with me, Diane, I looked out for her. I did what I could. Treated her good. When she left . . . What happened then, that's down to you, the pair of you, your concern, not mine. We understood?'

Vargas waited till the finger was withdrawn, the hand dropped down. 'Yes,' she said. 'We're understood.'

'Then I can go? Because I got calls to make, business to take care of, things needing to get done.' He was on his feet already, Vargas and Cherry following suit.

'These things,' Vargas said, 'they involve you leaving the city, you should be sure let us know. Once we've chased a few things down, we're going to want to be talking to you again, there isn't any doubt.'

Delaney smiled his slow smile. 'Something to look forward to. Both ways.'

◆

'You like him for this, don't you?'

Vargas looked up from her plate. The diner was down to a third full, far side of the lunch rush, one of the waiting staff relaxed enough to whistle 'Daniel' as he cleared tables. Vargas had never really got Elton John, hadn't seen the point.

'You all through here?' the waiter asked, indicating the sesame bun Vargas had carefully removed from around her burger, half an acre of coleslaw, a large dill pickle still untouched.

'Thanks. Sure.'

Cherry was still eating his way through apple pie, whipped cream.

'Any more coffee?'

'Please,' said Cherry.

Vargas shook her head.

'Delaney,' Cherry said again, once the waiter had moved away. 'You like him for this.'

'Don't you?'

They had already contacted the police department in Winchendon, close to the Massachusetts–New Hampshire state line and by now Mr and Mrs Stewart would have been informed about their daughter's death. The management at the Pierre had hesitantly furnished Kenneth Baldry's Phoenix address. Cherry had spoken to one of the local detectives, man to man: if Baldry were married, no sense unnecessarily fouling his nest. The detective would ask around, call back. Later Vargas and Cherry would go back to the Manhattan Lounge and enjoy more light-hearted banter with Howard Pearl, gain access to the staff records, begin making calls, knocking on doors.

'You think things got a little too physical?' Cherry asked. 'Out of hand?'

'I can see it happening.'

Cherry thought he could too. He stirred sugar into his coffee, ate a piece more pie.

'He must have a vehicle, right? Parked somewhere.'

'Delaney? Chances are.'

'I'd like to get a good look inside.'

'You think he drove her out to the Highway, dumped her there?'

'I think it's a good possibility.'

'His own car?'

Vargas shrugged. 'What else is he going to do? Call a cab?'

Cherry shook his head. 'Any chance you're right, he'll have had it stripped down, cleaned, sparkling like new.'

'So what are you saying, we should take his word, let it go?'

'What I think,' Cherry said, 'we should talk to the lieutenant. See how he feels about the two of us flying out to Phoenix. See how this Baldry shapes up, face to face.'

Vargas nodded, liking the way he was setting his own agenda, not too pushy, reining her in. 'Phoenix,' she said. 'Shouldn't be too hot, this time of year.'

19

THE TEMPERATURE HAD DROPPED at least five degrees. Sloane stopped for coffee near the corner of 22nd and Tenth, and pulled from his pocket the battered copy of *Another Country* he'd snapped up from a pavement entrepreneur on Sixth Avenue.

He had seen Baldwin once, the writer back from Paris and holding court in the White Horse Tavern, a small, bug-eyed man with a lustrous smile, who smoked continuously through a shiny holder and preached the gospel of black liberation with a logic and inevitability that to the nineteen-year-old Sloane had been both stirring and chilling in its implications. Ten or so years later, when the cities of America were burning, Sloane, from the relative safety of England, had recalled Baldwin's words, vividly remembered the occasion.

Now he finished the first chapter of the novel, turned down the corner of the page, left a mixture of dollar bills and quarters on the table and continued westward.

Rachel Zander's gallery was on the first floor of yet another warehouse conversion, the space divided into three rooms with a partly shielded office space at their center. Near the head of the stairs a young woman with silver close-cropped hair and a series of overlapping gold earrings sat squinting into the screen of a brightly colored VDU. A short sequence of dialogue, muffled, was being relayed from the video installation in the middle room. The same words, over and over. *He'll kill us if he gets the chance. He'll kill us if he gets the chance.* Through the opening to his right Sloane glimpsed a larger-than-life image of a young girl in a white dress standing in front of a computer-generated cornfield, crows circling. *Conversations with the Dying.*

'How may I help you?'

Sloane turned. 'I'd like to see Rachel Zander.'

'Is she expecting you?'

'I shouldn't think so.'

The receptionist blinked. Sloane stood his ground. 'Who might I say is calling?' There was something European in her voice, a stiffness lodged like phlegm at the back of the throat.

'A friend of Jake Furman's,' Sloane said. He had seen Jake's name lower-cased in green alongside the entrance, a list of the gallery's sometime clients: Jake nestling somewhat incongruously between Lucian Freud and Andreas Gursky, keeping company with Ellsworth Kelly and Sam Taylor-Wood.

'I'm not sure if Ms Zander's here at this moment,' the receptionist said. She reached for the phone and punched in a number. Beyond her, Sloane could see Rachel's hair, red against the pale wood of the office furniture.

After a brief conversation the receptionist replaced the receiver. 'If you wouldn't mind waiting?'

'Not at all.'

'Can I get you anything? Coffee? Juice?'

Sloane shook his head. 'Thanks, I'm okay.'

He wandered through the first two rooms into the calm of the third: cool abstractions in muted blues and grays. Sloane supplied the soundtrack for himself, Chet Baker in Paris: 'I'll Remember April'; 'Tenderly'.

'Hello.'

At the sound of her voice Sloane turned. Rachel was wearing a loose-fitting cream dress, slit high at the side, lilac pumps with a low heel; lipstick two shades lighter than her hair.

'I came to apologize,' Sloane said.

'Fine.'

Someone came several paces into the room, hesitated, coughed and then withdrew.

'Was there something else?' Rachel asked.

Sloane shook his head. 'No,' he said.

Still neither of them moved.

'My friend,' Rachel began. 'At the restaurant. Maybe he was a little out of line.' She shrugged. 'Wine, it affects different people in different ways.'

'So I believe.' Sloane smiled with his eyes.

'Look,' Rachel said quickly, 'Jake didn't send you, did he?'

'Send me?'

'Yes, you know. Send you to do this.' She laughed. 'Jake, he's forever trying to set me up.' She laughed again, unimpeded, drowning out the sound of murderous voices from the adjacent room. 'Jake doesn't take celibacy lightly, not even other people's. I think he finds it threatening.'

'And that's what you are? Celibate?'

'Just at the moment, yes.' A smile lingered at the corners of her mouth.

'Then it's by choice,' Sloane said and grinned, and for an instant Rachel saw him as he must have been years before, attractive and winning. Boyish, even.

'In this town,' she said, 'once you've passed a certain age it's difficult to find a man who isn't gay or married. Or both. Either that, or they're so seriously screwed up by something in their past it's not worth bothering.'

'Right.' Sloane drew a breath. 'You seem to have all that pretty well worked out.' A quick half-smile and he was turning away.

'There's a place called the Chelsea Commons, right around the corner from here, 24th and Tenth. I'll see you there at six. Six thirty. Up front, near the bar. Okay?' Without waiting for his answer Rachel pivoted on her heel and walked away.

◆

The Commons was across the avenue from a garage and a car wash. A waitress in fishnet tights, high boots and a skimpy black and white print skirt moved unsmiling between crowded tables. Rachel was sitting on a stool at the bar, laughing with the white-shirted bartender.

Sloane crossed the stained boards into the space beside her. 'Sorry if I'm late,' he said.

Rachel raised a hand to smooth the hair away from her face. 'I was early.' There was a wineglass in front of her, barely a quarter-inch of wine remaining. 'Harry,' she said, pushing the glass towards him, 'I'd better have another one of these. And my friend will have . . .' She looked at Sloane enquiringly.

'Black Label,' he said.

'Straight up or rocks?'

'Straight up. Water back.'

When Harry tilted the bottle, it overflowed the measure generously. He scooped two ice cubes up into a tall glass, two-thirds filled it with water and set it down alongside Sloane's Scotch.

Rachel was drinking Sauvignon Blanc.

'So,' she said, 'tell me how you know Jake.'

For the next half-hour they swapped small parcels of their lives, Sloane's late teens in Chicago, his days at art school, Rachel's obsession with horses growing up in Kentucky, her student days at Bennington. Nothing awkward, nothing difficult, no hard moves.

'And do you still paint?' Rachel asked.

Sloane shook his head.

'Not at all?'

'Not really.'

She let it lie. 'So what do you do?' she asked.

Sloane angled his head towards her and smiled. 'This and that.'

'Why all the mystery?'

'No mystery. I used to work in an auction house in London. Since then . . .' He spread his hands, palms up.

Rachel nodded and looked around.

The waitress leaned past Sloane and slammed a tray down on the bar top. 'Another four Sams for those assholes on table one.'

Rachel raised a hand towards a group of people in the doorway and waved.

'Time for another glass of wine?' Sloane asked.

'Thanks, but no,' Rachel answered. 'I'm going across the street for dinner with some friends. The Red Cat.'

'Maybe some other time,' he said.

But Rachel's friends were already alongside her, fashionable and fashionably young, milling around and kissing air. When she introduced Sloane he had forgotten their names before the obligatory shake of hands and they his. 'Enjoy the rest of your visit,' Rachel said, before they swept her up and out the door.

Adding some bills to those Rachel had left on the bar, Sloane swallowed down the remainder of his drink and followed them out on to the street. Turning left, he set off back towards midtown. If his conversation with Rachel had run on longer he might well have mentioned Jane Graham, said something of his reasons for being in the city. And it was Jane, more and more, who dominated his thoughts as, arms swinging loosely at his sides, he lengthened his stride.

20

A PARTY, JANE HAD said, University Place, why don't you come? Sloane had shaved, applied deodorant a little too lavishly and borrowed a button-down Brooks Brothers shirt from Stuart Hazel without giving away too much about where he was going.

When he arrived, music and laughter were bouncing through the open windows on the third floor. On the first-floor landing a couple were pressed into a hot embrace, the woman's face tilted upwards, pale in the half-light, lips parted and eyes clenched tight. A small knot of people had spilled out into the third-floor hallway and Sloane excused his way between them and into the apartment, where he was enveloped in a fog of cigarette smoke and loud, over-lapping conversation.

Men and women, mostly men, stood shoulder to shoulder, back to back, leaned against the walls. Courtesy of a gramophone near the window, alto sax and trumpet were chasing down the chords of 'I Got Rhythm'. As Sloane squeezed his way towards the center of the room, a voice close behind him rose above the rest: 'All I'm saying, all I'm asking, right, imagine this is possible, you can have either Sal Mineo or James Dean, who would you fuck first?'

Someone had thrust a glass of wine into Sloane's hand and he drank some of this before making his way towards what seemed to be an adjoining room.

Here it was calmer, less crowded, a couple slow-dancing to a tune that was playing somewhere inside their heads. A small crowd of four or five was standing near the window, smoking and passing a bottle of brandy between them as they argued over the merits of a foreign movie Sloane had never heard of, let alone seen. And among the haphazard piles of coats strewn over the bed, several people sat or lounged, deep in conversation, one of them Jane Graham.

Seeing him, only moments after he saw her, she excused herself and slithered towards him, skirt riding high along her thighs.

'You came.' Happily, she took hold of his arm and then, not quite an afterthought, lifted her face and kissed his cheek.

'Yes, didn't you think I would?'

'I didn't know. I wasn't sure.' Her fingers squeezed his arm. 'I'm glad you did.' She looked at his glass askance. 'Swallow that down, or, better still, use it to kill one of Frank's remaining plants. Come over and have a real drink.'

Sloane followed her and perched, less than comfortably, on the edge of the bed while Jane introduced her friends in a blur of names which he immediately forgot.

'They're married,' she added of one couple, 'but what makes them so very different from most everybody else, they're actually married to each other.'

Sloane saw an open face and friendly smile, brown hair that was brushed forward over the man's forehead; his companion, Sloane thought, could have stepped off the cover of *Vogue*, her classic features framed by dark hair, her mouth the perfect mouth.

The man unscrewed the cap from a bottle of Dewar's and tipped some of the Scotch liberally into Sloane's glass.

'We were just discussing,' Jane said, 'who's likely to get selected for the big touring shows now that Frank's in charge.'

Seeing the confusion on Sloane's face, she said, with a nod

towards the main room. 'Frank O'Hara, it's his party. He's responsible for what the Museum of Modern Art sends overseas. So far this year there've been shows in Tokyo and São Paulo, and none of us has had a look-in.'

'And we're his friends,' someone added with a laugh.

'That's Frank,' someone else said, 'always bending over backwards to be fair.'

'Not an uncommon position for Frank,' another man suggested from the far side of the bed.

'Bitch!' Jane said, laughing just the same.

Smiling at Sloane, she caught hold of his hands. 'Come on, I didn't invite you here to spend all night on the bed.'

'That,' the Dewar's man said with a wink, 'is what she'd have you believe.'

There was live music now, saxophone, guitar and bass, and Jane, slipping her arms about Sloane's waist, steered him round the room to a slow ballad and then a medium-tempo blues. Sloane had swallowed down the whiskey too quickly after the wine and things were beginning to move through a slight haze. A handsome young man, not much older than Sloane himself, fair hair falling forward across his face, came up behind Jane and, laughing, stage-whispered something about 'cradle-robber' in her ear. Jane elbowed him playfully away and pulled Sloane closer.

When the music finished she refilled her glass with Scotch but Sloane, reading the warning signs, shook his head.

'Come on,' Jane said, 'let's get you some fresh air.'

If possible, the main room was even more crowded than before.

'We ought to say goodbye to Frank,' Jane said.

Cigarette in hand, wearing a pressed blue shirt, creased pants and grubby sneakers, Frank O'Hara was holding court in the furthest corner of the room. Seeing Jane Graham approach, he broke off his peroration on Orpheus and Eurydice to wrap her in a quick, warm embrace.

'Aren't you going to introduce me to your friend?' O'Hara remarked, stepping away.

'Not a chance.' Jane laughed and, seizing Sloane's hand, led him towards the door.

'Larry,' someone shouted in the hall, banging on the toilet door, 'whoever it is you're blowing in there, could you just speed it up a little.'

'Cocteau,' pronounced a young man on the bottom step, 'understand him, you understand just about everything.'

'I feel the same,' his friend said, 'about Judy Garland.'

Jane Graham led Sloane fifty yards along the street, pushed him back against the wall and kissed him on the mouth, her tongue pushing hard between his teeth.

21

VARGAS CHECKED HER WATCH for the third time in as many
minutes, the official at the desk repeating her final call. American
Airlines flight 732 for Phoenix leaving out of gate fourteen. Where
in God's name was Cherry? Vargas hefted her carry-on on to her
shoulder and, ticket in hand, moved towards the gate. One other
passenger, breathless, in front of her, she swivelled her head for one
last check, swore beneath her breath, then there he was, slender
and unhurried, raising a hand in greeting as he crossed the departure lounge towards her. John Cherry, wearing a lightweight suit in
pale tan, pink shirt, two-tone deck shoes and no socks.

'Vacation?' Vargas queried, eyebrow raised.

'More undercover.'

'Blending in with the natives.'

'Something like that.'

If boyish could be handsome, Vargas thought, he was handsome
when he smiled.

Settled into their seats, Vargas found her place in the battered
copy of *The Shipping News* she'd started half a dozen times and set
aside, while Cherry riffled through the pages of that morning's *New
York Times*. Neither of them was to read a great deal. Instead they

talked of families and music, favorite movies, what made you want to be a cop. Cherry drank Cokes, three, one after another, Vargas a diet Seven-Up. She offered him her complimentary pack of peanuts and he accepted gratefully, eating them after his own. Vargas had three brothers, two older, one—the baby—still in his teens, the result of a second honeymoon her parents had taken in Europe, conceived on a waterbed in Amsterdam, fifty dollars extra and worth every dime. Her mother taught school till she retired, her father, a police officer like his father before him, pushed papers across a desk in the Denver police department, answered the phones, a hostage to angina. Cherry's dad had gone on a fishing trip to Key West fifteen years ago and neglected to come back; his mother worked part-time as a paralegal, rented out rooms in their 1890s house in Park Slope, painted watercolors, volunteered at the Brooklyn Museum. He was an only child.

Vargas had danced through her adolescence to Earth, Wind and Fire, Sister Sledge, 'Young Hearts Run Free', Grandmaster Flash and the Furious Five. Sang herself to sleep at night with Gloria Gaynor's 'I Will Survive'. Cherry had accompanied his mother to Tchaikovsky and Brahms, to free lunchtime recitals for piano and violin; listened on headphones in his room to Bowie and Patti Smith, Lou Reed and Talking Heads.

Vargas's top three movies were *Aliens*, *The Philadelphia Story*, *Thelma and Louise*. Cherry owned up to *E.T.* and *The Man Who Fell to Earth*; wisely, perhaps, kept *Terms of Endearment* to himself.

When Vargas told her father she'd be treading in his footsteps, showed him the forms, he cried; Cherry's mother had begged him to reconsider, wondered just where she'd gone wrong.

The temperature at Phoenix airport was high eighties, the sky a pearly blue. The uniformed officer detailed to meet them wore a shirt several sizes too large and spoke with a slight but perceptible stutter: 'Andy J-Jackson.' His smile was slew-toothed but sincere. Out of uniform, any self-respecting bar would have refused him a drink without ID. It was good to know, Vargas thought, that local law enforcement was taking their visit so seriously.

♦

Kenneth Baldry's house was on the western edge of Scottsdale, a sprawling retro-adobe with pink plaster walls that toned judiciously with Cherry's shirt. Beyond some fancy fencing, automatic sprinklers pandered to swathes of lawn. Vargas spoke into the microphone embedded into the high-arched gateway, opened her identification for the camera's scrutiny. Red dust puffed up from the thinly gravelled path as she and Cherry walked, veiling their shoes.

Baldry was wearing a green and white striped shirt, casual trousers, leather shoes. From behind contacts his eyes blinked out into the light.

Vargas introduced herself and then John Cherry. 'We'd like to talk to you about Diane Stewart,' she said.

At first she thought Baldry hadn't heard or properly understood. But then he stepped back and ushered them inside, across a broad hallway and into a long split-level room dominated by a wall of uninterrupted glass. Brightly colored Navajo rugs on pale recycled boards, low settees upholstered in gray and cream. A laptop, slim and black, open on a long table of dark wood, inches thick.

'You said Diane . . .' Baldry began.

'You were friends,' Vargas said.

The tense of the verb hit Baldry like a slap. 'What is it?' he asked.

'I'm afraid she's dead.'

Baldry's arms moved away from his sides, flapped and were still; his mouth worked strangely, like a fish yanked into air. 'But how . . . ? What . . . ?'

Vargas outlined the bare details, all that, at that time, he needed to know.

Baldry lowered himself on to the cushions of the nearest settee and sat there, head down, arms trapped between his legs, fingers close to the floor.

'Can I get you something?' Cherry asked. 'Some water?'

'No, no, I . . . Yes, yes, perhaps. Thank you. The kitchen, it's over there, to the right.'

Vargas listened to the clink of glass, the quick rush of water from the tap; through the wide screen of window she watched a pair of small birds playing tag among pale shrubs. Baldry didn't move until Cherry returned.

Vargas gave him a little time: not too much. 'How would you describe your relationship with Ms Stewart?'

Baldry blinked and looked away.

'Friends?'

'Yes. Yes, I suppose . . .'

'More than friends?'

'Yes. I don't know. I mean . . . Yes, yes, I . . .'

'Lovers, then?'

'Look, do we need . . .' Baldry let the sentence hang. 'Yes,' he said finally. 'Yes.'

'You knew she was living with someone else?'

'Of course.'

'And it didn't matter?'

Baldry laughed, bitter and short. 'Of course it mattered.'

'To you? To her? To him?'

'I wanted her to tell him.'

Vargas nodded.

'I wanted her . . .' For an instant Baldry's voice caught in his throat. 'I wanted her to leave him, come out here. Live with me.'

'You loved her,' Vargas said.

'Yes.'

'And you wanted her to tell Delaney that?'

'Yes.'

'Perhaps she did.'

There was silence and then the sound of Baldry sobbing. Cherry waited, lifted the unfinished glass of water and held it towards him.

'Did she ever say anything,' Vargas said, 'might have suggested Delaney would be violent towards her?'

Baldry turned away to the window, stared out. 'She was bruised once, high up on her arm, what could have been fingermarks, and here . . .' With his right hand Baldry reached round towards his kidneys. 'In the small of her back. As though she'd walked into something. As if she'd been hit.'

'And Delaney had done this?'

'Yes.'

'She told you?'

'Not in so many words.'

'But you weren't in any doubt?'

'No. I don't think so. No.'

'And yet you were happy for her to face up to him alone.'

'What do you mean?'

'For her to face the music, tell this man you'd every reason to believe had been knocking her around that she was leaving him for someone else.'

A vein was pulsing against Baldry's temple, a small and frantic wing-beat against the paleness of his skin. 'It wasn't like that.'

'No?'

Baldry looked across at Cherry and Cherry looked away. 'She said she would handle things,' Baldry said. 'In her own time. And I respected that.'

Vargas stared at him for several seconds more, then turned away.

Cherry waited until she was by the window before sitting next to Baldry on the settee and taking the empty water glass from his hand. 'Can I get you anything else?'

Baldry shook his head.

'You're sure?'

'Thank you. Yes.'

Cherry gave it one beat, two. 'The last time you saw Diane, that would have been when?'

Baldry blinked and fidgeted with the front of his shirt. 'Saturday. The Saturday before last. The fifteenth, is that what it was?'

Cherry nodded.

'She came to my hotel after she'd finished at the club where she was singing.'

'Your hotel, that's . . .'

'The Pierre.'

'Yes, the Pierre. And she left there when?'

'Two thirty, three. Closer, I think, to three.'

'By taxi?'

'Yes. I wanted to go with her, but she said no.'

'And as far as you know she was going home?'

Baldry nodded.

'But you don't know, I mean, for certain that's what she did?'

Baldry fingered loose one of the buttons of his shirt. 'No. But I assumed . . . That's where she said . . .'

'Of course,' Cherry said quietly. 'Of course. And you didn't see her after that?'

'No, I said . . .'

'Or speak to her?'

'No.'

'And you left New York when?'

'Six o'clock that morning. The first flight out.'

Cherry nodded again and, with a glance towards Vargas, eased himself back along the settee.

'The incident with bruising aside,' Cherry said, 'from what you knew about their relationship, Diane and Delaney. Would you say she was frightened of him?'

Baldry didn't answer right away. 'Wary, rather than frightened. Yes, wary. That's what I'd say.'

'And when she said she was considering leaving him and coming here to live with you,' Vargas asked, 'you think that was serious?'

'Yes.'

'Something she fully intended to do?'

'Yes. Oh, yes. She was going to do it. She wanted to. It was just a matter of choosing the right time, that was all.'

◆

Outside, the sun was higher in the sky and the temperature seemed to have risen ten degrees. Jackson was sitting behind the wheel of his car, door pushed wide, smoking a cigarette. There were several fresh butts on the ground close by. 'G-get what you wanted?' he asked, just a slight stammer on the 'get'.

'Hell, no,' Vargas said.

'Maybe,' said Cherry. 'Up to a point.'

Jackson nodded as if he understood. 'You want to head right back to the airport or what? I've got instructions, take you pretty much wherever you want to go.'

It was almost two hours till their next flight.

'Do you suppose,' Cherry said, 'you could recommend somewhere we could get a bite to eat? Mexican, perhaps?'

Jackson grinned. 'Sure thing.' He tossed down the last third of his cigarette, worked at it a little with the heel of his boot, swung the door closed and keyed the ignition.

They had chicken fajitas with refried beans, guacamole and jalapeno sauce, Cherry and Jackson tearing into key lime pie while Vargas watched them indulgently over her second cup of coffee. The jukebox didn't seem other than ornamental, but the house tape served up Steve Earle and a little Lucinda Williams, Gram Parsons with Emmylou Harris and James Burton and, as they were leaving, Tish Hinojosa singing 'Esta Cancion'.

At the airport Jackson shook their hands enthusiastically and waved them through the gate; as the plane rose towards its cruising altitude, Vargas closed her eyes and left Cherry to stare out at the steadily disappearing scenery.

Alongside her, Cherry shifted balance. 'Way I see it, there's one window.'

'Philosophy, John?'

'Opportunity.'

'Uh-huh.'

'Delaney and Diane fight . . .'

'Like he said.'

'Either she storms back out or he shows her the door.'

'Maybe slaps her around a little first?'

'Maybe he does. Maybe not. But Diane, she makes her way back to the Pierre, she could be there by what? Four thirty? Four?'

Vargas nodded.

'Baldry's pleased to see her, overjoyed; thinks it means she's left Delaney for good and all, nothing now to stop her following him to Arizona, but that's not . . .'

'That's not what she says.'

Cherry nodded. 'Right. Say she tells him she's sorry but despite everything she's not about to follow through. Go with him. Baldry gets mad, can't understand, things get way out of hand. Next thing you know there's blood on the sheets, Baldry's got a body to dispose of before he makes his early flight.'

'You suppose they offer that kind of service at the Pierre?'

Cherry grinned. 'Body, sir? Certainly, sir. And would there be anything else?'

Vargas shook her head and leaned back in her seat. 'John, you believe any of that?'

'She could have gone back there.'

'And Baldry could have killed her?'

'Not really, no.'

With a small sound of exasperation Vargas fumbled for her book; Cherry browsed an article on e-commerce in the in-flight magazine. The drinks trolley came and went.

'How about this?' Cherry said abruptly.

Vargas rolled her eyes.

'Diane leaves Delaney's apartment, real pissed, upset. Goes for a walk, get it out of her system. Maybe she's foolish enough to walk through the Park. Gets attacked, mugged, things go too far. Whoever it is drags her into their car, tosses her out on the West Side Highway.'

Slowly Vargas shook her head.

'Okay, then. She leaves Delaney's place, jumps a passing cab, no idea where to go, winds up in midtown, over on the west side. Thinks she'll take a walk down by the river, clear her head. Crossing the highway, not really looking where she's going—wham!—sideswiped by a truck.' But she could see his heart wasn't in it.

'You still like Delaney for it,' Cherry said.

'More than ever.'

22

SLOANE HAD FINISHED *Another Country*, bought a Philip Roth, second-hand, and left it, largely unread and not quite accidentally, in a diner on the Upper East Side. At the International Center of Photography, high on Fifth Avenue, he spent an hour or so looking at the work of Eugène Atget, sepia-toned studies of Paris in the early years of the last century: shopfronts and shaded interiors, baroque railings, statues shrouded in mist. Zigzagging his way back downtown, he caught himself thinking of Rachel, wondering if he would see her again and surprised to find that, yes, he wanted to if he could.

Earlier in the day he had sequestered himself away with Jake's telephone and his blessing, doing his best to track down Connie through a network of club owners and booking agencies. At one time or another between 1995 and 1997, she had played dates in Dayton, Ohio, in Sacramento, St Louis and the outskirts of Chicago. The last confirmed gig Sloane could trace was a week's booking at the Doubletree Hotel in downtown Philadelphia. When she failed to show on the third night they cancelled her.

That was April 1998. Since which time Connie seemed to have dropped from sight, leaving Sloane like someone treading water, biding time.

After a couple of beers with Jake he made the short walk to the Zander Gallery.

When he arrived, Rachel was deep in conversation with a rain-coated man who seemed to be on the point of purchasing one of the larger pieces in the main exhibition, a computer-enhanced photograph of a closed casket on a barren stretch of seashore, mourners standing knee-deep in water. Sloane backed away, nodded pleasantly in the direction of the silver-haired receptionist and browsed through some back copies of *Modern Painting*.

Twenty minutes later Rachel was warmly shaking the man's hand and escorting him to the head of the stairs.

Sloane got to his feet. 'Successful?'

'I think so. He wants another forty-eight hours to think it over and meantime we'll hold it on reserve, but he's a good customer. He runs some kind of financial operation; offices near Battery Park. I think he likes to impress his clients.'

'You mean he leaves the price tag on display.'

'Not exactly.'

She was wearing a trouser suit in what Sloane assumed to be silk, somewhere on the black side of midnight blue. Her hair was tied back from her face.

'The other night,' Sloane said.

'Yes?'

He shrugged. 'It just didn't feel right.'

'I'm sorry,' she said. 'It was just a quick drink after work, that was all.'

'Yes, I know.'

'And you wanted it to be more.'

'Yes. No. Yes, I suppose so.'

She smiled again: a real smile, broad and warm. 'You're not very good at this, are you?'

'Aren't I?'

Rachel shook her head. 'And I don't know if, at your age, this kind of artlessness really works.'

'That's a no, then?'

'A no to what? I mean, exactly.'

'Dinner, maybe.'

'Maybe?'

'Definitely.'

The receptionist had left her desk and was hovering at the edge of Rachel's eyeline. 'All right,' Rachel said. 'Meet me here, say, seven thirty, eight. But now I really do have to go.'

Sloane waited until she had turned away, then headed for the street.

◆

'Why didn't you tell me about Jane Graham?' Rachel asked.

They were in Raoul's on Prince Street in Soho, the two of them seated at a table three-quarters of the way back. Dark wood, silver cutlery, dim lights.

'What about her?' Sloane asked.

Rachel tilted her head a fraction to one side and treated him to a look that hinted at exasperation. Her hair was down now, framing her face in a Dante Gabriel Rossetti meets Toni & Guy kind of way.

'We never had that kind of conversation,' Sloane said a moment later.

'Then let's have it now.'

She reached for the bottle of Shiraz but the waiter was there before her, refilling both their glasses and then stepping smartly away.

'All right,' Sloane said, 'what do you want to know?'

Rachel laughed lightly. 'Anything. Everything. Jake told me the basics this afternoon, how you two were the hot item of the day.'

'I don't know,' Sloane said, 'it's difficult to know where to start.'

'How about where you met?'

'The Five Spot. It was a jazz club, Cooper Square. It's not there any more.'

'And you were how old? Twenty, twenty-one?'

'Eighteen.'

Rachel whistled softly. 'So Jane Graham must have been in her thirties, early thirties?'

'Something like that.'

'Good for her.'

'You think so?'

'You bet. All these guys in their forties, fifties, older, schlepping around with some bimbo on their arm, young enough to have graduated alongside their daughters. Why not have a little of it the other way around?'

Sloane smiled his wry smile. 'You think that's what I was then, a bimbo?'

'A boy bimbo, sure.'

'Thanks a lot.'

'Oh, come on, Sloane. What do you think? She loved you for your brain, your grasp of foreign affairs? Maybe your art?' Rachel speared a piece of veal with her fork and left it uneaten while she drank more wine. 'You were cute, I imagine you were cute back then, tall, strong; at that age you could could probably make love—what?—three or four times a night.' Seeing the expression on his face, she stopped. 'Now you're upset?'

'No.'

'Offended.'

'No.'

'Oh, God, Sloane, you loved her, didn't you? Of course you did. And you thought that she loved you, at least you wanted her to.'

'It doesn't matter,' Sloane said, not looking her in the eye.

'No, it does.'

'Look, let's forget it. Let's talk about something else, anything, the weather, the price of real estate, the Davis Cup, the . . .'

'Stop,' Rachel said. 'Just stop.' And then, 'What happened? When it finished, what happened?'

Sloane fiddled with his knife, readjusted the position of his fork.

'She went to France,' he said quietly. 'She got on a boat and went to France.'

'And that was that, the end?'

'The end, yeah. Pretty much.'

'You never saw her again after that?'

'Not till this year, no.'

'That's incredible.'

'Yes, maybe it is.' He paused. 'I saw her in Italy, a couple of days before she died. Held her hand. Watched her breathe. Just not for very long. Now can we talk about something else? And since you insisted this was all on you . . .' With one long swallow he emptied his glass. 'How about another bottle of wine?'

They didn't talk about the weather or the Davis Cup, but in a way they might just as well have done. They spoke about Rachel's gallery, Sloane's days at the auction house, a little about his trans-atlantic upbringing, Rachel's siblings, the quality of the food, the wine, how much longer Sloane thought he might stick around in New York. When Rachel said she was flying to London soon on business and Sloane said, 'Great, let's get together,' neither of them thought they really would.

It was a fine night, not cold, and they walked west along Prince Street until they came to Broadway, one short block to the corner of Houston, where Rachel caught her cab.

'Thanks for dinner.'

'My pleasure.'

Stranded between a goodnight kiss and shaking hands, they did neither. And Sloane, picking up the tempo, set off back towards his hotel, annoyed at the way the evening had gone, surprised at the extent to which Rachel's remarks about Jane had got under his skin.

◆

Jane's studio had been south of Canal, abutting the eastern edge of Chinatown, a cold-water loft she had originally shared with another artist; but since her work had begun to sell, to be seriously collected, she had taken on the burden of the rent herself, enjoying the privacy, the luxury of space. Most days she would rise early and walk towards the river, either passing in the shadow of the Brooklyn Bridge, or going up on to the bridge itself and far enough along the walkway to see the fish market on Fulton Street, the ferry terminal, the whole Lower Manhattan skyline. When the wind blew from the south-west she could smell the money accumulating on Wall Street.

Back in her studio she would set her battered coffee percolator on the stove while she washed, combed and brushed her hair. Wearing paint-spattered Levis several sizes too large, belted at the waist and rolled over at the ankle, a man's plaid shirt, tail out, buttoned over a white vest, her feet bare, she would pace between several stretched canvases in different stages of completion, coffee, warm and slightly bitter, cupped between her hands.

She had totally forgotten, this particular morning, concentrating on a large, rectangular painting that was relatively new, still finding its shape, its form, that she had said to Sloane, a moment between kisses snatched, reckless and laughing, out front of the Cedar Bar, 'Sure, come by, see where I work' and tattooed the address in ink along his arm.

And there he was, wide-eyed and tousle-haired, clutching a bag of sweet buns he'd bought from a Chinese bakery on Pell Street, wearing workman's dungarees and a torn blue shirt that matched the color of his eyes.

No way of disguising from him the surprise, the momentary annoyance that fired across her face.

'OK,' she said, stepping back. 'Come in. Come in and sit over there.' Pointing to the far side of the room. 'Sit there and don't say a word.'

So Sloane sat for almost two hours, shifting his weight from side to side, from one buttock to the other, slowly stretching his legs, then drawing them up to his chest, as Jane, blanking him out, worked on her painting, moving, moving, rarely still, pacing, walking back and forth, in then out, close and away. The wide canvas stretched across its heavy wooden frame and stapled fast, covered then with white paint applied in broad strokes, a white, stippled ground upon which she was adding blocks of color, gradations of alternating blue and yellow shading down to mauve and orange, their edges blurred and softened with a swab of cloth soaked in turpentine, each balanced in relation to what was immediately above and below, and to the painting as a whole.

Jane darting quickly forward now, a fast sweep of brush from right to left, a slash of darkling, curving red; and then another, finer, ending in a filigree of scarlet flecks like tracks in snow.

And Sloane, watching, in thrall, as the painting grew, took on a life, each element held in tension with the rest but all, somehow, and this the real art, the artistry, in harmony. Something he would rarely, if ever, himself achieve. Not like this. Beautiful. Thrilling. The act, the thing, the thing itself.

'Oh, shit! Shit, shit and shit!' Jane threw her brush aside, reached for an oily rag and wiped her hands.

'What?'

'You. Shut up.'

'But it's amazing, it's . . .'

'I said, shut up!'

Sloane scrambled part-way to his feet and with one bare foot she pushed him back, forfeiting her balance as she did so and stumbling, so that he reached up and grabbed her arm to prevent her from falling, but fall she did, awkwardly across his body, pinning his ankle painfully beneath him, her face close to his, his mouth, and suddenly she was kissing him, the smell of linseed oil in her hair and on her finger ends. 'Christ, Sloane!' Hauling herself round until she was straddling his thigh, pulling at his shirt as she kissed his face, his neck, tugging it free so that she could drag her hands across his chest and sink her teeth into his shoulder, as all the while, inexpertly, he tried to tug her vest free from her belt; Jane laughing as she unsnapped the fastenings on his dungarees and wriggled back, yanking them down below his knees, his erection tenting up beneath his pants; Sloane speechless, flushed, attempting to pull her back towards him, till, evading his hands, with two quick movements she uncovered him. Dipping her head so that she could touch the tip of his cock with her tongue, her hand cupping his balls and sliding up the smooth skin of the stem. Moments after she touched him he came, splashing thick across the front of her vest, her breast, Sloane blushing deep red and stammering out apologies, as Jane ducked her head again and licked away one drop that had landed high on his own chest. When she flattened herself against him and covered his mouth with hers he could taste himself, salt and slightly sour, upon her tongue.

◆

When Sloane woke next morning, sticky with sweat, he had Rachel's name upon his lips, Jane Graham's body on his mind.

23

CATHERINE VARGAS WAS BEGINNING to feel more at ease in her new surroundings at the 10th Precinct. A few of the guys had asked her along to help celebrate someone or other's fortieth and, gross as the evening had progressively become, it had been good to feel included. Even Phelan, something of a throwback when it came to women and gays, had acknowledged her the other morning with more than a grunt. Just as long as he didn't start buttonholing her with his jokes.

Somehow, these last few days, she had found time to do her laundry, collect her dry cleaning, remember her nephew's birthday and phone her folks like a dutiful daughter should, skilfully negotiating the end of the call seconds before her mother raised the ticklish question of going to mass. More important still, she had all but finished negotiating the rental on a studio apartment on the Upper West Side.

Between working other cases she had tracked down Diane Stewart's ex-husband, living now in an upmarket suburb of Boston with the requisite wife and kids, and suitably disturbed at hearing of Diane's death without giving the impression it was going to cost him overmuch sleep. He had answered Vargas's questions politely enough and asked a few of his own; he and Diane had not set eyes on one another for close on ten years. Vargas had thanked him for his time and ran a check on him as much to keep the paperwork straight as anything else: it had come as no surprise to find he was clean.

She rechecked the forensic report in case there was anything she'd missed; scanned the solitary witness statement, the interview notes from conversations with Baldry and Delaney. That done, she counted one to ten, put the file aside, sent the computer to sleep, switched off the VDU and took a trip back to the Upper East Side.

When she returned, less than an hour later, there was a definite gleam in her eye.

'What?' Cherry said, glancing up from his desk.

Vargas looked back at him and grinned.

'You look like the cat that caught the mouse.'

'Could be.'

Cherry pulled across a spare chair so she could sit down.

'The garage joining Delaney's building, where he keeps his car—I just talked again to the guy on duty the night Diane disappeared. He thinks it's possible Delaney might have used the car twice that night.'

'How come, all of a sudden, he remembers it differently?'

'I pushed a little harder.'

'You leaned on him till he told you what you wanted to hear?'

'Absolutely not.'

'Okay.'

'Seems some nights there's a poker game in one of the other garages, along the same block. Our man, he sneaks across there, three thirty, four o'clock. Everything's quiet. Only when he comes back he thinks it's possible Delaney's car, it's in a different spot.'

'Possible?'

'Probable.'

'How long was he away?'

'He says no more than an hour. Time enough for Delaney to smuggle the body down in the service elevator, straight to the basement, through the rear doors and into the garage.' She paused. 'You think that's enough, raise a warrant, let forensics loose on the car? Bring Delaney in again?'

'No.'

'No?'

'Even if it's true, on its own it doesn't prove a thing. And if you're right about Delaney, the last thing we want to do, haul him in, watch him lawyer up, walk out again a couple of hours later, laughing in our faces.'

All of the shine had left Vargas's face.

'Maybe there's another way,' Cherry said.

'Which is?'

'For now, we forget about the car. File it away, future reference. What we do, dig a little into Delaney's background, finances, see what we come up with.'

'Old-fashioned police work.'

'Exactly. Except now we have PCs.'

Vargas stood and stretched both arms above her head. If she didn't get to the gym again soon her joints were going to be so stiff she'd be like the Tin Man in *The Wizard of Oz*. 'You know what worries me,' she said. 'If Delaney did do this, beat Diane Stewart to death and dumped her body, chances are it's not an isolated thing. He's done it before, beaten up on some woman. And he will do it again.'

◆

Connie switched on the TV and clicked it off again; after half a chorus of Ella's 'Night and Day', good or not, she consigned the disc to silence: vodka, peppermint tea; she lit a cigarette and stubbed it out. There was the newspaper, smoothed out on the kitchen work top after she had rescued it from the bin.

UNKNOWN VICTIM IDENTIFIED

The body of a young woman, found over a week ago alongside the West Side Highway, was confirmed yesterday as being that of thirty-six-year-old Diane Stewart, a nightclub singer who, until the time of her death, had been performing at the Manhattan Lounge. Police sources revealed that, although the most likely cause of death was being struck by a passing vehicle whose driver failed to stop, they have not, as yet, ruled out the possibility of homicide.

Connie reached for another cigarette.

Delaney's voice: *Don't ask. You don't want to know.*

She thought about the black bags stuffed full of clothing in the basement, waiting for the super to push them into the incinerator; the lipstick that had rolled down between the cushions of the settee, the hairclips under the bed.

Thought about the other women who had been a part of Delaney's life, some of them, the ones she knew about. The weekends in Baltimore or Philly, the sudden wayward flings in Vegas or Atlantic City, the countless one-night stands. Marks on his body where one or other had dug in her nails hard; once, a bruise that lingered like a stain upon his skin. Half-veiled hints at blows that had been struck, lessons forcibly taught and learned. And each time, when he had come back, half amused, contrite, she had closed her eyes and ears, shut out her fears, accepted him. From love and need or fear?

Drawing deep on her cigarette, Connie opened the bottle of Absolut and filled a shot glass to the rim. When Delaney's key turned in the lock the clear spirit splashed across the fingers of her hand.

'Hi, sweetheart!' Delaney called and then, seeing the open

newspaper, 'Been catching up on the news, I see.' And, reaching past her, he tore the page in half and half again, before screwing the pieces to a tight ball in his hand.

Ash spilled from the end of Connie's cigarette on to the floor.

'What?' Delaney said, moving close. 'You think that was anything to do with me? Yeah? That's what you think?'

Her eyes, the small tremor along her cheek, told him that it was.

'Sure, I admit it. I waited till she was crossing against the traffic and stuck my foot down on the gas. Knocked her flying, sixty miles an hour. Smack! There, you feel better now? Now you know the truth.'

Connie shivered and turned her back. 'Vincent, don't.'

'Don't what?'

'Don't tease me. Don't lie.' There were tears in her eyes as Delaney carefully folded back the collar of her shirt and began softly to kiss her neck, one hand reaching for her breast.

'Vincent . . .'

'Sshh.'

24

EDDIE MACGREGOR WAS SITTING in the lobby of the hotel when Sloane walked back in, mid-morning, MacGregor wedged into one of the low-backed chairs, uneasy, toying with an unlit cigarette.

'Let's go outside,' MacGregor said. 'I need a smoke.'

The pianist's hands were not quite steady as he struck one and then another match, his face the gray pallor jazz musicians often tend towards in daylight.

'Pal of mine,' MacGregor said, 'bass player, got a call last night. Could he do a gig, short notice, backing some singer, place in mid-town.' MacGregor inhaled deeply, holding it down. 'It's Connie.'

'You're certain?'

'Less someone else's lookin' to fuck up their career, using her name.'

'Where?' Sloane said. 'Where is this?'

'The Mint. On East Forty-ninth, between First and Second. Supper club. Nothing special.'

Sloane nodded, aware of the adrenalin jolting through his veins. 'Thanks,' he said. And then, 'You want to come along?'

MacGregor shook his head. 'Life's too short to go that route twice.'

◆

Connie stood, front and center, cigarette trailing an inch of ash in one hand, all but empty glass of vodka in the other. Her eyes were half closed, her back to the two curved tiers of empty chairs and tables, whatever was going through her mind at that moment hers and hers alone. The three musicians, piano, bass, guitar, waited, silent, in the cramped space towards the back of the stage. The bassist, Eddie MacGregor's friend, leaned against the piano's curve, while at the piano itself a youngish black man, head shaved, swayed the upper part of his body lightly side to side and resisted the temptation to touch the keys. Angled towards them, the guitarist, swivelling on his stool, made minor adjustments to his amplifier's controls, smoke from the cigarette fixed between the strings of his instrument rising in a slow spiral to the ceiling. It was a little after four thirty in the afternoon.

Delaney came through the doorway between the kitchen and the bar, pulled out a chair and sat down.

Connie opened her eyes. 'Okay,' she said, 'why don't we try that again? And Wayne . . . is it Wayne?'

'Wayne'll do fine,' the pianist said.

'Okay, let's take it up a tad this time, huh? We don't want everyone dropping off into their hors d'oeuvres.'

Wayne nodded at the other musicians, beat in time with the outside edge of his left shoe, and set off at a pace that had Connie waving her arms, ash falling across her clothes.

'Hey, hey! A tad, I said, not a fuckin' gallop.'

With a grin Wayne brought them in again, medium tempo, eight bars that ushered Connie into the melody, 'Day In, Day Out', the fifth time they'd run through the tune that afternoon without ever once getting it right. This was fine until they came to the bridge, Connie stumbling over the words and knocking the microphone aside, cursing as she stalked off the stage towards Delaney's table and slammed down her glass. 'I need another drink.'

'I know what you need,' Delaney said, even and calm.

'That asshole, he's fuckin' me around.'

'Wayne?'

'Yeh, fuckin' Wayne.'

'I don't think so,' Delaney said. He knew the last time Dee Dee Bridgewater had been in town and her regular pianist, the French guy, Eliez, had been taken sick, it had been Wayne she had asked for. Wayne, who had just come off a week at the Blue Note with Ron Carter's band and was only doing this gig because of what he owed.

'Don't you worry,' Delaney said, 'I'll talk to Wayne. Meantime, why don't you go back, check out your dressing room? Might find something, help the mood.'

As Connie slipped from sight, Wayne pressed his thumb up against first one nostril then the other, sniffed loudly and laughed.

Instead of laying out the two lines of coke on Connie's dressing table horizontally, Delaney had crossed them in the shape of a kiss.

◆

The door was open to the street and Sloane stood listening as the sounds spilled out, a guitar solo swinging to a close. Even before he had entered, all the way back along the street, his stomach had been alternately turning some crazy loop or clenched tight in a knot. And now, before he set eyes on her, there was the voice, taking up the tune from the beginning of the middle eight and riding it almost jauntily home. 'I Cried For You'. Pretty much the way Billie had sung it back in 1936, except there was no Johnny Hodges, no horns at all and the voice was lighter, thinner, distilled from a different draught of pain.

He had stared at Connie's picture, framed in the window—*Opening Tonite*—slender shoulders pale against the straps of a black dress, a face Sloane searched for signs of her mother and found in the eyes, the nose perhaps a little also, but certainly the eyes. For the rest, if this were to be trusted, Connie was thinner-faced, cheekbones sharp against her skin, closer to the Jane he had seen in Italy than the vivacious woman he had known in his late teens.

You loved her, didn't you? Of course you did. And you thought that she loved you, at least you wanted her to.

As the music started again Sloane eased the door wider and stepped inside.

Connie was leaning over the keyboard, talking to Wayne; the pianist using a pencil to make notations on the sheet music spread along the top of the piano; bassist and guitarist laughing quietly at something one or other of them had said. Wayne relaying instructions now, the others nodding as Connie lit a cigarette, moved towards the microphone and stared out across the empty room.

Watching, Sloane held his breath.

The first sound came from Connie's voice alone, an exhalation, one note sliding towards the next. The bass then, descending and ascending, a rhythm over which, wistful and slow, she drew the words. The guitar joining in, its chords adding texture, an extra bounce and spring, the tempo gradually increasing till, midway through the song, the pattern resolved and about to repeat itself again, the piano entered with a mazy, skittering run that buoyed Connie over the edge and carried her on, stronger now, towards the chorus end.

Standing at the back, in shadow, only the stage lights on, Sloane's mouth was dry, the skin at the back of his neck and along his arms electric and cold.

'Good, isn't she?' Delaney said, his voice barely above a whisper, and when Sloane, surprised, spun round, Delaney stepped out of the near-dark, not quite as tall as Sloane but thicker set, his suit expensive, tie just so, rings on the fingers of both hands.

Sloane nodded, said nothing.

'First show's at ten tomorrow,' Delaney said amiably. 'Come along, tell your friends.' Deft as a dancer, he swivelled sideways, allowing room for Sloane to pass.

Sloane didn't move.

'Okay,' Delaney said, smile still in place but impatience in the voice, 'you've had your freebie, now let's go.'

'I need to talk to her,' Sloane said. 'Connie.'

'You say.'

'I thought maybe after the rehearsal . . .'

'Anyone wants to talk to Connie, first they talk to me.'

'This is private,' Sloane said. 'Personal.'

Delaney looked at him carefully, studying his face. On stage the trio were working their way through a medium-tempo blues, Connie sitting on the edge of the stage, smoking, listening. Delaney gestured towards the lobby and, with one last backward glance, Sloane followed him back through the door.

'So what is it you need to talk about?' There were photographs on the wall behind Delaney, framed and signed, some beginning to fade: Nancy Wilson, Jimmy Scott, Freddy King.

'Her mother,' Sloane said.

'Her mother's dead.'

'And she knows?'

'Of course she knows.'

'Then it shouldn't be a problem, my talking to her.'

'About the money?' The beginnings of a smile now in Delaney's eyes.

'What money?'

'Whatever she left. The will.'

'I don't know anything about any money,' Sloane lied.

'Then what?'

'Messages she wanted me to pass on, things she wanted to say.'

'Shame she left it so fuckin' late.'

'She'd tried getting in touch before.'

'Then she should've tried harder.'

'Sometimes those things work both ways.'

Back inside the body of the club, Connie was singing again. Miles Davis: 'All Blues'. Sloane knew the melody, had never known it had words. 'Look,' Delaney said, changing tone, a reasonable man.

'Connie, hearing when she did, it came at a bad time. I'll be honest, I'm not sure how she felt. Whatever it was she kept it to herself. She's been goin' through some stuff, you know? Tryin' to put herself back together. This job here now, it means a lot to her, first time back in the city in I don't know how long. She's under a lot of pressure. This stuff you're peddling, opening old sores, it's not what she needs, okay?'

'Maybe that's for her to say, not you.'

Delaney stared at Sloane and Sloane stared back. Distant, the piano was rolling out a phrase, rubato, deep in the left hand.

Delaney's expression changed. 'You want to come in here, you pay your cover, listen to the show, eat your steak, whatever. That's fine. But you keep away from Connie. Right away. That clear enough?'

Sloane looked down at Delaney's right hand, which was pointing, fingers extended, towards the center of his chest. Gave him a look Delaney understood.

Slowly, Delaney stepped back and smiled. 'Maybe you'd be better off trying somewhere else. Stacey Kent's at the Vanguard; I hear she's pretty good.'

Sloane held Delaney's gaze for just long enough, turned and left, not looking back.

Fifty yards along the street he stopped and leaned sideways against the wall, eyes closed, hearing again the brittle emotion in the voice as he tried to recapture the movement of the hands, the face. Jane's daughter, yes, but his child? *When you find her, then you will know.* But what if you did not, for certain? And if he were not certain, why the chill in his belly, the trembling in his hands?

25

THE REMAINS OF A Chinese meal sat in its waxed containers on the table. Connie never liked to eat before a show; with Delaney it was the reverse. Wearing dark suit trousers and a pale blue shirt, he sat slumped in the armchair, fidgeting a piece of shredded pork from between his teeth while he watched a rerun of *The Crossing Guard* on TV. Jack Nicholson and Angelica Huston slugging it out as if they meant every word.

When Connie came in from the bedroom, still wearing her robe, he turned the sound down with the remote, bit his tongue about the time. Opening night and she was looking to be late.

'Okay, sweetheart?' he said, stroking her rear as he crossed to the drinks trolley, poured a small J&B for himself and for Connie an Absolut with a drizzle of tonic, a slice of lime. As many as half the apartments in the building opposite were brightly lit, no curtains drawn, no blinds—*Rear Window* without, as far as he could tell, the murder, the body in the trunk.

'Vincent?'

'Huh?' Turning to face her, reading the anxiety in her eyes.

'I don't know about tonight.'

Delaney set down the drinks, went slowly towards her. 'You know what Wayne said to me, earlier? You know what he said?'

'Uh-huh.'

'Said he'd no idea just how fine you were.'

'Then he's a liar,' Connie said.

'No, he's not,' said Delaney, who was.

Like stroking a cat, he felt the knots along her spine, taking pleasure from the way the skin slid over them beneath his fingers. 'It'll be better'n fine,' he said. 'It'll be terrific.'

Releasing her, he picked up her drink and took it to the kitchen for ice. Connie lit a cigarette and stood there, watching the screen: Nicholson loud-mouthing with his friends in some cheesy bar, jowly and overweight. Did he have to be that way for the part, she wondered, or was that how he really was?

Coming up behind her, Delaney slipped the glass down into her free hand.

'Who was that I saw you talking to earlier?' Connie asked. 'At the club.'

'Just some guy.'

'Some guy?'

'Some guy wandered in off the street.'

'That was all?'

'You know,' Delaney said, with a glance down at his watch, 'it's not that I want to hassle you or anything . . .'

'I know, I know, I should be getting myself in gear. Here . . .' Handing him the cigarette. 'Finish this for me. I'll be fifteen, twenty minutes, tops.'

Delaney knew that meant thirty, forty-five. He would phone ahead, warn them.

'Con?'

'Yes?' Her head poked back into the room.

'We're okay together, right? Back together and everything?'

'Sure.'

'Good,' Delaney said. 'That's good.'

As long as she believed it enough; as long as he could convince himself, keep things on an even keel. The last thing he wanted right now, the last thing he needed, Connie coming apart at the seams.

◆

Sloane caught the last set, Delaney nowhere to be seen.

Visibly nervous, Connie took the stage to polite applause, the club little more than half full. For the first couple of numbers she was uncertain, straining for effect, pushing her voice too hard; and even though she relaxed a little, by the time she thanked the trio for all their hard work, some thirty minutes later, Sloane had heard nothing to compare with the best of that afternoon.

Uncertain whether or not to go backstage, wondering if Delaney were in her dressing room, Sloane ordered another Scotch and waited. Less than fifteen minutes later Connie came back into the main room alone, intercepted a waitress on her way towards the bar, went to an empty table and sat down.

When the waitress had brought Connie's drink and a fresh pack of cigarettes, Sloane left his table in the upper tier, walked down the short flight of steps and across the floor. A ballad was playing through the house stereo, tenor sax and organ, and a couple were dancing in the small space in front of the stage.

Sloane stood alongside Connie's chair and waited for her to look round. So close, he wondered she couldn't hear the sound of his breathing. When she didn't move he bent forward and said, 'Do you mind?'

Taking her shrug for assent, he sat down. Up close, she looked tired, all of her forty-odd years. She'd started to wipe off her make-up, then changed her mind. There was a lipstick smear at the corner of her mouth and mascara smudged around her eyes.

'I enjoyed your show.'

'It sucked.'

'I don't think so.'

'What do you know?' She looked at him for the first time, little more than a glance. The flesh around her eyes was swollen and Sloane wondered if what had ruined her mascara was tears.

'You were talking to Vincent,' Connie said. 'This afternoon.'

Sloane nodded, thinking that's his name, Vincent. 'That's right,' he said.

'You had business?'

'Not with him.'

Connie glanced sideways, waiting for the pitch.

'It's about Jane,' he said, 'your mother.'

'What about her?'

'I was with her when she died.'

For a moment Connie looked as if all the air had been sucked out of her, cheeks hollow, lips apart. Then she tore open the seal on the pack of cigarettes, lit one with a match and, eyes closed, drew the smoke deep into her lungs. Sloane watched as she swallowed down her drink and signalled for another, vodka tonic.

'Not being able to see you, before she died. Talk to you. Know how you were. It upset her a lot.'

'I'll bet.'

'It's true.'

'So how come I didn't hear squat from her in ten fuckin' years?'

'I don't know.'

Connie looked at the wall.

'She asked me to find you,' Sloane said. 'Try and explain. Give you her love.'

'Fine,' Connie said. 'Fine.' Still not looking at him, refusing to. 'Consider it done. Now get out of here and leave me alone.'

'Look . . .'

'Leave me a-fuckin'-lone.' Her voice ragged and loud, and close to tears.

Sloane took one of the hotel's cards from his top pocket and wrote his name quickly on the back. 'That's where I'm staying. I'll be there for a few more days. If there's anything else you want to know about your mother, how she died, anything at all, you can reach me any time.'

Sliding the card along the table towards Connie's hand, he got to his feet. Delaney was heading for them from the far side of the stage.

'I thought I told you,' Delaney said, 'to keep away.'

'And I told you there were things I had to say.'

'Things to say? From her mother?' Delaney moved closer, his voice pitched low. 'I'll tell you this about her precious mother. When Connie needed her, really needed her, that bitch, what did she do? Spat in her face, that's what. And now you think she wants to hear a last few dying words?'

'Like I said before, I don't think that's for you to decide.'

In the corner of Sloane's eye, as he moved away, he saw Connie slip his card safe inside her pack of cigarettes.

26

CATHERINE VARGAS WAS WEARING a skirt, heavy blue
corduroy: a rich rust chamois-cloth shirt from L.L.Bean over a
faded blue-gray T-shirt she'd found one day in her laundry. White
Keds on her feet. John Cherry was at his desk, Oxford brogues
pressed up against the bevelled wood as he leaned back in his chair,
speaking evenly into the telephone. His suit jacket was folded
across some papers to his left, folded neatly that is; you could have
peeled an apple on the crease of his pants. . .

'Absolutely,' she heard Cherry say. 'You have my word.' And,
'Yes, ma'am, the minute I hear anything. Yes, right away.' Swivel-
ling towards Vargas, face opening into a smile. 'Thank you, ma'am.
Thank you. And a fine day to you, too.'

Setting the receiver back in place, he returned all four legs of his
chair to the floor and studied Vargas's face. 'What news?'

Vargas grinned. 'I've been doing a little of what you suggested,
old-fashioned police work. The Manhattan Lounge, Delaney's
more involved than we thought. He doesn't just book the talent, he
just about owns the place.'

Cherry raised an eyebrow. 'Something Mr Pearl omitted to
mention.'

'Too busy concentrating on labor relations.'

'You think we should go talk to him again?'

'Absolutely.'

Cherry reached for his coat.

'But wait, there's more. That fancy diner on the edge of the meat market, Kozinsky and Kelly. Blue-plate specials for the price of haute cuisine. Guess who's the silent partner? Thirty per cent share. Then there's a supper club on East Forty-ninth, the Mint. To say nothing of a small chain of restaurants near the Jersey shore.'

Cherry whistled appreciatively. 'Wonderful, isn't it?' Cherry said. 'Given a little patience, what you can find out on the Net.'

◆

Howard Pearl was venting his displeasure into a cordless phone. 'Linguine with clams on the menu, I need fuckin' clams. Which is what you're supposed to deliver. . . . No, no, wait. You hang on a fuckin' minute. . . . That's right, I want 'em here by tonight. I want 'em here this afternoon. I want 'em here inside the fuckin' hour. And don't think about passin' off none of that small shit, need a fuckin' microscope to find 'em on the plate. Yeah, five. Five o'clock. After that, as a supplier, you're history.'

He slammed the phone down on the counter hard enough to chip away some of the plastic trim. Looking up, he saw Vargas and Cherry, and was on the brink of dispatching them with a piece of his mind when he remembered who they were.

'Fuckin' job,' he said, buttoning his shirt. 'Ain't worth twice what I'm gettin' fuckin' paid.'

'Maybe you should ask your boss, Delaney, for a raise,' Vargas said.

Pearl paused in what he was doing, then hitched up his belt, a smile greasing across his face. 'Been doin' a little diggin', a little homework.'

'Time you could've saved us,' Vargas said.

Pearl shrugged and gestured back along the bar. 'Drink?'

'No,' Vargas said with a firm shake of the head.

'Coke,' said Cherry. 'Lemon and ice.'

Pearl clattered ice into a long glass and set to slicing a fresh lemon with a small, serrated knife. 'The girl. What you were askin', it was about the girl. Him an' her.' He speared a wedge of lemon and dropped it down into Cherry's glass, uncapped the bottle, tilted both bottle and glass, and poured.

'It didn't occur to you,' Vargas said, 'we might be interested in the rest? The wider picture.'

'Look,' Pearl said, 'I'll be honest with you. Vincent, he don't appreciate folk knowin' his business. Don't encourage, you know, chit-chat.'

'Really?' Vargas said. 'I wonder why that should be?'

'Comes in here, far as everyone knows, he's just the guy takes care of the floor show, pays the band. Diane, I doubt she even knew, no matter how close they were.'

'Don't you think that's strange?' Vargas was leaning one elbow on the bar, addressing her remarks to Cherry now. 'This is a guy drives an expensive car, wears look-at-me clothes, no shrinking violet, yet when it comes to part-owning a place like this suddenly he's all shy, Mister Modesty.'

'You're not suggesting,' Cherry said, 'he has something to hide?'

Vargas made a 'who knows?' gesture with her hands.

'Some people,' Pearl said, 'where money's concerned, they like to keep things to themselves. And I respect that.'

Vargas nodded solemnly. 'Delaney, he keeps a tight hold on the finances, how does that work?'

Pearl wriggled his tongue against the underside of his mouth, fidgeting with a piece of bacon trapped, since breakfast, between his teeth. 'I been here six years. Six, seven days a fuckin' week. Sometimes Vincent he comes in and checks the money himself, runs through the receipts, mostly he leaves everything to me. I'm the one settles up, pays the suppliers, banks the rest.' He looked square into Cherry's face. 'Anything shady going on, underhand, that the way your mind's workin', you think I wouldn't have noticed? I'd've noticed, right?'

'Right,' Vargas said emphatically.

'Right,' Cherry agreed.

'So,' Pearl said, rubbing his hands together as he stepped back. 'We through here? 'Cause if we are, I got things need seein' to . . .'

'No,' Vargas said, 'I think that's it for us. For now. Unless there's anything else you'd care to tell us about Mister Delaney, that is.'

Pearl fidgeted with the front of his shirt. 'Like I said, Vincent, he don't take kindly to people talkin' 'bout him behind his back.'

Vargas and Cherry exchanged glances and turned towards the door.

'You both take care now,' Pearl said, watching them till they were out of sight, then, from memory, dialling Delaney's number on the phone.

◆

Kozinsky was in his fifties, no more than five six or seven tall and weighed somewhere in the region of two hundred pounds. His hair was tied back in a ponytail, throwing into relief a round, flattish face with a thin mouth and watery eyes.

He offered Vargas and Cherry coffee, and took them into the office alongside the kitchen. Behind the desk he presumably shared with Kelly, there were the usual pictures of the two of them, proprietorially smiling at the camera as they glad-handed celebrities: Jack Nicholson, Christopher Walken, Michael Jordan. Kelly looked younger than his partner, taller and neatly bearded. There were no pictures of Vincent Delaney.

'These questions you're asking,' Kozinsky said, 'they involve this place here directly? This business?'

Cherry shook his head. 'Background,' Vargas said. 'Strictly background. Nothing more than that.'

'Okay.' Kozinsky leaned back in his chair, a little more relaxed. 'I first met Vince Delaney ten, eleven years back. I was running this place out on Long Island, nothing so special.

'Vince, he starts coming in a few nights a week, couple of drinks at the bar, never stays too long. Turns out he's got some involvement with this Italian restaurant close by, taking the reins while someone else is out of the country, I never caught the whole thing and, anyway, it doesn't matter, we get to talking, this and that, I tell him my idea, you know, a place like this, blue collar but for a different crowd, bump the profit margins till they mean something, stay in for eight, nine years, maybe ten, sell out big and retire to the Bahamas, Grand Cayman, one of those. Vince, he turns around, real serious, says I'm ever fixing to do more than break wind, let him know, could be there's some capital he wouldn't mind investing, strictly hush-hush.'

'Go on,' Vargas said.

Kozinsky swallowed some coffee, took a drag at his cigarette.

'A few months later this place came on the market. Great location, cost to match. Delaney checks out the property, runs his eyes across the books, forty-eight hours later he's got the contract drawn up and ready to sign. Before the ink's dry on the paper the money's in the bank.'

'His own money?' Vargas asked.

'Unless you're going to tell me something else.'

'He's not fronting for anyone?'

'It's possible.'

'But you don't know?'

Kozinsky shook his head.

'He leaves you to run things your own way?' Vargas asked. 'You and your partner.'

'He made a few suggestions early on, good ones, too. But since then, nothing. Long as his payments are coming through okay, far as he's concerned that's it.'

Vargas got to her feet and Cherry followed suit. 'Thanks for your time, Mr Kozinsky,' she said, holding out her hand.

'My pleasure.'

'You believe all of that?' Cherry asked, once they were back on the street.

'Bare bones, maybe.'

'What didn't you like?'

'The way it rolled off his tongue.'

'Like it had been rehearsed, you mean?'

'Like Delaney was backstage, working the strings.'

They crossed the avenue to where Vargas had illegally parked the car.

'So,' Cherry said. 'A little more digging, what d'you think?'

Vargas ducked her head and swung her legs round beneath the wheel. 'I think, one hell of a lot.'

27

SLOANE HAD FINALLY FALLEN asleep with an image of Connie firmly in his mind and woken in the small hours, sheets damp with thoughts of her mother, the moment of entering her piercing his memory like a knife.

Showered, dressed, he laughed at the absurdity of it, a man of his age paddling in the wet dreams of his youth. Lust recollected in tranquillity. Great fucks from the past. Dreams of fatherhood. The thought that on the sagging couch in someone's apartment, or down among the turpentine and paint of that studio floor you had made a child. You. The pair of you.

Over breakfast he tried to marshal his thoughts about Connie, to untangle what he felt. He had heard of families separated at birth, a mother and child who had known each other instantly after almost twenty years; a father who had recognized, in a crowded school playground, the daughter he had never previously seen. But encountering Connie for the first time the cold shock that had jolted him, that had not been the shock of recognition merely, but what he had heard, the music, one of those rare times when everything— the voice, the instruments, the melody, the words—had come together and made something special, unique. And later, recollecting their brief conversation, adrift in her silences and her sullen anger, what he felt more than anything was anger at her stubbornness and the situation he was being drawn deeper into.

Back at his hotel, there was no word from Connie .

That afternoon, restless, he headed back to MoMA and sat in front of Jane's painting, *Trinkle Tinkle*, remembering watching her put the finishing touches to it one long morning. The night before they had been back at the Five Spot, listening to Monk amidst jugs of beer and lurching conversation, the pianist's broken rhythms still resonating as she trod her familiar patterns forwards and back, towards the canvas and away, shifting an edge of color so that it overlapped, a small dissonance that sparked the eye, then, with the quickest movement of the wrist, a final curve of brilliant blue went arcing from the tip of her smallest brush, a glittering cadenza.

'It's finished,' Jane had said.

'For good?' Sloane asked.

'Yes.'

'How do you know? I mean, how can you be certain?'

She looked at him, then back at the painting, wondering if there was any way to explain in words. 'I know,' she said. 'That's all.'

As Sloane continued to sit in front of the painting now, other visitors moved around him, breaking his concentration, his vision. He was on the verge of going when, in the block of orange near the painting's center, he saw Connie, in reflection, walk towards him. Breath caught in his mouth, he swung round and, wearing a slender button-through dress in apple green, a small, soft leather bag hanging from one shoulder, it was, of course, someone else entirely. Brushing past her, Sloane hurried from the museum.

When he turned the corner on to West 11th less than an hour later, there she was again, Connie or a likeness of her, coming down the steps outside his hotel and Sloane, not wanting to be fooled again, only quickened his step when he realized, her hand on the waiting cab door, that it was in fact her.

Calling her name, he ran.

Connie's face, sharp and drawn, dark beneath the eyes.

'Wait,' Sloane said, slowing. 'Hang on. I'm sorry I . . .'

'I can meet you tonight,' Connie said. 'After the show. Vincent's got stuff to do, he won't be around.'

'All right, where shall I see you?'

Connie pointed back the way Sloane had come. 'There's an all-night diner on 45th, between Second and Third. I'll meet you there. Two-thirty, three.'

'Okay.'

A quick movement, a slamming of the cab door and she was gone. And Sloane, standing there, wondering how far the dryness of his mouth, the acceleration of his heart were due to his hundred-meter sprint along the street or something else.

◆

There were booths front and back, a counter midway along; Sloane sat in the rear section and told himself not to keep looking at his watch. A foursome, occasionally loud and trendily dressed, was taking time out from clubbing near the door; closer to Sloane a fiftyish woman with thinning ginger hair was crying soundlessly over her fried eggs. Behind the counter an olive-skinned young man in a spotless white coat assiduously polished glasses with a soft cloth, while the waitress, a large woman with freckled arms, sat on a stool opposite him, filling in the answers in a puzzle book and drinking Seven-Up.

He was on his second cup of coffee by the time Connie arrived, a long coat, black and shiny, tightly belted over a dark skirt, a gray and white striped top. It was a quarter past three. Slipping off her coat, she leaned back and stretched, then looked around, flinching at the sight of her own face, pale, in the mirror opposite.

'He'd kill me if he knew I was here, talking to you.'

The words set off an echo in Sloane's head, the source of which he couldn't immediately trace.

'You think I'm kidding, don't you?' Connie said.

And when Sloane didn't answer, just gave her a look, assuming exaggeration, she shook her head. 'Well, you don't know. You just don't know.'

'Then maybe you should explain.'

Connie laughed abruptly, then coughed. 'I wouldn't know where to start.'

'Vincent, that's his name?'

'Vincent Anthony Delaney.'

'And you live together.'

'Ten years, off and on.'

'A long time.'

'I suppose.'

'A long time to live with a jealous man.'

'Is there any other kind?' Connie asked.

'I think so.'

She leaned towards him, sardonic, playful. 'Are you living with anyone, Sloane?'

He shook his head and Connie laughed. 'Maybe if you'd shown a little jealousy yourself, showed her what you felt, she'd still be around.'

'It wasn't like that,' Sloane said, defensive.

'Yeh,' Connie said. 'Right. It never is.'

The waitress had left her puzzle book and was standing at the end of the table, patiently.

'I'll have tea,' Connie said, 'Black. Tea with honey, can you do that?'

'Don't see why not.'

'Okay. And an omelette. Plain. No fries, no coleslaw, no garnish. Nothing.'

'You want a plate?' the waitress asked, straight-faced.

Connie stared at her hard.

'How 'bout you?' the waitress said to Sloane, unperturbed. 'You want to eat?'

Sloane shook his head. 'No, thanks.'

'More coffee?'

He shook his head again and the waitress moved away.

'My mother,' Connie said. 'I really don't have a whole lot of time.'

Sloane told her what he knew about Jane's illness, how she had been when he had seen her, not embellishing, telling it as straightforwardly as he could, the days, the hours before Connie's mother died.

By the time he had finished, the waitress had brought her omelette and it lay there on the plate, losing heat. Sloane drank the last of the water from his glass.

'You know,' Connie finally said, 'it's a funny thing. There you are sitting watching TV news, Ted Koppel or whoever, I don't remember, and suddenly there's this painting on the screen, one of those abstract things, and a voice going on about early fame and later obscurity and just before her picture comes up I realize it's my mother they're talking about and she's dead, and then before I can start to take it all in, it's sports and football and I'm left sitting there, thinking what the fuck, what the fuck?'

'She wanted to see you,' Sloane said, 'more than anything, I think.'

As if she were no longer listening, Connie cut away a piece of omelette with her fork and lifted it to her mouth, and Sloane had to resist a sudden urge to reach across and shake her, make her pay attention.

'Do you care?' he said, his voice sharp and hard.

'What?'

'Do you care? About any of this?'

She raised her head towards his, slow-eyed and insolent, and he wanted to slap her.

'She loved you, you know that. She really did.'

'You don't have to shout,' Connie said.

When Sloane moved abruptly she flinched. Squeezing past the end of the table, he went quickly to the rest room at the back and leaned his head forward against the speckled glass of the mirror, angry with himself for getting so worked up, surprised at the ease with which she had got under his skin.

When he got back to the table, Connie was sitting angled in the corner, resting partly against the seat back, partly against the wall. Her plate had been cleared away and she had a cup of tea in her hand.

'You okay?' she asked, a lot of the bitterness gone from her voice.

'Yes, thanks. Fine.'

'I thought maybe you'd gone to throw up.'

Sloane shook his head. Turning in his seat, he signalled to the waitress for more coffee and when it came, Connie said, 'You and my mother, I mean, what was the deal? You never said.'

'I knew her,' Sloane said. 'A long time ago. Here in New York, as a matter of fact.'

'You knew her?' Connie asked.

'Yes.'

Connie narrowed her eyes. 'You mean you were screwing her. That is what you mean, isn't it?'

'I suppose.'

'What d'you mean, you suppose? You either were or you weren't.'

'Okay, then. Yes.'

Connie had the same sardonic glint back in her eyes. 'You're a little old to be coy, Sloane, you know that? And besides, from what I hear about that crowd, everyone else would have been screwing her, why not you?' She stopped short, recognizing the look that passed across his face and laughed. 'It still hurts, doesn't it? After all this time. The thought that there might have been somebody else. And you were the one sounding off about jealousy, how it was such a bad thing.'

Sloane drank his coffee, avoided her amused gaze.

Connie looked at her watch. 'Why don't we get down to it?' she said. 'The rest of it.'

'What rest?'

'The money. I mean, if I'm forgiven, everything's lovey-dovey, then I'm back in the will. That's right, isn't it? Whatever there is, my share, I've got it coming.'

'There will be money,' Sloane said. 'There isn't yet.'

'What do you mean?'

'Your mother's estate, it's mostly in the form of paintings to be sold. Auctioned. The bulk of what's raised goes to set up a foundation in her name, scholarships for young artists, that kind of thing. Anything that's left, it gets divided between Valentina and yourself.'

'All that could take years,' Connie said in disgust.

'I can put you in touch with Valentina . . .'

But Connie was already on her feet.

'Here,' Sloane said, 'take this.' He pulled an envelope from his pocket. 'That's all the information, you should get in touch, let her have an address for you at least.'

Connie screwed up the envelope and pushed it down into the pocket of her coat. Sloane dropped some bills on the table and followed her out.

On the street, Connie pulled her collar up around her neck.

'Which way you headed?' Sloane asked.

'Uptown. You?'

'Down.'

'I'm gonna walk over to Third,' Connie said. 'Catch a cab.'

'Right.'

For a long moment neither one moved.

'Your father,' Sloane said, 'are you in touch?'

'Difficult, when I don't know who he is.'

'Jane, she never said?'

'When I was growing up I used to go on and on at her. She wouldn't answer. In the end I just stopped asking.'

'And now?'

Connie looked at him with tired eyes. 'Now who cares? Who the holy fuck cares!'

Hands in pockets, rejection like a swallowed stone inside him, Sloane watched her walk away.

♦

Waking after too few hours' sleep, Sloane remembered what Connie's first words in the diner had reminded him of—the installation at the Rachel Zander Gallery, the recorded voice, slightly distorted, repeating over and over, *He'll kill us if he gets the chance.*

At ten thirty he called Rachel, to be told she had flown to London on business the day before. Inside twenty-four hours that was where Sloane would be himself. He had done what he could, what he had promised. There was nothing, he had convinced himself, to detain him further in New York.

28

IT WAS RAINING. LONG, slanting lines which blurred the out-
lines of the airport buildings and turned the runways into slick gray
ribbons, water ghosting the surface like a skin. Sloane lugged his
baggage along line after line of interconnecting corridors, up esca-
lators and down stairs, until finally he joined the slow line through
passport control and then the empty customs hall, out into the press
of faces, anxious relatives and friends, bored drivers holding names
high across their chests. The Heathrow Express was crowded and
stalled for ten minutes outside Paddington Station while the
backlog of trains, distressed by the weather, untangled itself. The
queue of taxis was impossible and Sloane took the Tube, elbowing
his way against the current of commuters as he changed platforms
at King's Cross.

The distance between Kentish Town station and home was
enough for him to be soaked through several layers of clothing and,
once inside the door, he stripped off everything and let it lie in a
bundle where it fell, dried himself with a towel and pulled clean,
dry clothes from the old mahogany chest of drawers. At the sink he
rinsed a glass and tipped in several fingers of whiskey, half of which
he drank at a swallow. A few new spiders' webs aside, a suggestion

of damp in the bricks below one of the upstairs windows, the interior seemed secure, unchanged.

By late morning the rain had stopped and the sky was a sudden, unexpected blue. Walking round the corner to the café, Sloane found himself shivering in the freshness of the air.

Dumar greeted him with his rich laugh and threw an arm round his shoulders, almost knocking him down. 'Great to see you. Even looking like you do.'

'Which is what?'

'Tired, cold, about to come down with something bad.'

'Thanks,' Sloane said, attempting a grin.

Dumar was already ladling soup into a bowl, hacking off a hunk of bread. 'Sit. Eat. Then go home and rest. I will come later.'

Sloane needed no second bidding. The soup warmed him and he ate it greedily, aware for the first time of his hunger. Some thirty minutes later he lay down on his own bed and, within moments, was fast asleep.

He was still sleeping, sheets and pillow damp with sweat, when Dumar arrived. Disorientated and bleary-eyed, he started to apologize, but Dumar brushed him aside. 'This I will leave on your stove to heat. I still have a few things to fetch.' *This* was a large earthenware pot, a tagine of chicken and chickpeas, flavored with cinnamon and cumin.

Sloane threw cold water on his face, combed his matted hair, brushed his teeth; rummaged for clean clothes. The smells coming from across the room were enough to revive his appetite, bring him back to some kind of normality. Dumar returned with a small tape player, bread and wine and aspirin, a pot of cream which he stirred into the stew.

'You have a fever,' Dumar said. 'Take two of these, then eat. We will talk later.'

It was not so long before Sloane was wiping a piece of bread around the inside of his plate and, having set Ali Farka Toure's 'Niafunke' rolling, Dumar was in the process of rolling the biggest joint Sloane had seen since the days of Cheech and Chong.

Dumar grinned. 'A feast.' The grin became a laugh. 'When I was at school we used to read these old books, very old. Patched together with tape and glue. Grayfriars, you know?'

Sloane shook his head.

'British public school. Harry Wharton. Tom Merry. Billy Bunter, the Owl of the Remove. Oh, crikey! Ow! Yarooh! Midnight feasts in the dorm.' He took a toke from the joint and passed it across to Sloane.

'And that's what you thought England would be like?' Sloane said. 'Grayfriars writ large?'

'Not really, no. These were stories, old stories. I knew things would have changed.'

Sloane shook his head. 'Not so much. Harry Wharton, was that his name? Merry. Others like them. They're all here. All the same.'

Dumar took the joint between his fingers, drew smoke down deep into his lungs. African voices rang, slow and hypnotic, around the room. 'Mali Dje'. Spiky guitar, dejembe and conga drum.

'Tell me about your journey,' Dumar said. 'Your daughter, you found her?'

'Maybe.'

'How can you be not sure?'

Sloane leaned forward. 'Connie, I found. Jane's daughter, certainly. That doesn't mean she's mine.'

'You talked with her?'

'I tried.'

Dumar laughed and shook his head. 'What? You thought she would throw herself into your arms? Be grateful after all these years?'

'No, no. I don't know.'

'But she rejected you, is that what happened?'

'Not exactly.'

'Perhaps you were expecting too much.'

Sloane pointed an accusing finger. 'You were the one. You. When you see her you will know. Well, that's crap, because I didn't know then and I don't know now.'

'Ah,' Dumar said, angling back his head so that the smoke drifted upwards, 'maybe deep down you do. Simply you are too frightened to say it is so.'

'And that's bullshit, too.'

Dumar's smile spread wide across his face.

'What?' Sloane asked.

Dumar shook his head.

'What?'

'Remember,' Dumar said. 'If she is not your daughter she is somebody else's.'

'So?'

'So she may need your help.'

'Oh, no. Someone else's responsibility, not mine.'

'Perhaps.' Dumar's eyes were bright and alive.

'Christ, Dumar! What d'you think I am? Some avenging bloody angel? Some knight on a white fucking horse?'

Dumar smiled. 'We will see.'

Time passed. The bottle of wine was two-thirds empty. Dumar passed round another joint.

'My daughter . . .' For several moments Dumar rested his face in his hands. 'You know she is here in England. At the university. Manchester.'

Sloane nodded.

'The police, last week they came to see her in her room. Demanded papers, proof of identity, passport, visa. Asked questions.'

'What about?'

'Her family.'

'About you?'

'About me.'

'But everything was okay? Her passport and everything, it was all okay?'

'They said there may be irregularities. With her visa. Told her to report to the police station. Took her papers away.'

'And?'

'Nothing. When she arrives as told, she is given an envelope, her passport, everything is inside. No one says a word. No explanation.'

'And since then?'

Dumar shook his head. 'Also nothing.'

Sloane didn't know what else to say. The music drifted on. When the wine was gone and the joint smoked down, Dumar rose, not quite steadily, to his feet and collected what was his. 'I will see you tomorrow.'

An hour later Sloane woke, cramped and stiff, and realized he had fallen asleep where he was. He drank some water, swallowed two more aspirins and went to bed.

29

SLOANE SLEPT BADLY, TROUBLED by dreams. His covers were tangled, his sweat-soaked pillow thrown to the floor. At six he got up, head spinning, tipped whiskey into a glass of warm milk and took it back to bed. When he woke again it was past noon and the worst of his fever seemed to have passed. His head no longer ached. Carefully, taking his time, he washed and dressed.

The day was mild, the sky a mottled gray. After a couple of slow turns round the park he thought it made sense to try and eat. But the door to the café was locked and inside the chairs were still stacked on the tables in pairs. Of Dumar there was no sign, no note fixed to the door. The windows of the flat above where he lived were closed, the curtains partly drawn.

Sloane asked the first few passers-by if they knew anything, but all they did was shrug and shake their heads. 'These people,' one said, 'you know what they're like. Nomads, ain't they? Here today, scarpered the next.'

It wasn't what Sloane believed.

He made more inquiries in the neighborhood, the greengrocer's and the butcher's on the high street which Dumar used, the cash-and-carry where he bought basic supplies. No one had seen him that morning; no one knew where he had gone. What next, Sloane thought? Phone the hospitals? Go to the police?

Dumar's daughter was standing outside the café when he turned back into the street and, without ever having met her or seen a photograph, he knew immediately who she was. Medium height, slender build, she was wearing loose trousers, silver-gray with dark bands above and below the knee, a multi-colored top with baggy sleeves, a thin patterned scarf loose at the neck, her dark hair braided with strips of ribbon, purple and gold. Silver rings on her fingers. Adidas trainers on her feet.

'You looking for your dad?' Sloane asked.

She tilted back her head a little, looked at him warily but unafraid.

'You are Dumar's daughter?' Sloane said.

'Yes.'

'From university?'

'Yes, how did you know?'

'My name's Sloane,' he said, holding out his hand. 'Your dad and I, we're friends.'

'Olivia.' Her voice was clear, her grip firm and strong. 'I think he mentioned you.' She was what, Sloane wondered? Twenty? Twenty-one?

'I phoned him last night,' Olivia said.

'He was with me.'

'I didn't know. I wanted to tell him I was coming down to London today, arrange to meet.'

'When I got here an hour or so ago,' Sloane said, 'the place was like this.'

'And you don't know where my father is?'

Sloane shook his head.

'He didn't say anything last night?'

'See you tomorrow, that's all.'

The concern was clear on Olivia's face.

'The flat,' Sloane said. 'You don't have a key?'

'No.'

'How about his girlfriend, couldn't he be with her?'

'Angie. Yes, I suppose so.'

'Could we phone?'

'It's not so far from here. Why don't we go round and see?'

Angie lived in a two-room conversion on the upper floor of a mid-Victorian terraced house adrift of the Caledonian Road, dormer windows let into the roof front and back. She proved to be welcoming, concerned, clearly fond of Olivia, a fondness that seemed warmly returned. She was possibly fifty, Sloane thought, silver-haired and slender-hipped, amply bosomed. There were posters of Pablo Neruda and Miriam Makeba on her walls, plants vying for space with books on every flat surface, a rather expensive-looking laptop and matching printer on a corner table.

Angie made tea while they talked, quick to seize on the unwelcome visit Olivia had had from the police, wondering if there couldn't be some connection with her father's disappearance.

'I don't see how,' Olivia said. 'As far as I know he's never had that kind of trouble before. Immigration. He's been here a long time, yeah. Got his own business, bank account, credit cards.'

'Then he's untouchable?' Sloane asked.

'We don't know,' Angie said.

Olivia looked at the floor.

At Angie's suggestion they telephoned all the hospitals in the area, checking both admissions and accident and emergency, and then the police stations at Holmes Road and Haverstock Hill.

Nothing.

When they left almost an hour later, Olivia and Angie promised to keep in touch and contact one another the moment they heard anything at all.

There was still no sign of life at the café, so they went around the corner to Sloane's place. Standing in the center of the big room Olivia nodded her head approvingly. 'It's like one of them lofts, right?'

'I suppose.'

She accepted water instead of coffee or more tea, peered restlessly at this and that, unable to settle.

'What's up here, then?' Olivia asked, turning her head towards the stairs.

'Nothing. Nothing, special. Don't . . .'

But already her young legs had taken her up out of sight, Sloane following in her wake.

'Wow!' Olivia exclaimed, looking around at the canvases that lined three sides of the walls in piles of four or five or more. 'Whose are these? Are these all yours?'

Without waiting for an answer she moved from one to another, pulling canvases out, then sliding them back. 'They're brilliant, right? I mean, the colors . . .' She stopped, sensing Sloane's uneasy silence, the near embarrassment on his face. 'What?' she asked. 'You don't like them or what?'

'They're okay. Better than the others, at least.'

'What others?'

He gave her a wry smile. 'The ones I burned, painted over, threw away.'

'Now you're joking, yeah?'

Sloane shook his head.

'Then you're crazy. Got to be. Look, look at this.' She lifted a squarish canvas high off the ground, a flurry of squiggly, expanding technicolor lines exploding across a deep blue, almost black ground. 'That on your wall, you'd never tire of looking at it. See something different every time.'

'Take it,' Sloane said.

'What?'

'Take it with you, put it in your room.'

'I couldn't afford . . .'

'It's a gift.'

'I couldn't . . . You can't just . . .'

'Olivia, please . . .'

'No, I can't.'

Sloane laughed. 'Then you were just being polite, being kind.'

'No way.'

'Have it then. Please. Say it's for your father if that makes it easier. Something against his return. But take it when you go.'

She was smiling at him with her eyes, sizing him up anew. 'All right. I will.'

'Good. Now can we go back downstairs? It depresses me up here. Besides, I'd like some food.'

They walked to an Italian restaurant on the high road and ordered pasta and salad, a bottle of house wine.

'Wherever my dad is,' Olivia said, 'he's all right.'

'How do you know?'

'I just know.'

Over the meal, Sloane asked Olivia about the university, her courses, friends, the student house with its shifting population where she and her friend Nicky lived. It was Nicky, whose parents lived relatively close, that she had come down with that day.

'Do you still paint?' Olivia asked, accepting more wine.

Sloane shook his head. 'Not really. Hardly at all.'

'Why not?'

'I just don't.'

'You should.'

He shrugged, willing her to change the subject; reached for his glass.

'Think of all the people who'd give their right arm to be able to paint like that.'

'Perhaps not exactly like that.'

'You know what I mean.'

Despite himself, Sloane was smiling.

'What?'

'Nothing.'

'You're laughing at me.'

'No. No, not for a minute. I promise.'

'Good.' She reached up and pulled her sweater over her head, sleeveless T-shirt snug against her breasts, white cotton against metallic brown skin. Then laughed as Sloane caught himself staring and quickly looked away. 'Here,' she said, lifting the water glass, 'have some of this, old man. Cool yourself down.'

Back at the studio he surrounded Olivia's painting in bubble wrap and then two large sheets of brown paper, taping the edges carefully down before tying it all with string.

'You sure you're going to be able to manage this?'

'Sure.'

Nicky's parents lived somewhere off the Holloway Road and that was where Olivia was going to stay. Sloane had already phoned for a taxi. There was coffee on the stove.

'What you said about your dad, his being okay,' Sloane said. 'I hope you're right.'

'Thanks.'

He had barely poured the coffee when the taxi arrived.

'I'd better go.'

'Yes.'

At the door, holding it open for her, the painting awkwardly between his arms and hers, Olivia leaned quickly towards him and kissed him on the cheek. 'You know what you ought to do?' she asked.

'Besides paint?'

'Besides paint.'

'What's that?'

'Find yourself someone, before it's too late.'

He watched the taxi drive away, the quick blink of the brake lights before it turned from sight, shut and locked the door, and leaned back against the wood, eyes closed.

30

SLOANE WAS UP AT five thirty, pulling on dungarees, splashing cold water on his face and combing his fingers through his hair. Through the upstairs windows the sky was limpid gray, waiting for the light. He selected a canvas he'd begun work on years before, a dull catechism of uneven squares, gray and muddy cream, rising one above the other without belief or reason. It was wider than the span of his arms, above head height when he raised it off the floor and secured it to the wall. He levered the lid from a large can of matte white paint, stirred it strongly with the handle of a long brush before pouring some liberally into a large tray and using an ordinary household paint roller to cover up what was there before. In some places he rolled the paint on more thickly, not waiting until the first application had dried, the edge of the roller making faint over-lapping horizontal lines in the process, some of which he eased away, leaving the remainder as they were. Towards the lower right section a smudge of gray, no bigger than a hand, showed through and this, too, he left.

When finally he stepped back, the first task done, his arm ached, the light had changed in the sky and what he was looking at resembled a painting by Agnes Martin, a parody of it at least, without her hand-drawn geometric lines, without her mystery.

He went downstairs to make coffee. Carried it back up and began collecting tins and tubes of paint, arranging them in a rough cluster on the floor and then shaking, stirring, squeezing, sorting through, daubing samples on to a piece of wood; shades of purple, shades of gold.

The adrenalin firing through him, the muscles of his stomach contracted, knotting, bending him forward, cramped, where he stood.

At the last moment he moved away, searching for a color he had seen in his mind and had yet to find. A pale violet, pale yet clear. He found something comparable, brighter, darker, and decanted some into an empty tin, adding linseed oil to lighten it.

Only when he was satisfied he had the right shade did he reach for a fine, sable-tipped brush and, after stepping back to judge the necessary balance with the existing smudge of gray, make the first fresh mark, a curve of violet tapering away, the size and shape of a feather on a magpie's wing, the shade of skin seen by certain eyes in failing light.

Where previously he might have gone barrelling in, taking out his frustrations, his anger, on the canvas, now he made himself wait, reined himself in.

When he was certain, and only then, he fired up a four-inch brush with gold and made a broad stroke, high up, right to left, angling in. Another above. Another below. Then purple, no, not the purple, not yet. White. More white. White on white. Shiny, this, and thick, laid on with a palette knife, then worked at with a sponge, textured and teased. Moved around. He seized a tube of paint, pinkish hue, rose pink, and squeezed it directly on to the center of this new white mass, letting it slide slowly down before attacking it with a turpentine-soaked piece of cloth, blending the two till the pink had all but disappeared.

He wanted breakfast, he wanted something, he wanted lunch.

What he found were a tin of sardines soaked in oil, another of cannellini beans, a jar of sun-dried tomatoes, as yet unopened, and, hiding behind the marmalade, a slim, black and silver tin of anchovies.

All of these he emptied into one large bowl, stirred with a fork, added a splash or two more of olive oil, then took the bowl upstairs and sat cross-legged on the floor opposite the painting, eating with fork and fingers both, finally licking his finger ends. Finished, he set the bowl aside and continued to sit.

His intention had been to add the purple gradually, spray it, possibly, from the end of a brush held an arm's distance away. A flick of the wrist. A technique he remembered Jane practicing to great effect. All the more reason, perhaps, for not doing it now.

Instead, he ferreted for the largest of his brushes, almost a hand's breadth wide, and plunged it into the purple paint, quickly lifting it, dripping, to the top of the canvas, right of center, and drawing it smoothly down in one long descending motion that took it, color perceptibly thinning, to within inches of the bottom frame, missing the original gray by a whisper as it slid past.

He hadn't heard the knocking at the downstairs door and, when he did, had no idea how long it had been going on. Dumar, he thought, or Olivia. Both together.

When he opened the door, paint splashed here and there across his overalls, along his arms, tattooed in fine lines across his face, it was to find Dutton and Boyd on the pavement, a third man, taller, one he did not recognize, standing in their wake.

'Been hard at it, I see,' Dutton said, nodding towards Sloane's dungarees.

'Rolling on the canvas, is it?' said Boyd, the Swansea lilt more pronounced than usual. Either he'd been home for a few days, or his mam and dad were staying. 'Marvellous, that contiguity with the actual surface. No substitute for a bit of actual skill, of course. Control. Perspective. Someone like Rembrandt now, brushstrokes fine as a hairline fracture.'

'Always bothered me, that,' Dutton said. 'How come, when you can obviously paint properly—that Singer Sergeant forgery, for instance—how come it is you waste your time on the sort of shit you do?'

'Fuck off,' Sloane said.

'No way to take a smidgen of constructive criticism,' Boyd said.

'You can fuck off, too.'

'I think,' the third man said, speaking for the first time, 'we've had just about enough of this Edinburgh Fringe badinage, don't you?'

'Right, Mr Elms,' said Boyd, properly deferential.

Sloane thought Elms had the sort of accent that went perfectly with his suit and tie, the kind of public school vowels, supercilious and slightly menacing, that set you up for a life in merchant banking or cricket commentating. Sloane didn't think that Elms, however, was currently following either of those career paths.

'Perhaps,' Elms said, addressing Sloane directly, 'you'd care to invite us in.'

Sloane didn't budge.

'What Mr Elms might have said,' Dutton offered, 'is that although we'd have been happy to invite you round the corner with us, stand you egg and chips, a mug of tea, our understanding is that the café's closed, due to unfortunate circumstances.'

Bastards! Sloane thought. You bastards!

He stepped aside and waited while they walked, one, two, three, through the door. Elms went immediately to the far end of the settee and sat down, arms lightly folded, knees together; Dutton and Boyd, true to their nature, took advantage of the chance to snoop in corners, commit to memory, admire.

'Open plan, very nice,' Dutton remarked. 'Bit like wandering round Ikea—except for the furniture, of course.'

Boyd was on the first tread of the stairs before Sloane stopped him with a shout.

'Later, perhaps,' Boyd said, attempting a bashful smile in his retreat. 'At your invitation, of course.'

Sloane took a seat facing Elms. 'Dumar,' he said. 'Where is he?'

'Quite safe,' Elms replied, overriding Dutton's attempt to circumlocute.

'Where?'

'Near Salisbury. A former army barracks, spartan, but given the deprivations your friend is used to in his own country, not uncomfortable. One of several facilities currently in use for asylum seekers and the like.'

'Is that what he is, an asylum seeker?'

'Oh, my, I hope so. I mean if not that, then what? His documentation, such as it is, is niggardly in the extreme.'

'Illegal,' Dutton said. 'Your pal, Dumar, an illegal immigrant ripe for transportation, that's what Mr Elms means.'

'How about a victim of police harassment?' Sloane said, temper in control but only just. 'Him and his daughter both. And you . . .' He was looking at Boyd now, pointing in his direction. 'If you open another one of those drawers, I'll break your fucking arm.'

Boyd made a move towards him, bristling, but Dutton stopped him with a warning. 'He just might, you know. Remember what he did to Parsons's nose.'

'Oh, yes,' Boyd said, beginning to chuckle. 'The parson's nose.'

'How come,' Sloane said to Elms, 'you're at the beck and call of these clowns?'

'Wonderful, isn't it?' Dutton said. 'All the departments of the law pulling together. One of the triumphs of New Labour, I think it'll be seen as, greater police powers, computerized intelligence gathering, DNA banks, saying bollocks to the jury system.'

Sloane ignored him. 'What's the deal?' he said to Elms. 'I suppose there's a deal.'

By way of an answer Elms nodded at Dutton, who pulled an envelope from his pocket and from that removed a number of photographs, grainy for the most part, the result of working with a fast slim telescopic lens.

Parsons, of course, Sloane identified instantly, but the woman . . . Smart in a loose-fitting linen suit the color of pale wheat, her hair recently shaped and cut, Valentina Ceroni looked altogether different from the person he had known in Italy.

'When were these taken?' Sloane asked.

'Six days ago, seven. Ceroni was in London for a series of meetings. The Jane Graham Foundation—you know about that, of course—setting up a board of trustees.'

'And Parsons . . . ?'

Dutton smiled a thin-lipped smile. 'Other interests, we think. A stash of paintings for sale, Pollock, Kline, you know the kind of thing.'

'Parsons,' Sloane said, 'wouldn't know a Franz Kline if it stood up and bit him in the ass. You know what he specializes in as well as I do.'

'Nevertheless, rumor has it he's offered to broker the whole deal. And put ten per cent of his fee back into the Graham Foundation.'

'Then he's set to make a lot more some other way,' Sloane said.

'Don't altogether believe in his altruism, then?' Boyd said. 'I must admit I found it a little hard to buy into myself.'

Dutton shuffled the photographs back into a neat pile. 'One way or another, Parsons has been slipping through our hands for years. No thanks to you on that account. If we can move on him here, proof positive, there's a lot more he'll fall for, mark my words. Put him out of business for a long time, maybe for good.'

Sloane looked at the photo uppermost, Valentina with her face angled towards Parsons, listening intently; Parsons himself, smooth, confident, self-assured. 'Like I said before,' he said, addressing Elms, 'what's the deal?'

'It's simple,' Elms replied. 'In the matter of Parsons, you agree to help our friends here obtain a conviction. Cast iron. We recommend the tribunal looks favourably on your friend's application for asylum. Quid pro quo.' Elms paused, watching Sloane's face.

'Dumar,' Sloane said, 'he'll be able to stay permanently, officially? Not some bloody carpet you can yank out from under him the minute you've a mind.'

'I think you can rest assured.'

'And his daughter?'

'A fine student, I believe. Lively mind. The kind of citizen we need.'

'All right,' Sloane said, after a long moment's thought. 'All right.'

Behind Elms's back, Dutton and Boyd were exchanging smug grins.

31

HE CAUGHT UP WITH Parsons at an opening, the Shirin Neshat at the Serpentine. Large black and white photographs displayed sparingly on the walls, *Women of Allah*, faces defiant, beautiful: one woman in particular, a gun held close against her cheek, the barrel end staring out, mirroring her eye, calligraphy covering every inch of her skin, words in Farsi she can only think, not speak. And moving between them, these fashionably dressed, articulate people, women and men with glasses of Shiraz or Chardonnay in their hands, all chattering at once, all avoiding their accusing gaze.

In the dark of separate rooms, Neshat's videos were playing, Iranian men and chador-clad women side by side on separate screens, voices that are insistent, keening.

It was coming out of the third of these that Sloane saw Parsons, a soured expression on his face, one hand cupped against an ear to shield it from the sound.

Seeing Sloane approach, he flinched, as if expecting to be hit.

'Don't worry,' Sloane said, hands carefully at his sides. 'I'm over that now.'

Outside the gallery, on the broad flagged stones, the lawn leading out to the edges of the park, people stood in twos and threes, cigarettes bobbing like fireflies. Sloane was wearing a loose black designer suit and collarless white shirt, both bought that morning at the Hampstead Oxfam shop, all the better to blend in, deep pockets to house the tape recorder Dutton had issued him more comfortably.

'Let's walk,' Parsons said. 'It's a lovely evening.'

They crossed the road, the soft sanded strip on which horses are daily exercised, down through the crowded car park towards the lake. Looking back, the gallery resembled a ship, all sails alight. Parsons chose a seat some little way along. In silhouette, ducks threaded their way up and down the lake. The music from the gallery could still be heard above the movement of water, the occasional cry of birds.

'That bloody row,' Parsons said.

Sloane said nothing.

Parsons lit a cigarette, leaned back and held the smoke down in his lungs. 'I'm rather pleased to have bumped into you, actually. If we have really put all that silly unpleasantness behind us.'

'I was angry.'

'Out of control.'

'I'd just come out of prison, remember.'

'And now you feel differently.'

Sloane stared out into the near-darkness of the lake. 'You can't stay angry forever. Even with you.'

'Dear chap.' Parsons smiled and touched Sloane lightly on the arm, and Sloane caught himself wondering if Parsons and Elms might have gone to the same college, the same school. Harry Wharton and Tom Merry, too.

Parsons flicked the remainder of his cigarette towards the water. 'The thing we've never done,' he said, 'never capitalized on, is getting you to do something in your own style.' He moved closer, lowering his voice. 'There's a small group of Abstract Expressionist stuff coming on to the market, a private collection. Big names, Pollock and the rest . . .'

Sloane was already shaking his head. 'Attribution on that work's too clear-cut. We'd never get away with it. It'd be Vuillard all over again.'

'No. What happened there was sheer chance. One in a million. It couldn't happen again.'

'Easy for you to say. You weren't the one doing time.'

'Listen,' Parsons urged. 'You're right, of course, I'm not suggesting we come up with some gigantic new Pollock canvas, too many complications all round. But imagine this instead: a number of small paintings, five or six. Pieces he did when he was getting into his Jack the Dripper period, test runs, if you like. Transitional. God, he used to trade those things in at the general store for bourbon and cigarettes, give them to women he met in bars as a way of getting into their drawers.'

'And as far as potential buyers are concerned, you came across them where?'

'Part of the collection, of course. Personal gifts, treasured, never displayed. Till now.'

Sloane stared out across the water at the shapes of the trees on the other side, empty of definition as a series of Rorschach blobs. He wondered to what extent Valentina was involved, how much detail, if any, she knew.

'These pieces,' Sloane said, 'you think the money would be there? Serious money?'

'Dear boy, if anyone had bottled them, I could get you serious money for one of Pollock's farts.'

Sloane got to his feet and Parsons followed suit.

'I'll have to think about it,' Sloane said.

'Of course.'

'If I go along,' Sloane said, after several moments, 'I'll need start-up money, cash in hand.'

'A thousand,' Parsons said airily. 'Something along those lines?'

Sloane laughed.

'Two, then.'

'Five.'

Parsons breathed deeply, akin to a sigh. Lit another cigarette. The music from the gallery seemed, temporarily at least, to have stopped and, in its place, laughter rolled down the slope towards where they were standing. 'All right,' he said. 'But I need to know soon, within a couple of days at the most.'

'Tomorrow or the day after,' Sloane said, starting to move away.

'Good.'

'And you'll have the money ready?'

'I doubt,' Parsons said, smiling, 'I could afford to risk another Giacometti.'

They set off towards the gallery, side by side, but at the car park Parsons paused.

'You're not going back in?' Sloane asked.

Parsons shook his head. 'I don't think so.'

They shook hands and Sloane watched as Parsons crossed towards his car. Safe from sight, he reached inside his jacket and switched off the small recorder, aware of the sweat thinly layering his back and scalp.

Moments later he was brought up short by the sight of Rachel Zander, in a full-skirted turquoise dress, cream shawl across her shoulders, standing just inside the main entrance to the gallery, quite alone.

◆

She was staying at a hotel in Covent Garden, close by the Royal Opera House. In the taxi she suggested supper at Joe Allen's. 'Unless you're sick of the place, that is.' Sloane had never been. Sitting at the bar while they waited for a table, Rachel talked with enthusiasm about the show at the Serpentine and of a young artist whose work she'd seen earlier, paint and collage mixed with video and sampled sounds. Sloane nodded, listened, drank his Beck's from a glass—drinking beer from the bottle an affectation too far.

They were shown to a table by the far wall, beneath a signed poster for Liza Minnelli in *Cabaret*. Sloane ordered the lamb and

Rachel the Caesar salad and a portion of fries on the side. Finding a Cline Mourvedre on the wine list seemed to give her inordinate pleasure.

'You know,' she said, 'I haven't exactly been handing you an easy row to hoe. Always rushing off somewhere. Never relaxed.' She laughed. 'I made a promise to myself, if the chance came up, I'd make amends.'

'And that's what this is? Making amends.'

'We'll see.' The light catching the green in her eyes just so, making it shine.

They talked easily about very little, titbits of conversation, inconsequential scraps. Movies, writers, art world gossip. Drank and ate. When the waiter came to take away their plates and inquire about coffee or dessert, Sloane asked when she was going back to New York.

'Soon. A couple of days. A few more people to see, a couple of plays.' She looked at him across the top of her glass. 'I might not see you for quite a while.'

'Don't be so sure.'

'You're coming back over?'

And without having intended to, he told her the whole story, more or less. Jane and Connie. Delaney. Rachel sat there listening, transfixed.

'When I left,' Sloane said, 'I thought that was the end of it, I really did. I'd carried out my promise to Jane as well as I could and that was that.'

'And now?'

'Now I have to go back.'

'Even though you're not certain if she's your daughter or not? Connie.'

Sloane nodded. 'Yes, that's right.'

Back up on the street, Rachel linked her arm through his. 'Care to walk me home?'

'Why not?'

Within minutes they were outside Rachel's hotel.

'I've had a nice evening,' she said.

'Me, too.'

'You know,' Rachel said, 'after we talked about Jane Graham I went to look at some of her work.'

'And what did you think?'

'She's great. Stronger than I'd remembered. Generous. Sensual.' A smile played at the corners of Rachel's mouth, crinkling the skin around her eyes. 'I bet she was a wonderful lover.'

Sloane surprised himself by kissing her, Rachel freezing just for a second or two, then kissing him back. One of his hands pushed up beneath her hair, fingers tracing small circles on her neck.

'Don't you think we're a little old for this?' Rachel asked when they broke apart.

'What?'

'Necking in public like a couple of kids.'

'Probably.'

So they did it again.

'This isn't the point,' Sloane asked, pausing, 'where you invite me up for a drink?'

Rachel shook her head. 'No way. But I could be free for coffee tomorrow, around, say, eleven, eleven thirty.'

'Then come to my place,' Sloane said. 'There's something I want you to see.'

◆

Rachel stood in front of the canvas, not too close, not too distant, quite still. Above the unbroken hum of traffic from the nearby road, the sound of a train slowing into the station.

'Remember, it's not . . .'

'Sshh.'

Sloane turned away to the window and looked out: the train that had just arrived was already pulling away; two magpies and a crow doing battle around the chimney stacks; of course, he was stupid to have asked her to look at the damned thing so soon—Sloane, you idiot, you fool!

'Look, why don't we . . . ?'

'Stop fussing!' Rachel said.

He went downstairs and pottered, washed his breakfast things in the sink. He could hear her moving around now, imagined her looking at other canvases with increasing dismay as she struggled for something polite, not too damning, to say.

And then there she was, facing him at the foot of the stairs. 'I think you may have something,' she said. 'Of course, it's too early really to know, but there's a life to it, real promise. And the colors—the colors are really strong and unlike the others, the earlier work—I mean I only took a quick look—instead of crowding out all the light, here it's letting it come in.'

Sloane was blushing, a grown man, sixty years old, actually blushing at praise.

Rachel laughed. 'Of course, there's always time for you to screw it up.'

'Thanks!'

She looked at him and raised her hands, fingers spread. 'Christ, Sloane, you bring me here, stick me in front of your painting like I'm some oracle and expect me to pronounce.'

'It's okay.'

'What?'

'What you said.'

Rachel smiled. 'Good. I'm glad. And I'm grateful for letting me see what you're working on, I really am. And now I must go.'

The taxi taking her to her meeting with the director of the Whitechapel was waiting outside. Sloane kissed her lightly and she squeezed his hand. 'See you soon,' she said and as the cab turned out of sight at the corner of the street, Dutton and Boyd sidled into view.

Inside, first one, then the other listened to the tape on headphones, nodding contentedly, even smiling once or twice.

'So?' Sloane said, anxious for them to be gone. 'It's what you wanted?'

'It's a start,' Dutton said.

'You'll meet him again,' said Boyd.

'Tomorrow, probably.'

'Good.'

'And Dumar?' Sloane asked.

'All in good time.'

'I need better than that.'

'The wheels of bureaucracy . . .' Boyd began.

'Fuck the wheels of bureaucracy,' Sloane said. 'If Elms doesn't follow through on his promises about Dumar, you won't get a word out of me in court and without that these tapes won't fly.'

Dutton looked at him with sharply, eyebrow raised. 'Something's put lead in your pencil. Wouldn't be that redhead, sailing off in the cab, I suppose?'

Sloane held the door open for them to leave.

32

SLOANE WORKED ON THE canvas for eighteen hours solid, eating only when he remembered, alternately drinking bottled water and Scotch whiskey, cat-napping, fully clothed, in a chair he had dragged upstairs. The telephone he had unplugged; he was oblivious to any hammerings on the front door. Through all of this process the basic shape of the composition, what he had achieved on the first morning, remained the same; other sections he labored over, trying this shade, this shape, always moving close, stepping back, wiping away, covering up and starting again. Building. Remaining true to the same basic core colors, purple and gold. Remembering what Rachel had said about the light, the importance of letting it shine through.

Parsons he met in the restaurant on the upper floor of the National Portrait Gallery, views out across the rooftops towards Nelson's Column and Whitehall. Sloane asked for more details of the pieces Parsons wanted, sizes, frames; the dealer would need to be setting up accreditation before they were all finished, contacting likely buyers, oiling the necessary wheels.

'This means working fast,' Sloane said.

'When did you work any other way?'

A waiter drifted close, then drifted away.

The envelope Parsons passed across the table was plump and pleasingly heavy in the hand.

At the exit they went their separate ways, Parsons south towards his club on Pall Mall, Sloane cutting through to meet Dutton at the ticket booth on the south side of Leicester Square, a quick handover of the tape, then the Tube and home.

The telephone was ringing when he arrived.

Rachel's voice was slightly breathless, the ambient noise from the airport lounge busy and loud.

'Mason Ranch,' Rachel said, 'that name mean anything to you?'

Sloane remembered a friend of Jane's, a short, portly man with a shock of hair he was forever pushing away from his face when he read his poems, Monday nights at the Five Spot, poetry and jazz, the cadences of a Southern accent undisguised.

'Yes, of course. Why?'

'I'm going up to see him next weekend. I thought, just as long as you're going to be around, you might like to come along.'

Sloane ran it through his mind, sensing Rachel's slight anxiety, her eye running down the departure screens, seeking out her flight. 'Can I let you know?'

It wasn't exactly the answer she'd been expecting to hear. 'Sloane, you're not blowing cold on this, are you?'

'No,' he said, 'I shouldn't think so. There's just a few more things I have to do.'

'Like finish that painting for one.'

'Exactly,' he said, though it was only part of the truth.

'Good luck,' Rachel said. 'And call me. Okay?'

'Okay.'

And she was gone.

Sloane made coffee, strong, and carried it upstairs to where the canvas waited. An hour later—or was it two, or four?—pleased but not yet satisfied, suddenly hungry, he went to the nearest shop for milk, butter, bread, eggs and cheese. Made himself an omelette and ate it with a fork, straight from the pan. His mind drifting back to

Mason Ranch, he recalled one night in particular, a conversation about poetry and painting between himself, Mason and Jane, which had started, as so many conversations did, in the Cedar Bar and continued in one of the coffee houses on Bleecker or MacDougal. Jane loving the oils Grace Hartigan had done, incorporating lines and phrases from O'Hara's poems. Out of that evening, Sloane believed, had come collaborations between Jane and Mason Ranch that he had never seen.

He threw cold water on his face and went back to work.

Not allowing himself to rush, to overcrowd, pacing back and forward, forward and back, this brush, this rag, this color, that. Back aching, a vein throbbing low on his left leg, he stopped, he smiled, it was finished, he knew. Nothing more he could or should do.

Below, he took a long bath before crawling into bed and falling, almost immediately, asleep.

Someone was tapping at the window when he woke.

Olivia and her friend, Nicky: Nicky, a slender girl with Doc Martens and stubbly pink hair, her white skin laced with studs and rings; Olivia smiling excitedly when Sloane, having pulled on shirt and jeans, finally opened the door.

'My dad,' Olivia said. 'It's gonna be okay.'

Sloane smiled and Olivia threw her arms round him and held him tight.

'It's okay,' Nicky said, sly smile in her gray-green eyes. 'She's always doin' that. Grabbin' hold of old men an' snoggin' 'em.'

'Thanks a lot,' Sloane said.

'He rung me this morning,' Olivia said, releasing him. 'Dad. These fellers from the Home Office been down to see him, about asylum. He reckons it'll all be fine. Should be home here in a week or so, maybe less. He said I should thank you for what you done.' Her face lit up with a smile. 'I thought we could, you know, have a drink, celebrate.'

'What time is it?' Sloane asked. 'I've lost track.'

'Half-four,' Olivia said uncertainly. 'Five?'

'Five twenty-three.' Nicky looking at her watch.

They went to the pub on the corner of Holmes Road and sat outside, drinking beer, chatting about nothing in particular.

'You know,' Nicky said when Olivia had gone to the toilet, 'when Livia come round mine the other night, the way she was going on and on about you, I thought she had this crush, right?'

'And now?'

'Bollocks, i'n'it?' Nicky said and grinned.

Back in his studio the painting still looked finished, its colors vibrating across the canvas, brushstrokes live and strong. Perhaps he wasn't fooling himself this time. Hoping it wasn't too late, he phoned Rachel at home and then the airline.

He thought it wouldn't be easy to sleep again, but when he woke early next morning, the lamp was still burning and the book he had been reading lay open where it had fallen. In the small park behind the station the railings gleamed damp, dew was silver on the grass and above the light was gathering in the sky.

◆

One of the runways was out of action at JFK and planes were stacking up the length of the eastern seaboard. Sloane's flight finally landed a good fifty minutes behind schedule, its passengers whey-faced and irritable, and punching the buttons of their phones the moment they were freed into the terminal, alerting family and friends, altering arrangements. Sloane shouldered his carry-on baggage through the terminal and stood in line, waiting for the cab that would take him to the hotel.

33

VARGAS HAD PROMISED HERSELF a new bed. After spending weeks on a borrowed couch and, before that, an antique hand-me-down with a metal cross-piece that regularly woke her from sleep with dreams of crucifixion, she owed it to her body to purchase something better. Pliant but firm. A bed to which, when and if the occasion arose, she could invite a close companion without fear of discomfort for them both; a bed to which that companion might return. Yet a bed which, this being a studio apartment, could be folded away each morning, opened out each night.

After a diligent search she found the perfect one. Of course, it was several hundred dollars more than she'd intended to spend and delivery would take, the sales clerk had told her, six to eight weeks. Minimum. Until then she'd be sleeping on the floor.

'Is this the last?' Cherry called, hefting a box on to his shoulder and heading for the stairs leading to Vargas's new apartment.

'I doubt it.' She followed him with two brimming bags in each hand, clothes draped over both shoulders and round her neck.

They had been at it since early morning, loading the U-Haul truck, first with her possessions from the Bronx, then the East Village; finally carrying everything up five stubborn flights.

'Next time,' Cherry said, unburdening himself inside the front door, 'try a place with an elevator.'

'You know how much extra an apartment with an elevator would cost?'

Twenty minutes later they were sitting on a pair of folding chairs, surrounded by bags and boxes of every shape and size.

'You want a drink?' Vargas asked.

'I'd give my life for a cold beer.'

'How about champagne?' Jumping up, Vargas disappeared into the tiny square of kitchen and, after much foraging, found paper cups. It was only when the bottle was two-thirds empty that either of them spoke Delaney's name.

Vargas sat with a legal pad open on her lap, ballpoint in her hand; Cherry, using boxes as a table, had layered several pages of computer printout, one over the other, and topped these with a pocket-size, leather-bound notebook.

'You want to go first?' Vargas asked.

'You. It's your place, after all.'

Vargas didn't need asking twice. 'Okay, Vincent Anthony Delaney, born Las Vegas, nineteen forty-nine. His old man was a gambler, worked the casinos, dealing faro. Hung around the coat-tails of the mob. When Delaney was born it looks as if the mother skipped town. Whatever the reason, he was brought up by his dad. Whether his father had ideas of Delaney following in his footsteps or not, Delaney clearly had plans of his own. Left Vegas for the coast and got himself a law degree.'

Cherry whistled in appreciation.

'Joined an LA firm specializing in entertainment, media, all the glitzy stuff. Junior partnership in the bag, seemed to have it made. Except he overreached himself.'

'How so?'

'One of his clients was stuck in a recording contract she wanted out of. Delaney, wanting to cover his back, had a quiet word with the judge.'

'Is this the plain brown envelope story? Unmarked bills? The briefcase left under the table, beside the men's room stall?'

'Something like that,' Vargas said. 'Only Delaney either didn't offer enough, or tapped the wrong judge. Either way, he ended up disbarred.' She turned another page. 'Exactly what happened after that I have no clear idea, except a year or so later, he's running a club in West Hollywood.'

'Sounds familiar.'

'You want familiar? How about this? In nineteen eighty Delaney's arrested in South Pasadena, charged with assaulting a woman with whom he'd been having an affair. Marianne Burris, a banker's wife. Case gets to court but no further; the woman changes her mind about giving evidence, denies all previous testimony, Delaney walks free.' She looked over at Cherry, waiting for him to speak.

'Okay,' Cherry obliged, 'the woman, she was either threatened in some way or paid off. Has to be. And Delaney, this is what you're suggesting, this is the beginning of a pattern.'

'Right again. Seattle, nineteen eighty-seven. Beat a woman within an inch of her life.'

'You know this?'

'I know this. I talked to her, on the telephone, several times. Mary Jane Flood. Charming, runs an animal sanctuary. What happened with Delaney, it's behind her. She talked about it, though, albeit grudgingly. Seems ninety-eight per cent of the time Delaney was a perfect gentleman. A tad overprotective, maybe, but that's what some people seem to need. She was an accountant when they met, doing the books for a supper club Delaney was managing. Everything running smoothly until Mary Jane decides she's had enough.' Vargas shook her head. 'One thing you don't do easily to Vincent Delaney, walk away.'

'She didn't press charges?'

'Says she was too traumatized. Too afraid. But now I think she could be persuaded to go on record.'

'Corroboration, it's what we need.'

'Wait, there's more. One of the reasons Mary Jane wanted out, she'd been becoming more and more convinced everything wasn't above board at the club.'

'Delaney had been skimming off the top?'

'A distinct possibility. But that wasn't her main concern. What was, the amount of money passing through, the revenue, it always seemed in excess of the business being done. I mean, she'd go in there some nights and the place'd be less than a quarter full, but according to the books things were booming.'

'Then Delaney was using the place to launder money.'

'Somebody was.'

'At the very least, Delaney must have known.'

'It's not credible he didn't.'

'Your Ms Flood, did she ever pick him up on this, confront him?'

'No.' Vargas shook her head.

Cherry was on his feet, leaning first this way and then that, loosening up muscles he seldom used and could feel beginning to tighten up. 'Is it stretching the imagination to suggest the reason he took up with her, one of the reasons, was he thought she might turn something up and figured if they were together, comfy-cosy, the less likely she was to spread it around?'

'Intention or not, seems it worked.'

'Till now.' Cherry reached down and picked up the printouts. 'Delaney's got four bank accounts I've been able to trace, all pretty healthy. Not only does he own the apartment he's living in, as in own outright, he owns another in the same building, which he rents out. Oh, and then there's the yacht.'

'The what?'

'Well, it isn't actually a yacht, it's some kind of power boat he keeps out on Long Island. State-of-the-art. Cost six months' salary, yours and mine combined.'

Vargas put her head in her hands and rubbed her eyes. She was tired; it had already been one hell of a day. 'All of which means, chances are Delaney's still laundering money.'

'Through the Manhattan Lounge and all the rest.'

'Despite what we've been told.'

'Precisely.'

Energized, Vargas was on her feet. 'If he's doing it in any serious way, it's got to be the Mob.'

'Possibly.'

'Christ, John!'

'What?'

'Who else needs to bury large amounts, shift them coast to coast?'

'You want me to count them? The Russians, Chinese, the Vietnamese.' Cherry ticked them off on the fingers of one hand.

'But if I'm right and it all goes back to Vegas . . .'

Cherry nodded. 'Yeah, I see what you mean.'

Vargas poured out the last of the warm champagne.

'I've got a friend in the Department of Justice,' Cherry said. 'I'll get in touch, see if Delaney rings any bells.'

'Sounds like a plan.'

Cherry finished his drink, set down his cup. 'Feel like getting something to eat?'

'I don't think so. I'm going to go through a few of these things, call it a night.'

'Till tomorrow, then,' Cherry said, heading for the door.

'John . . .'

'Yeah?'

'Thanks for everything.'

'My pleasure.'

Vargas slid the bolt into place and surveyed her new home.

◆

Cherry met Pat Holland, his friend from the Department of Justice, in the restaurant of the St Regis, 7.30 a.m., Holland's choice. Holland was there early, already well into his fresh fruit, low-fat yogurt and no-cal muffin by the time Cherry arrived.

'What's that you're drinking?' Cherry asked, pointing suspiciously at Holland's glass.

'Hot water.'

Cherry ordered scrambled eggs, bacon, rye toast, coffee.

'Your friend Delaney,' Holland said, 'his connections go back a long way.'

'Vegas?'

Holland nodded. 'Via LA. Nothing big time, nothing that was ever going to draw much attention. Low profile.'

'Flying under the radar.'

'Exactly. The kind, oh, we'd look at him once in a while, figure, hey, bigger fish to fry. Fronting for guys on the fringes of the Mob, made guys, money laundering, that's his steady number. Nothing spectacular. Nothing greedy.'

Cherry shook Tabasco on to his eggs. 'And he doesn't step out of line?'

Holland pushed away his empty plate. 'There was something in Reno, seven years back. Nothing I could get to the bottom of, but it seems he messsed up somehow. Frozen out for a while. This guy, Marchetti, brings him back in. Sets him up, running this small network of clubs. Delaney, as you might say, he's expanded his portfolio from there.'

'But he's still Marchetti's boy?'

'For sure.'

'Sticky fingers?'

'If his hand wasn't in the till for a little, they'd figure something was wrong. So, yeah, within reason. But that's a guess, speculation.'

'And reason is what? Ten per cent? Fifteen?'

'Again, I'm guessing, but fifteen seems kind of high.'

Cherry spooned sugar into his coffee and stirred it. 'Your connections, any way you could put it around he was getting greedy, taking more?'

Holland smiled thinly. 'So that Marchetti heard?'

'So that Marchetti heard.'

The Department of Justice man ran the pattern in his head: names, faces, links in the chain. 'Absolutely.'

'And soon?'

'Consider it done.' Holland was on his feet, *Times* in one hand, clapping Cherry on the shoulder with the other. 'Next time it's on me.'

Which was what he'd said the previous time, and the time before. Cherry glanced at his watch, signalled for more coffee, finished off the last of his bacon and eggs.

34

RACHEL PREFERRED NOT TO talk while she drove. Instead, she punched the pre-set buttons on the radio of the rented Saab until she came to something palatable and kept her own counsel, Sloane alternately dozing and gazing at the scenery. At Southampton they stopped for coffee, cinnamon Danish for Rachel and for Sloane, eggs over easy on wheat toast.

'How much further?' Sloane asked.

'Not far. Another twenty miles, twenty-five. Just past Amagansett, where the Fork starts to get really narrow.'

'Mason's place is on the shore?'

'Inland. And beautiful, great views. From the upstairs you can see the Atlantic to the south, Long Island Sound to the north.'

Thirty minutes later they were back on the road.

'Long Island Sound', Sloane thought, the tune title surfacing on the tide of his brain. Jimmy Raney? Stan Getz? A bit more of his adolescence that wouldn't stay down.

They turned off the highway on to a dirt track that took them up through a rough meadow, before levelling out to pass through an apple orchard with Mason Ranch's white clapboard house beyond. Ranch was on the porch to greet them in a creased blue cotton suit, his hair still full but now completely white, face deeply lined, his belly seeming to have survived while the rest of him had shrunk. An antique golden Labrador barking as it hobbled arthritically down the steps, wagging its tail, and while the dog brushed unsteadily against their legs, Mason Ranch waited at the top of the porch steps, arms outstretched. Rachel he kissed on both hands and then both cheeks, before shaking Sloane's hand, then clasping him in an earnest, clumsy embrace.

'You, my dear,' he said to Sloane, 'I've hardly seen since you were barely weaned. And beautiful. You wouldn't believe'— addressing Rachel now—'how beautiful this boy was when he was eighteen.'

'Oh, I think I might,' Rachel said, close to smiling.

'And, his saving grace, entirely oblivious of the fact.'

There was little Sloane could do, other than stand there awkwardly, an object of appraisal.

Chuckling, Ranch led them inside into a large room with broad windows on three sides, pale polished boards and faded rugs, high-backed wicker chairs and a low settee strewn with cushions. Books, floor to ceiling, occupied one wall; newspapers and magazines lay haphazardly across occasional tables and, here and there, on the floor. Opposite the settee a grand piano stood, lid raised, and behind it a painting which Sloane thought could have been by Jane Freilicher, though at this distance he couldn't be sure. There were vases of flowers everywhere.

'A little refreshment after your journey,' Ranch said. 'Mimosas, I think.'

Rachel went with him to the kitchen, leaving Sloane to cross towards the painting, which was indeed a Freilicher, oil on canvas, a splash of marsh flowers, cream and pink and purple, rising above green leaves from a rich, reddish-brown jug on the table end: and through the window beyond, fields of green and yellow-gold leading down to a solid blue finger of sea, the shifting, paler blue of sky.

'She lives out here, you know,' Ranch said, coming back into the room. Behind him, Rachel was carrying three tall glasses on a tray. 'Water Mill. That's one of the views from her studio.'

'She was as much in love with color as the rest of us,' Sloane said. 'She just used it in a different way.'

There was a book of Chopin nocturnes open at the piano, which Sloane paused and glanced at as he passed.

'You play?' Ranch asked.

Sloane shook his head. 'No.'

'Me either. Not any more. Not with hands like these. The best I can do now is sit there in the afternoons and read the score, hear the damned thing in my head.' Slowly he lowered himself into one of the chairs. 'It's so shitty getting old, the way your body makes you give up on things, one by one. And you, Jackson . . .' He gestured towards the Labrador which was making courtship gestures against one of Sloane's legs. 'You're in pretty much the same boat, so you can stop pretending and go lie down.'

The dog half raised his head and sniffed the air, then waddled away.

'Time was,' Ranch said, 'he'd try and fuck anything if he thought he had half a chance.' He chuckled. 'Why we called him Jackson, I guess.'

For a while they sat and drank their mimosas, Sloane mostly listening while the other two chatted back and forth.

'You're still happy here, though?' Rachel queried at one juncture. 'You wouldn't think of moving?'

'Only every other day when some developer drops by with his chequebook and offers me more money than I could shake a stick at.'

'And you'd take it? You'd go? Mason, you've been here half your life.'

'I know, but the way this area's changing, smart money moving in more now than ever, I scarcely feel I belong here any more. This artist feller, Schnabel, for instance. Neo-Expressionist, I think that's what he calls himself. Just recently bought a place further down the Point. Ten bedrooms, seven acres. An eighty-foot pool with a goddam island in the middle of it sprouting cherry trees.' He looked across at Sloane. 'When you and Jane Graham stayed out here, I wouldn't mind betting you pumped water straight from a well and used a crapper in the outhouse.'

'Just about.'

'I was sorry to hear about her dyin'.'

'Thanks.'

'You and her, you lit up the sky for a while.'

Sneaking a glance across at Rachel, Sloane nodded.

'I've got some of her pieces, you know,' Ranch said, 'things we worked on together, if that's what you can call the way we did it. Airmail, for the most part. One time I did get over to see her, when she was still living in Paris, but that was all.'

'These are the paintings based on your poems?' Rachel asked.

Ranch nodded. 'The ones you're here to offer me a good percentage on, I'm hoping. I wouldn't have sold one of 'em when she was still alive, but now, well, if I am goin' to hang on to this place, I've got to realize any assets I can find.' Slowly he shook his head. 'Got in touch with my publisher a while back, same imprint I've been with more'n thirty years. Finally got to speak to this youngster, fresh out of college by the sound of him. Polite, once he'd recovered from the shock of realizing I wasn't good and dead. Told him I just about had enough poems for a new collection and would they be interested. Wow, he said, that's wonderful and yes he was absolutely sure they would. Just give him a few minutes to log on to the computer, check a few sales figures and he'd get right back to me. Haven't heard a damned word since.'

Ranch laughed savagely and the laughter became a cough, which doubled him over and sent Rachel hurrying for a glass of water.

Recovered, he apologized before walking slowly upstairs to fetch the pieces he wanted Rachel to sell. Jane Graham's style was immediately apparent, her brushwork, her use of color, the paint merging here with the words of Ranch's poems; sometimes these had been stencilled directly on to the surface, in others his own handwritten version had been cut around and pasted on, partly painted over. Each piece was clearly numbered and signed, one through six.

'You sure you can bear to part with these?' Rachel asked.

'I have one I'm keeping, upstairs. Jane was never totally happy with it herself, that's why it's not numbered as part of the set.' He smiled lopsidedly. 'Maybe it's a love of waifs and strays that makes me like it best.'

'I almost hate to say it,' Rachel said, 'but since her death Jane's star's been rising. I can get a good price for these.'

'Thirty pieces of silver plus inflation,' Ranch said caustically. 'I shall do well.'

Afternoon, Sloane read silently from the canvas closest to him, *the light falling softly in the northern sky. These trees . . . And you, your heart, the best of you, is still.*

'Now why don't the two of you go for a walk, drive down to the beach?' Ranch said. 'Let me rest.'

◆

It was just warm enough for them to have dinner out on the porch, smoked chicken and sesame noodles, a green salad with lime dressing.

Looking across at Ranch, Sloane remembered him at the quay-side, kissing Jane goodbye, waving her off flamboyantly, hair falling across his eyes.

'When Jane went to Paris,' Sloane said, 'did you know she was pregnant?'

Instead of answering immediately, Ranch chewed thoughtfully for several moments longer before wiping his mouth with a napkin. 'I take it you didn't.'

'No.'

'I think I only knew more or less by default. She had to tell somebody and, well, with my history I wasn't about to lay claim. Wasn't likely to try and talk her out of it, either.'

'Out of what?' Rachel asked, though she must have known.

'This young woman she knew, she'd gone to France and had an abortion. Stayed away a year, did the grand tour and returned, leaving most of her kith and kin none the wiser. Jane figured she could do the same.' He speared a piece of lettuce with his fork. 'It didn't work out that way.'

'Do you know why?' Sloane asked.

Ranch shook his head. 'She never said. Not directly. A hint, maybe. My guess, the nearer it came, the harder it was to go through with it. After which the time it would have been safe had passed.' He drank more wine, emptying his glass. 'I sometimes wonder if somehow Connie knew what her mother had intended; if maybe that didn't account for the way she turned out.'

Sloane sat forward, alert. 'You know her then, Connie?'

'Right up until she and Jane had their big falling-out. Oh, I wouldn't say we were ever bosom pals. But if I went into the city and she was performing, I'd go along. No hardship there, she was pretty good. Maybe still is. Once, just once, she came out here. Got pretty bored and couldn't wait to leave.'

Close by, a bird called and was still, and Sloane stepped into the silence. 'Did Jane ever say who the father was?'

'Connie's father?'

'Yes.'

'Not in so many words.'

There was no disguising the disappointment on Sloane's face.

'But then,' Ranch continued, 'I never really considered it necessary.' His already creased face creased even deeper in a grin. 'The way the two of you were at it every conceivable opportunity, I'm only surprised it wasn't twins.'

After coffee and brandy, which they drank indoors, Ranch showed Rachel and Sloane to a pair of rooms across the landing from each other and bade them goodnight, leaving them to work out whatever arrangements they wished.

Rachel caught Sloane looking past her, almost wistfully, at the turned-down bed and, smiling, kissed him lightly on the lips. 'All that good fresh air. Even if I don't need a good eight hours, you do.'

She squeezed his hand, turned into her room and closed the door and, after a few moments, Sloane did the same.

Tired or not, neither could sleep.

Rachel fidgeted with her pillows, kicked off the covers, pulled them back; tried reading a magazine. After an hour or so she heard the sound of a piano from below and, getting out of bed, reached for her robe.

Sloane was at the keyboard, feeling his way, albeit tentatively, through 'I Let a Song Go Out of My Heart'. When the last chord had faded he lowered the lid and slowly turned towards her.

'I thought you didn't play,' Rachel said.

They sat back out on the porch, a bottle of wine between them, listening to the wind rousting the trees and, distant, the ocean breaking slow against the shore.

'At dinner,' Rachel said. 'When you asked Mason about Jane. You heard what you wanted to hear.'

'Did I?'

'I thought so.'

Sloane didn't answer, sat staring out.

'Whatever it is that's worrying you,' Rachel said, 'frightening you, even. I thought you'd dealt with all that when you decided to come back.'

He looked at her through the almost dark. 'Maybe it's not that simple.'

'Oh, Sloane,' Rachel said with a shake of the head. 'It rarely is.'

He leaned forward and flexed his fingers. The wind seemed to have dropped and there was only the sound of water, rolling up, then back. 'I had this long time,' Sloane said. 'I was forty, I suppose. Forty-five. Moody as can be. Sneaking glances at other people's babies on the street. Maybe you know the kind of thing?' He looked quickly across at Rachel, then away. 'One reason or another, it never happened and the thoughts went away. I had a life and I got on with it. Came to terms, the way people do.'

'So now you should be pleased.'

'At the prospect of getting everything turned upside down?'

'God, Sloane! What do you want?' Rising fast, Rachel spilled wine across her hand. 'Forty years down the line, an easy birth? Smiling babies with blue eyes and blonde curls? Grateful little girls? This isn't some fantasy, it's real. She's real. Real and pretty messed up, from what you've said. Connie. Maybe she needs your help, maybe she doesn't. Could be she'll tell you to stay out of her life. That's a risk you have to take. But, Sloane, you have to give her the chance. Give yourself the chance.' Close enough, she reached out her hand towards his face. 'I don't see what else you can do.'

35

HE TOOK A CAB across town, the evening warm, windows part-way down; Sloane wearing the suit he'd bought for the opening at the Serpentine, blue cotton shirt, plain leather shoes. Inside the club he sat and drank two whiskies at the bar. The house system was playing a mixture of ballads, Sinatra, Dean Martin, Nat Cole, a few innocuous instrumentals thrown in. A little over half the tables were full. Stage lights still down, the musicians took their positions on stage. When the barman gestured towards Sloane's glass, he shook his head. A few testing notes from the bass, a quick shuffle on the snare. The music faded and, as it did, the piano player leaned into the mike alongside his keyboard and spoke Connie's name. A pause and then she appeared, stepping into the spotlight to sparse applause.

For the third number Wayne introduced 'Why Was I Born?' from the piano, slow-medium tempo, Connie squeezing out the words like sour fruit.

Sloane thought he would have another drink after all.

The set over, he waited five minutes before negotiating his way backstage and knocking on the dressing-room door.

'I wondered,' Connie said, 'when you'd come sniffing round again.'

'No Delaney this evening?' Sloane asked.

Connie laughed a harsh, dry laugh. 'Vincent's got other things on his mind.'

For two days now he'd been like the cat on the proverbial roof, jumping at shadows, bad-mouthing all and sundry to their faces and behind their backs. Something to do with the business, Connie knew that much, somebody asking questions, poking their nose into the trough. When she'd asked him what was wrong, earlier, he'd lashed out and punched her in the face. Tonight he was over in Jersey and good riddance, asking a few questions for himself.

'I thought maybe a drink?' Sloane said. 'Somewhere we could talk.'

'Oh, God, why not?' Connie reached for and lit a cigarette. 'Give me ten minutes, okay, I'll see you out front.'

They went to the bar at the top of the Beekman Tower and sat out on the balcony, the lights of the city veiled in thin mist and cloud. When Connie shivered, Sloane took off his coat and slipped it around her shoulders.

'What happened?' Sloane asked. Reaching slowly and with care, he turned her face towards him: what had been hidden beneath her stage make-up was just visible now, the bruise spreading across the left side of her face, cheek to jaw.

'Lamp post?' Sloane said. 'Door?'

Connie said nothing, lit a cigarette. The waiter brought their drinks.

'It was him, wasn't it? Delaney.'

Connie shrugged. 'People argue.'

'People get killed.'

When she shivered this time, it wasn't the cold.

Sloane leaned in closer. 'When we met before, you remember what you said? He'd kill me if he found out. And you were right, I didn't really take you seriously, figured it was just one of those things people said.'

Connie was looking at him over the top of her glass. 'And now?'

'Leave him,' Sloane said.

Connie shook her head and looked away. 'I can't.'

'Why not?'

'You wouldn't understand.' She drank, dragged deep on her cigarette.

'I'll help,' Sloane said.

'You?'

'Why not?'

'You got the hots for me or something? That what it is?'

'No.'

'What then? Prince Charming? Saint George? My Fairy fuckin' Godfather?' Seeing something in his eyes, she stopped. 'Oh, fuck! That's it, isn't it? How she got you to come chasing after me waving some goddamn olive branch. Said you were my fucking daddy.'

Sloane felt as if he had been struck hard, his skin numb, the air sucked out of his lungs.

Connie laughed, caustic and rough, the laughter overlaid with tears, a succession of short, breathless sobs. Blindly, she scrabbled for a tissue inside her bag. 'It's crap,' she said, when she could catch her breath. 'You know that, don't you? You, my father. Bullshit, it has to be.'

Sloane waited until she was looking at him again. 'Suppose it's not?'

Connie held his gaze. Traffic noise rose muted from below; the sound of a piano, staid and genteel, from the lounge behind them; sirens on Second Avenue. She scraped back her chair. 'I have to go to the bathroom.'

'You'll come back?'

'Yes. I'll come back.'

When she did, she seemed more settled, calm; she lit another cigarette and slowly released the smoke into the air. 'I want to tell you a story,' she said. 'About Vincent and me.'

A nerve set up its erratic pulse at the corner of Sloane's eye.

'The first time he met me, I was about as low as it was possible to get. Least, that's what I thought. He got me working again, set me straight. Gave me an inch of self-respect. So then, when he turned around after that and walked out after someone else, quit me cold, I came apart. The drink, everything got out of control. By the time the affair was over and Vincent found me again, I was working for this guy in Portland, Oregon, the Triple X Escort Agency. A cellphone and a bunch of business cards he'd leave around the airport and hotels, in the back of cabs. Hooking, more or less.'

She glanced at Sloane, then closed her eyes.

'Vincent went crazy. Slapped me around, knocking some sense into me. Made me take him to where the guy lived. The two of them, they got into this fight. Vincent finally smashed the guy's head against the wall and then he beat him and kicked him and beat him some more and, God help me—I don't know, I must've been high—I joined in. And when we were through he was dead.'

Connie took a long drag on her cigarette. She looked at Sloane through the waft of smoke, but his face was giving nothing away.

'I think he was dead a long time before we stopped.' She reached for her drink. 'I helped Vincent clean up the room, every mark, every spot of blood. The body we took downstairs in the service elevator and stuffed in the trunk of Vincent's car. We'd wrapped it in plastic bags, sheets and towels. We must've driven around for hours, looking for a place to dump it. Ended up in some part of the city I never knew existed. Projects, places boarded up. Finally stopped by this piece of wasteland, dogs roaming around in packs, barking, making a hell of a din. Vincent chased them off long enough for us to tip the body out, drag it into the middle.' Ash fell from the end of her cigarette. 'By the time we were driving away and I looked around, you could see the dogs coming back.'

She shivered and Sloane took the glass from one hand and set it down, took the cigarette from the other and stubbed it out. He put his arms round her and held her close.

'So you see,' Connie said finally.

'What?'

Their voices were quiet, hushed.

'Why I can't ever leave him. Why he can keep leaving me and then keep coming back.'

'No,' Sloane said.

'We killed someone. Together. Murdered him.'

'No.' A slow shake of the head. 'You didn't kill him, he did that. You were—what?—an accessory at worst.'

'I could still go to prison.'

'Maybe.'

'And besides, if Vincent ever thought there was the least chance I'd talk to the police or anyone . . .'

Sloane started as a face appeared on the other side of the glass, but it was only the waiter, looking out to check that they were all right. Seeing his reaction, Connie caught hold of his hand.

'If it weren't for this,' Sloane said. 'What you just told me. Could you walk away?'

Connie looked at him and shook her head.

'You love him?'

'No. I don't think so. Not any more.'

'Then why . . . ?'

'I need him.'

'No.'

'What do you know?'

'Look,' Sloane said. 'One way or another, you've got to get Delaney off your back. Which either means going to the police and telling them what you told me . . .'

'I can't do that.'

'Then come back to England with me.'

She looked at him sharply, then laughed. 'Now I know you're crazy!'

'I don't see what's so crazy about that.'

'What the fuck would I do in England?'

'The same as the rest of us, sit around reading Jane Austen, eating crumpets for tea.'

'Funny!' But she was smiling, just a little.

'Either way, you get some space, get yourself some counselling, go into detox, whatever it needs.'

'And what do I do for money while all this is going on?'

'We'll come up with something. Your mother's Foundation maybe, some kind of loan, advance.'

'God! You've got it all figured, haven't you?'

'Not till this minute.'

'And if I say no?'

Sloane took his time. 'Maybe you'll live to regret it. Maybe.'

He got to his feet.

'I'm going to stay here,' Connie said. 'Have another drink.'

'Okay. You know where I'm staying, same place as before.' On a napkin he wrote down Rachel's name and address. 'If I'm not at the hotel, try here.'

Scarcely bothering to give it a second glance, she folded the paper and pushed it down into her bag. 'Thanks for the drink.'

Sloane hesitated only a moment before stepping off the balcony back into the building, leaving her alone. Down on the street he hailed a cab and paid the driver to sit idling until she came out and then, at a distance, followed her home.

36

RACHEL HAD BEEN AT her desk for the best part of an hour, sorting through the mail. She was leafing, amused, through the miniaturized portfolio of a young photographer from Port Arthur, Texas—*No, I am not Janis Joplin, nor have I ever been*—when the receptionist interrupted her.

'There's someone in the main gallery I think you ought to see.'

Rachel read the concern in her eyes.

Delaney was standing in front of a larger-than-life portrait of a child's face, the face a collage of overlapping newsprint.

'Rachel Zander?'

'Yes.'

'Vincent, Vincent Delaney.' A smile creased his mouth and was gone. 'It's good of you to spare me a little of your time.'

He was wearing a dark suit with a purple shirt, purple and black tie. Black leather shoes that shone. His hair, cuffs, everything about him just so, except he looked somehow out of place, out of time.

'I believe you know a friend of mine,' Delaney said.

'It's possible.'

'Connie.'

'I don't think so.'

'Connie Graham.'

'Oh.'

Delaney took a pace forward, just one but it was enough to have Rachel glancing up at the security camera in the top corner.

'You do know her, then?'

'No.' A quick shake of the head, a step away.

'That's strange. Your address, it was in her purse.'

'This address?' The response too fast, the voice pitched too high.

Delaney slowly shaking his head. 'Not here,' he said, 'your apartment. Private. Personal. Safe.' Smiling now, smiling with his eyes, the cruel curve of his mouth. 'The one place you can lock all the windows, bolt all the doors. Keep out the bogeyman.'

The pre-recorded voice echoed around them: *He'd kill us if he got the chance.*

Rachel's legs, the backs of her arms, were like ice.

Delaney snaked out a hand.

There was a movement in the space behind them, visitors to the gallery. Delaney broke the tension deliberately, moved towards one of the canvases on the side wall, closer to where Rachel was standing. Painted with meticulous attention to physical detail, it showed the trunk of an eviscerated body in a field. A tableau of body parts arranged against a sunlit, storybook background, leaves and actual pieces of grass and weed stuck to the edges of the frame. Little Gray Rabbit meets Hannibal Lecter.

'You like it?' Delaney asked.

Rachel shook her head. She didn't know. She did. She saw it for what it was, not what it was pretending to be.

'It's here. Your gallery. Your choice. Or so I suppose.' Delaney's voice a gentle croon, persuasive.

'It has certain qualities . . .' Rachel began. 'It speaks to . . .'

'To who?' Delaney asked, close enough to touch. 'Maybe that should be to whom, I was never sure.' And then he laughed a surprisingly musical laugh. 'To people like me, I'd suppose.'

His fingers brushed her arm and she jumped back, eyes closed.

When she opened them again, seconds later, he was behind her and she turned, searching for him, betrayed, bemused.

'You know what this all lacks,' Delaney said, sweeping his arm through an arc to encompass the room. 'This stuff on the walls. The excitement. The thrill. The pleasure in the pain.'

She stood there for a long time after he'd gone, unable to move. And only when her staff had assured her they had searched the building twice and that he was nowhere in sight did Rachel permit herself to step back inside her office.

◆

'For Christ's sake, Sloane, you gave him my address. This address. Whatever were you thinking?'

'I didn't give him anything,' Sloane said defensively.

'He had it in his goddam hand.'

'I gave it to Connie, just in case . . . I'm sorry. I didn't think.'

'No, you didn't.'

He reached for her and she shrugged him off.

Sloane and Rachel alone in her apartment, early evening as arranged. Come around, why don't you? A glass of wine, a bite to eat. It wasn't intended to be like this. The minute he had arrived, Rachel had launched it at him in the cool space of her living room, unburdening herself of the fear. Trying to.

'At least,' Sloane said, 'let me try and explain. If Connie's ever going to leave Delaney she has to have somewhere to go. Otherwise it'd never work . . .'

'And so you told her to come here.'

'No.'

'What then?'

'All I said, if I wasn't at the hotel, she might contact me through you. Was that so wrong?'

'Yes, of course it was wrong. You had no right.'

'I only thought . . .'

'You had no fucking right.'

Sloane rocked back in his chair and swung himself to his feet. Faint, the sounds of Brazilian music from the apartment below. 'Okay, okay, I'm sorry.'

'It's a little late for that.'

'Rachel, I don't think he'll do anything. Not to you.'

'You don't *think*?'

'That's not what it was about. It was his way of telling me what he could do if I don't back off and leave Connie alone.'

'And is that what you're going to do?'

He looked at her steadily. 'You were the one, Rachel, telling me to face up to my responsibilities, remember?'

'Jesus, I don't believe this. I get threatened where I work and you're putting the blame on me.'

Sloane pulled on his coat and she followed him to the door. 'What do I do now? Change all the locks? Hire private security? Tell the police?'

'I'll handle it. I'll handle Delaney. You'll have to do whatever you want.'

'Sloane . . .'

But he had gone. Rachel slid the bolts across, slipped the chain in place and turned the key. Back in the easy chair, she sat with her arms held tight between her legs, fingers locked, elbows pressing hard against her womb as she rocked slowly back and forth and back and forth again.

◆

Sloane went first to the apartment block on Second, but neither Delaney nor Connie was home. The doorman had seen them leave almost an hour before by cab, Mister Delaney's car was still in the garage. At the club, Connie was backstage getting ready for her first show, Delaney had been and gone. Was he expected back? Most probably.

Suddenly hungry, Sloane bought a bowl of chicken and vegetable soup at the nearest corner store and ate it in the shadow of a doorway. Having threatened off and on throughout the day, rain began to fall. At intervals cabs drew up outside the club and customers, usually couples, middle-aged, hurried inside.

When Delaney himself arrived, Sloane stepped forward and called his name clear and loud, and Delaney spun fast, ducking as he did so, shoulders hunched. When he saw who it was, relief flooded his face and he laughed.

Sloane was level with him in a moment, staring hard. 'Rachel Zander, keep away. You don't go near her. Where she works, where she lives. You don't even look in her direction. Understood?'

Delaney looked back at him almost carelessly, amusement bright in his eyes. 'Got your attention, didn't it?' he said.

'This is no fucking joke,' said Sloane.

'I can see.' Delaney smiling still, taunting.

'Rachel, you leave her alone.'

'And Connie?'

'What about Connie?'

'She doesn't need you, Sloane. She doesn't want you. All this crap about the past, her mother, some pathetic little fortune she might come into. It throws her off, gets under her skin. Keep away, Sloane, okay? Right away.' No hint of amusement now, Delaney with fists clenched, elbows by his sides, voice low in the hiss and bounce of rain. 'If you don't, remember how easily I can get to anyone, anyone you care for, anyone you love.'

The rain falling heavily now, the light from the club doorway reflecting back from the pavement, illuminating both their faces.

'Lay a finger on either of them,' Sloane said, 'Connie or Rachel, and I'll make you pay.'

Delaney's eyes focused in on him hard and Sloane tensed, waited for whatever was to come, but then Delaney was laughing again and stepping away, shaking his head as if to clear the rain from his eyes and, still laughing, disappeared through the doorway and into the club, leaving Sloane alone.

When he turned and crossed into the street, Sloane was shaking. A car he'd failed to see braked hard and honked, and Sloane raised a hand in acknowledgement and waved the driver past. He was on the opposite pavement, walking away, when a second car slowed alongside him, windows down.

'Get in,' a man's voice said from the rear.

Blinking through the rain, Sloane shook his head and continued to walk, picking up his speed. The car kept pace and this time a woman leaned across from the driver's seat. 'Come on, don't be such a hard-ass, get in the car.'

Sloane could see now the shield the man in the back was holding up towards the light. The car stopped and he climbed into the vacant front seat.

'Detective Catherine Vargas,' the driver introduced herself. 'And this is my partner, Detective John Cherry. Let's go somewhere we can talk.'

37

THE SQUAD ROOM WAS quiet, almost empty. Vargas sat with her chair pushed back on to its hind legs, boots resting on the edge of the desk, blue jeans and a black turtleneck. Cherry had folded his suit jacket neatly over the back of his chair, but failed to notice when it slid to the floor. Sloane, faded blue shirt pushed back to the elbows, sat diagonally across from the pair of them, sipping a cup of stale coffee and waiting.

'You and Delaney,' Vargas opened, 'it looked as if you were having an interesting conversation.'

Sloane said nothing.

'What you might want to do,' Vargas said, 'run down your basic relationship, the two of you.'

'Why would I want to do that?'

'Because,' Vargas said, 'Vincent Delaney is the subject of an ongoing police investigation.'

'And because,' Cherry said affably, 'we can't imagine you've anything to hide.'

Sloane took a breath and told them, as succinctly as he could, about Connie and Jane, about Rachel, the reason for that evening's confrontation with Delaney. Not wanting to incriminate Connie unnecessarily, he didn't say anything about the incident in Oregon.

The detectives listened patiently, not interrupting, one or the other occasionally scribbling down a note.

'Your friend,' Vargas said, 'Rachel. Delaney didn't actually threaten her?'

'Not in so many words.'

'Offer violence? Raise his hand?'

Sloane shook his head. 'He got to her, though. Frightened her. And Rachel's not a timid woman; I doubt if she frightens easily.'

Vargas swung her feet down from the desk and settled her chair squarely on all fours. 'And Connie—she is your daughter or she isn't?'

Warily Sloane smiled. 'It's not that simple.'

'Surely it is. Either she isn't or she is.'

'I don't know. Not for certain. I mean, it's possible. More than possible. But I don't *know*. Not for a fact.'

'There are tests,' Cherry said. 'Maybe not cheap, but thorough. And quick. Way it works, far as I know, you just walk in off the street. Give a little blood, a little this and that, maybe.'

'A few hundred bucks,' put in Vargas. 'They sift your DNA through the computer. Wave a couple of wands. A few hours later, a day at most, you know the truth. If, that is, you want to know the truth.'

'Why wouldn't I?' Sloane asked.

'I suspect,' Cherry said, smiling slightly, 'this isn't the time or place for that conversation.'

Somewhere back along the corridor a door was opened and slammed shut.

'There are a few things about Delaney,' Vargas said, 'we should share with you.'

Eschewing unnecessary detail, they laid out the bare bones of the case they were building against Delaney. First, they were increasingly convinced that for years he had been steadily laundering illegal funds through a number of establishments that he either part owned or managed. And second, he was responsible for serious assaults on two women, Marianne Burris and Mary Jane Flood, and the murder of a third, Diane Stewart.

'You can prove this?' Sloane asked. 'Any of it?'

'Not exactly,' Vargas replied.

'Not yet,' Cherry said.

'On one hand,' Vargas started to explain, 'it's a matter of resources. Personnel. Time. The only way we could hope to go after Delaney on the money laundering, for instance, would be to convince the Department of Justice to set up a strike force. FBI, ATF, DEA and ourselves. And chances of that are slim. In their book Delaney's just so much small potatoes.'

'As to the rest,' Cherry said, 'without clearer evidence we'd be laughed out of court.'

'We wouldn't get into court,' Vargas said. 'Not even close.'

'Which means what?' Sloane asked. 'Delaney carries on as before, scot-free?'

Vargas and Cherry exchanged glances.

'Not exactly,' Cherry said.

The misinformation he'd arranged to have fed down the line to Delaney's associates seemed to have taken its effect. The watch he and Vargas had been able to keep on Delaney these last few days, partial as it was, had shown a man with troubles, real and imagined, on his mind; someone who was forever looking over his shoulder in the clear expectation of more. A man whose mood changed faster than the weather: who could never be still.

'Which way d'you think she'll jump?' Vargas asked. 'Connie.'

'I'm not sure,' Sloane said.

'Do you think she'd ever give evidence against him?' Vargas asked.

Sloane shook his head. 'I doubt it. Not unless something changed.'

'Okay.' With something of a spring, Vargas was on her feet and holding out her hand. 'Thanks for the co-operation. I'll give you a card. Anything else that occurs to you, anything happens, be in touch.'

Sloane told them where he could be reached and shook both their hands. 'Connie,' he said. 'You think she's in real danger?'

'While she's with Delaney?' Vargas replied. 'Oh, yes. Don't you?'

They watched Sloane walk away along West 20th, slender and tall, head lowered slightly against the wind, which seemed to have cleared the earlier rain away.

'You think he told us everything?' Cherry asked.

'No more than he had to.'

'And Connie, you think she's really his daughter?'

'I think right now he wants her to be. Maybe that's more important.'

Cherry moved away from the window, back towards the center of the room where a telephone was ringing unanswered. He made no attempt to pick it up.

'Connie,' Vargas said, 'I think she might need a little nudge. I'll try to get her on her own, see what I can do.'

'You don't think that might be pushing her too hard?'

Vargas raised an eyebrow. 'It's a risk you take.'

38

CONNIE WAS IN HER dressing room when Delaney came in; one set to go and she was exhausted already, smoking a cigarette, legs crossed, eyes barely open.

'Jesus!'

'What?'

'You look like shit, that's what.'

Connie swivelled in her chair and stubbed out the cigarette. 'You're a charmer, Vincent, you know that? A real way with words.'

For a split second, when she saw his arm move, she flinched, waiting to be struck, but all he did was take a small opaque tube from his pocket and shake a couple of pills out on to the dressing table near her arm.

'What are those?'

'What do you care? Just swallow them. And for God's sake make yourself look like something, after you close we're going out.'

Connie hung her head. 'Not tonight, Vincent, I'm bushed.'

Delaney gripped the sides of her chair and slowly swung her round. 'Marchetti's out front. He's taking us to dinner after the show.'

'Vincent . . .'

'He loves you, you know that.' Carefully, Delaney tilted up her face with the tips of his fingers, kissed her bruised cheek. 'Connie, I need this.'

When he stepped back, she reached for a bottle of water and swallowed the pills.

'You were good tonight, sweetheart,' Marchetti said. They were sitting in a back booth, the same restaurant Marchetti had been going to for close on fifty years.

'Not really,' Connie began. 'I . . .'

'Listen.' Marchetti reached across the table, seizing her hand. 'I've seen them all and believe me, you're good. Among the best.' He chuckled deep in his throat and gave her fingers a squeeze. 'Then I've always loved you, you know that.' He winked and leaned back into his chair, wiped the corners of his mouth. 'I keep waiting for Vincent here to really screw up, know what I mean? Then I can move in, take you down to Grand Cayman, just the two of us, what do you think?' And he winked again. A network of tiny veins criss-crossing his nose, loose flesh hanging off his neck, yet his eyes still clear. Sixty-seven years old.

Connie smiled. 'I think that might be nice.'

'Nice? Nice is right. You just make sure he keeps treating you right. You treating her right, Vincent, huh?'

Delaney nodded and kept his head down, eating his way through a plate of veal with Parma ham. Before they'd got into the car there had been this kid with a wall eye and a swagger, Marchetti's driver—twenty? twenty-five?—leering at Connie like she was old meat, breathing garlic all over Delaney as he patted him down.

'Back in the old days,' Marchetti was saying, 'I knew Vincent's old man. I ever tell you that?'

Connie shook her head, though he had told her, several times.

'Jeez, what a fuck-up, what a loser!' He pointed his knife across the table. 'First time I saw you, Vincent, remember? First time we did business. What I said. Keep out of your old man's shadow, you don't want to end up the same way.'

'Fuck you,' Vincent said beneath his breath. He kept the thought to himself.

At the end of the meal the waiter brought brandy, cigars. 'Connie, sweetheart,' Marchetti said, 'why don't you go and powder your nose a while, let me and Vincent talk a little business here?'

Squeezing out a smile, Connie did as she was told.

Marchetti clipped the end from his cigar. 'Vincent,' he said, 'you playing straight with me?'

'What else?'

'Dipping your hand into the till, skimming off the cream?'

'No more than usual.'

Marchetti looked him in the eye and laughed. 'I've got your word on that?'

'Of course you've got my word.'

'Only I've been hearing all kinds of things . . .'

'What kinds of things?'

'All this bullshit about how you're looking to get rich at my expense. Offshore accounts, who knows?'

Delaney leaned across and lit the older man's cigar. 'It's garbage, what can I say? Someone stirring trouble, the fuck knows why.'

'And that's all?'

'I swear. And I'll get to the bottom of it, you see. Watch it all go away. Nice and peaceful, like it was before.'

'I hope so.'

'Like I say, you got my word.'

Marchetti drew on his cigar, swirled brandy around the bottom of his glass. When he saw Connie heading back, he leaned forward. 'That bruise on her cheek, Vincent, I don't like to see that. A man can't keep his woman in line without hitting her, he's a weak man. That's what I've always believed.'

And then, half rising from his chair, 'Connie, sweetheart, we were just talking about you. Sit yourself down, have some brandy. Relax. Vincent, why don't you pour the lady a drink?'

◆

The next day, afternoon, Connie was in the basement of HMV uptown, fingering her way through the racks of jazz CDs. For days now she'd been carrying a folded-over piece of paper in her purse, a list of people Wayne thought she should listen to. Joshua Redman. Dave Douglas. Brad Mehidau.

'These are singers?' she'd asked and Wayne had shaken his head. 'That's not what you need. You already know how to sing.'

Connie had found herself smiling; now that things had settled down on the bandstand, Wayne was one of the few people who could make her smile.

'Like, it's a matter of a sensibility,' he had said, 'a way of phrasing, sounding now. What you don't want to risk, getting caught up too much in this nostalgia thing. The whole lounge bit. Next thing you know, you'll be playing cruise ships round the Bahamas care of Club Med, Alzheimer's Division.'

Connie had laughed and pushed the piece of paper down into her purse. She didn't think cruising round the islands with an inexhaustible supply of vodka tonic was such a bad idea.

Standing there now in front of the 'M's, Connie recalled the pressure of Wayne's finger against her skin, the closeness, the scent of him as he leaned towards her face.

'Hi!' Vargas said brightly, stepping alongside Connie and lifting an album out of the rack. *Mingus Ah Um*. 'Know anything about this? I think maybe I could use a little advice.'

Connie shook her head and moved away, Vargas following.

'Hey,' Connie said, 'what is it with you? This some kind of pick-up scene, 'cause if it is . . .'

'Marianne Burris,' Vargas said, 'that name mean anything to you? Mary Jane Flood?' She took a photograph from her bag and held it out. 'Diane Stewart, Connie. You know who she was, don't you?'

Cold shivered across Connie's skin and wrapped itself tight.

'What happened to her, you know that?'

'She was hit by a car,' Connie said. 'A truck, whatever. Hit and run.'

Vargas smiled. 'Who told you that, Connie? Delaney?'

Connie jumped at the sound of his name.

'Is that what he told you, hit and run?' Vargas reached towards her bag. 'I've got more pictures here, Connie, you want to take a look?'

Connie angled her head away.

'I was the first detective at the scene, you know that? It wasn't pretty. Down among all the cement, all that junk. She was a mess, a real mess. He beat the shit out of her, then tossed her out of his car like the piece of crap he thought she was.'

'No.'

'No? Why don't we go across the street, Connie? Get some coffee. Talk.'

Vargas watched as Connie lit her cigarette, inhaled. Eyes flickering this way and that. 'All those women,' she said. 'I just don't want you to be next.'

She reached for Connie's hand and Connie snatched it away.

'Connie,' Vargas said, 'if you wanted to leave him; if you were afraid and wanted to leave, I could help. Offer protection. Make sure you were safe, stop you from getting hurt.'

Connie looked back at her, tears pricking at the corners of her eyes. Pale skin tight across her face, she looked like her own ghost.

'Think about it, Connie. Before it's too late.' From her top pocket Vargas took a card on which her name and numbers were printed, nothing else. 'Call me. Any time, day or night. And think about this—a little help from you and we could put Delaney away for a long time. Make sure he never hurts you or anyone else again.' Rising, she gave Connie's arm a gentle squeeze, then walked, without looking back, towards the door.

Connie sat perfectly still, watching her go. For several minutes she didn't move, what Vargas had said replaying over and over inside her head. When, finally, she lifted her cup to her lips, some of the contents spilled down her front; as she tried to light a fresh cigarette her fingers fumbled so much that the waitress took pity and came to her aid. She willed her mind to stop racing, playing tricks.

She knew about the other women, of course, the ones Delaney had left her for, the younger ones, the smart ones, the ones he had to get out of his system before coming back. Affairs that had lasted their course. Lovers who had gone back to their husbands, left the country, moved to the other coast—women who were road kill, hit and run.

And there was Sloane and now this cop saying leave him, leave him, leave him . . . as if she had the guts, as if she had the will.

Too much that bound them together.

Too much fear.

39

CONNIE HAD ALL BUT finished changing when someone knocked, none too loud, on her door and her first thought was Sloane, but then when the visitor knocked again and called her name she knew it was Wayne. After a quick check around the tiny room, she told him to come ahead.

'Hey.'

'Hey, yourself.'

'I thought we were pretty good tonight.' Wayne, leaning against the open doorway, leather trousers, black shirt, smiling, looking cool.

Smiling a ragged smile, Connie shook her head. 'You were good. I managed to keep up.'

'Don't,' Wayne said.

'What?'

'Put yourself down. Plenty others do it for you, give 'em a chance. Know what I'm sayin'?'

'I suppose.'

'Damn it, girl.'

'Okay, yeah. I know what you mean.'

It took only half a stride for Wayne to reach the center of the room, close enough to take the lower part of Connie's face in one hand and tilt it gently up towards his own. 'After me,' he said and then, pronouncing each syllable with exaggerated care, 'I was good.'

'I was good,' Connie said quietly.

'C'mon now, again,' Wayne said, releasing her. 'This time like you mean it.'

'I was good,' she almost shouted and laughed. 'There, that better?'

Wayne grinned. 'You gettin' there.'

She could still feel the warmth of his fingers on her neck and cheek, their strength.

'We're going to go get somethin' to eat,' Wayne said. 'Check out some music later. Figured you might like to tag along.'

Connie shook her head. 'Wayne, this *is* later.'

'Bullshit.'

'I can't.'

'Sure you can.'

'Wayne, Wayne. Just don't pressure me, okay. Some other time, maybe.'

He shrugged and stepped back through the door.

'Hey,' Connie said.

'Yeah?'

'I'm glad you asked.'

Wayne nodded and was gone.

After a minute Connie turned back towards the mirror, lit a cigarette and looked at herself through the blue-gray skein of smoke. She thought about what Wayne had said and knew that he was right, they had been good tonight, the two of them. Bass and drums as well, sure, no question, but really it was Wayne, pushing her along, throwing in a few unexpected chords, making sure she was on her toes, on her game.

Maybe once this gig was finished they'd work together again.

Get better still.

She smiled at herself, quickly, in the glass. Maybe things were going to be okay, pretty much the way they were. No need to make a change. Slipping on her coat, she stubbed out her cigarette, picked up her purse, put out the light.

◆

Crossing the lobby, she wondered what kind of mood Vincent would be in. Distracted? Morose? Something was winding him up real bad and for once, thank God, it wasn't her. When the elevator came to a halt with a small shudder and the door slid back, she stepped out into the corridor and began fumbling for her key.

It was silent inside the apartment, almost dark, just a small light shining from the galley kitchen and the muted glow of the city slanting through the blinds. No Vincent settled in front of the TV, watching some old movie, the way he'd usually be this time of the night.

Pushing the door closed behind her, she dropped her key back into her purse and stepped into the apartment. 'Vincent, you here?'

Dropping her purse down on the settee, Connie slipped off her coat and carried it towards the bedroom. At first her eyes didn't make out the shape on the bed and then they did. 'Jesus, Vincent! You startled me!' Her coat had fallen from her grasp.

Delaney was stretched out on top of the covers, pillows pushed up against the headboard supporting his head and shoulders.

Connie turned and reached for the light switch on the wall.

'No,' Delaney said. 'Leave it.'

Connie did as she was told. She could see more clearly now, her eyes adjusting to the levels of light, Delaney wearing a pair of boxers and a T-shirt, nothing else.

'Come on over here,' he said.

She went and stood beside him and he ran his hand upwards along her leg. So that's what it was, she thought, Vincent feeling horny and, reaching down, she dragged her nails lightly through the dark hairs of his forearm. Fingers of the one hand spread across her buttocks, he used the other to pull her down on to the bed, finding her mouth with his. Connie wriggled a little, adjusting her position, kissing him back as he half turned and his thigh pushed up between her legs. 'Vincent,' Connie said. 'I should go to the bathroom.'

He grunted something that might have been no and kissed her all the harder.

'Vincent . . .'

He rolled over on top of her, tugging at the fastenings of her clothes, tearing impatiently. She knew how hard he was, how hard he would be. She was still a little dry when he pushed inside her and she cried out, but not loud, and then he was driving into her, abrasive at first, not really hurting, not too much, then finally sliding, sliding, his chest and shoulders above her rising, one hand reaching underneath her and pulling her even closer towards him, Connie's head going back, mouth open, her back arching, starting to scream his name as Delaney's whole body suddenly shuddered and he came, shouting, inside her, Connie caught there on the very edge and pushing herself impossibly against him, already knowing it had gone, her moment, tears welling in her eyes as she wrapped herself around the sweated bulk of his body, spent inside her.

She slept and when she woke he was sitting on the side of the bed, showered, fully dressed, gray slacks and a pale green shirt, a small, square envelope in his hand.

'Vincent . . .'

'Shh. Stay there.' A hand on her shoulder, keeping her down. There was sorrow in his eyes.

'I love you, Connie. You know that.'

'I know. You don't have to . . .'

'Why I keep comin' back to you, no matter what.'

'Vincent, I know.'

'All this shit been goin' down. I've been wanting to talk to you about it. 'Stead of it all hammerin' round inside my head. Get, maybe, some sense of perspective, you know? Some bastard's goin' round, spreading stories that ain't true, putting me in bad with Marchetti. Fuckin' lies!'

Connie shifted a little on the bed. 'He's your friend, Vincent. He'll believe you.'

Delaney went on as if she hadn't spoken. 'An' all the while I'm wondering how it's happenin', who it is knows enough to make this crap sound kosher? And finally I figure it's Howard, Howard Pearl, got to be. He's envious, mercenary, far enough inside, just, to know some, guess the rest. Maybe he figures, I don't know, with me out of the way, the spot is his. Poor shit! I had him down on his knees, sucking on the barrel of a little Smith and Wesson .38 while I spun the chamber like somethin' outta the fuckin' *Deerhunter*. Bastard pissed hisself an' worse, stank like a toilet in there. And you know what, Connie, it wasn't him. Cryin' an' screamin' and wishin' it was, just so's he could tell me somethin', make me pull that gun outta his mouth before I squeezed down on the trigger one more time. It wasn't him.'

Connie shivered and wrapped her arms across her chest, cold.

'Here,' Delaney said and flicking open the envelope he shook out a small batch of Polaroids, four or five, and let them fall across the bed.

Connie and Catherine Vargas, photographed through the glass door leading to the jazz and blues section of HMV.

Connie and Vargas, emerging out on to the street.

Connie in the diner, her head turned towards Vargas as the detective speaks.

Vargas standing, her hand stretched out towards Connie, fingers brushing her sleeve.

In the bedroom the only sounds, breathing aside, were those of Connie's choked crying as she covers her face with her arms the way she did when she was a little girl, pretending she wasn't really there at all.

40

SLOANE WOKE, FLOUNDERING, OUT of sleep, and grappled with the telephone. The clock beside the hotel bed told him it was 4:24.

Sloane identified himself, then listened, face tightening.

'Yes,' he said. Then, 'Yes, I understand.'

He let the phone fall from his hands.

A moment, then he was pulling on his clothes.

At the corner of 11th and Sixth Avenue he hailed a cab. 'New York Presbyterian Hospital,' Sloane said, slamming the door closed. 'Sixty-eighth and York.'

The reception area of the ER was a maze of bodies: anxious relatives and friends, strident, nervous, angry, close to tears; uniformed nurses weaving in and out; doctors who, to Sloane, looked impossibly young. He heard three, possibly four languages other than his own. Anxious, he pushed his way through the crowd and grabbed the attention of a tall Asian at the desk.

'Connie Graham,' Sloane said. 'She was brought in—I don't know—forty-five minutes to an hour ago.'

The receptionist glanced round at the white board behind him, checked a sheaf of pages by his hand. 'And you are?' he said.

'I'm her father.' The words there without thought or hesitation.

'This corridor,' the receptionist said, pointing left. 'Next to the last room on your right.'

Vargas was sitting in the corridor outside, head bowed, arms resting on her thighs. Like a boxer who'd just gone five rounds and didn't want to get up for the sixth. As Sloane approached, however, that was what she did.

'Connie,' Sloane said. 'How is she?'

'Alive.'

As Sloane moved towards the curtain, Vargas intercepted him. 'Wait. Let me get the doctor,' she said.

Sloane glimpsed overhead lights, monitors, people crowded around a bed, a body swathed in white.

A few moments later Vargas re-emerged with a tall, willowy blonde, tennis shoes on her feet, wisps of hair straggling loose from where it had been pinned, blood speckled faintly down one side of her white coat. 'Doctor Sullivan,' she said, holding out her hand.

'No jargon,' Sloane said. 'No lies.'

Sullivan breathed in and held it for a count of three. Her eyes were the palest blue, the shadows around them purple shading into indigo. 'The right cheekbone is fractured and so is her jaw. The retina has become partly detached from the right eye.'

'Christ!' Sloane said softly, an exhalation of breath.

'There's other damage to the head—it's too early to say how much is serious, how much is superficial. Bruising to the body. Lacerations. Internal bleeding. She's lucky we got to her when we did.'

'But she'll be all right?'

'We need a surgeon to work on her eye. Then we'll look at the results of the X-rays, tests.'

'She's going to be okay?' Sloane persisted.

'We'll do everything we can.'

'Fucking answer me!'

Sullivan sighed. 'I am answering you, Mister Sloane, as best I can. But it's not an answer you really want: it's a promise I'm not in a position to give.'

Sloane opened his mouth and let it close, thought unspoken.

'If you want to see her before she's moved, there's just time.'

He stood beside the bed while staff busied around him, Connie's face a welter of bruised flesh and bandages, one side protected by a wire cage from which a damson stain spread around the closed and swollen eye. Tubes and electrodes. Fluids feeding into her broken body, keeping her alive.

Sloane searched for words but again they refused to come.

Lightly, the doctor touched his arm. 'It's time.'

He stood aside as the bed was wheeled towards the elevator. He needed to talk to Vargas, but Vargas was nowhere to be seen. Back at the reception area he phoned Rachel. He needed to talk to someone.

When they were through, Sloane looked at his watch; it was still not six o'clock. He pushed back out through the doors of the ER, seeking air, and there was Vargas coming towards him, John Cherry by her side.

'What happened?' Sloane said. 'I need to know.'

'Absolutely,' Vargas said. Cherry's words had been haunting her since the first call had come through: *You don't think that might be pushing her too hard?* And her own reply: *It's a risk you take.*

They found a table in the cafeteria one floor down. The coffee was bitter and stewed, Cherry's Danish stale.

'It was Delaney?' Sloane said. 'You know that for a fact?'

Vargas nodded. 'For once in this city, someone acted instead of simply turning up their TV. Hammered on the door and called 911. Probably saved her life. By the time the first squad car arrived, Delaney had gone. But, yes, there doesn't seem to be any doubt.'

'The bastard,' Sloane said. 'I should've killed him when I had the chance.'

Cherry shook his head. 'If you mean the other night, I don't think that's what you had.'

'I should have tried.'

'Don't blame yourself,' Vargas said.

After that, no one spoke for some little time.

'There's something I should have told you,' Sloane eventually said.

They looked at him. 'What?'

Sloane repeated Connie's story of the Portland murder unembellished.

'And this was when?' Vargas asked.

'Seven or eight years ago.'

'And they drove round with the body in the car, looking for a place to pitch it out?'

'That's what Connie said.'

Another image rose clear in Vargas's mind: Delaney driving round the city in the Lexus with Diane Stewart's body in the trunk, finally pushing her out off the West Side Highway. 'Why didn't you tell us before?' she asked.

'Would it have made a difference if I had?'

'Possibly.'

'I wanted her to tell you herself.'

'And you didn't want to be responsible for maybe sending her to jail,' Cherry offered.

'That's right.'

'Depending on the way it fell,' Vargas said, 'her willingness to speak out in court, it's unlikely that would happen.'

'And now?' Sloane asked.

'After what's happened,' Vargas said, 'Delaney can't assume Connie won't give evidence against him. Not any longer. Which means as long as he remains at large we have to assume Connie's life is in danger. So until he's in custody, or we know for certain where he is, there'll be a guard on Connie, either police or hospital security, twenty-four hours a day. Meantime we'll check out all his known associates, places he might go. We'll find him, don't worry.'

They left Sloane at the table with his cold coffee and headed for the stairs.

'You really believe that?' Cherry asked, pushing through the door and holding it open behind him. Stairs and then a corridor.

'That we'll find him?'

'Yes.'

'We better.'

'He had—what?—ten, fifteen minutes' start. The Lexus has gone from the garage. By now he could be a few hundred miles along some interstate. Aboard a plane. Anywhere.'

'His description's gone out, details of the car . . .'

'So he switches cars, dyes his hair . . .'

'No,' Vargas said, 'I think he's still here, in the city.' A set of double doors and they were at the front of the building.

'You think he'll try to get to her again?'

'Don't you?'

◆

Connie lay amidst the alternating hum of machinery, oblivious. Brief intervals aside, Sloane sat beside her through the day, occasionally resting his hand alongside hers on the surface of the bed, letting their fingers overlap. Once he thought she tried, weakly, to squeeze his hand, and he spoke her name aloud, but almost certainly it had been a reflex gesture made, unbidden, in her sleep.

Sloane phoned Rachel and she looked in once during the afternoon, returned in the evening with soup and sandwiches.

A uniformed guard sat outside the door, reading the paper, checking visitors' ID.

Sightings of Delaney's vehicle were reported up and down the eastern seaboard and as far inland as Cleveland; Delaney himself was in Newark, in Boston, riding the airport shuttle to La Guardia, bold as brass buying shirts in Bloomingdale's.

According to the Portland Police Board, the broad details of

Connie's story checked out: the body of a known pimp and small-time criminal had been found, badly savaged by dogs and almost unrecognizable, in the North Precinct, seven years before. No one had ever been charged with the crime.

Vargas spent part of the day at the hospital, part at the precinct, much of it on the streets. By midnight she was bushed. At an all-night coffee shop she talked to Cherry on the phone, apologizing for waking him, ordered a pastrami on rye and lacked the energy to eat more than half.

Cursing the lack of an elevator, she climbed the stairs to her apartment; the bulb on the upper landing had blown. She was bringing her key towards the lock when she sensed, rather than heard, something in the darkness at her back. Turning fast, she ducked low, right arm angled out in self-defence. The first swing of the bat broke her arm at the elbow, the second caught her smack on the right temple and sent her careening into the wall.

A smile on his face, Delaney dropped the bat and caught her before she hit the floor.

41

JOHN CHERRY RANG VARGAS'S apartment at seven fifteen and then again at seven thirty; assuming she'd gone in early, maybe to catch up on her paperwork, he went straight to the 10th Precinct. When she wasn't there he contacted the hospital. No joy. Less than twenty minutes later he was gaining access to her apartment building, the supervisor complaining his way up the stairs as he did half a hundred times a day, fumbling with a large ring of keys before he finally pushed the door to Vargas's apartment open. The covers on the bed were untroubled, the undersheet felt cold; there were no signs of coffee having been made that morning, breakfast eaten; the shower floor was dry. There was a small, alphabeticized address book by the phone; Vargas's family, Cherry remembered, lived in Denver. Even in an extreme emergency, though, one of her parents, say, suddenly taken ill, she would have found time to phone the department before leaving, phone him. Checking the interior again carefully, slipping the catch on the door, he went back out on to the landing where the supervisor was still standing.

'How long's that been missing?' Cherry asked, pointing to the empty light socket above his head.

'Some cheap bastard steals 'em, I swear.'

'How long?'

'It was fine and dandy yesterday.'

'Yesterday when?'

'Yesterday around five.'

Cherry crouched down and began to examine the floor.

'And as for keepin' the place clean . . .'

'Move,' Cherry said.

'If I mop these floors once a day, I . . .'

'Move!'

'Hold your horses, no call to shout.'

Cherry was bending lower, face almost against the tiles; there, faint against the worn pattern, dark specks of what was certainly blood.

◆

Connie had been transferred to a room on the eleventh floor of the main building, a single window looking out over the FDR Drive on to Roosevelt Island and the East River. An armed guard staring off along the corridor from a chair outside.

Connie had been awake a little earlier; she had seemed to recognize Sloane and tried to smile. That morning he had read to her, uncertain whether she could hear him or not. A couple of Hemingway short stories, the ones about Nick Adams.

Now that she was sleeping, he went along the corridor and phoned Rachel as promised. When he arrived back at the room the doctor was standing beside Connie's bed.

'How's she doing?' Sloane asked softly.

'Well, I think, don't you? Her blood pressure's stable, pulse close to normal. Another day of rest and we can start working on her jaw.' She smiled. 'Poor thing, she looks like a quarterback got sacked once too often.'

'If it were only that,' Sloane said.

The doctor touched his hand. 'She will be okay, you know.'

Sloane nodded, still a little bewildered at how much he needed that to be true.

'One of the nurses said you were reading to her earlier.'

'Yes.'

'From this?' She lifted the paperback Hemingway from near the foot of the bed.

'Not what you'd prescribe?'

She laughed. 'I'll bring in some Margaret Atwood, next time I call.'

When the doctor had gone, Sloane moved closer. Connie's eyes were closed, a ripple of movement across the darkened lids, and then they were open, looking directly at him.

'Connie.'

The eyes widened slightly as he leaned towards her, reaching for her good hand.

'You're going to be okay,' he said, squeezing her fingers and feeling, no illusion this time, a small pressure in return. 'You're going to be fine.'

Connie smiled and let her eyes fall closed.

'You're going to be fine,' Sloane said again to no one but himself.

◆

Cherry sat at his desk and stared at the phone, willing it to ring. All precincts had been alerted, a search of buildings and alleys in the vicinity of Vargas's apartment had begun. So far no sign. And Delaney, all those sightings having been checked out and yielding nothing, seemed to have successfully disappeared.

Of course, there was as yet no proof Delaney was involved. It could have been a random attack, a rapist lying in wait, someone desperate and after the contents of Vargas's purse. But in either case Vargas's body, dead or alive, would still have been there, stretched out along the landing at the head of the stairs.

What the fuck was Delaney up to?

Cherry bit into an almond Danish and forced his brain to think.

◆

'You look exhausted,' Rachel said when she arrived, resplendent in red and peacock-blue, bags of expensively prepared food from Dean and Deluca in each hand.

'Do I?'

'Here, take one of these.'

He set one of the bags on the floor near the bed.

'She's all right?'

'Yes.'

Rachel put down the other bag and began to rummage inside. 'And you're hungry?'

'I expect so.'

'Good.'

She had small pastries stuffed with goat's cheese and fennel; others with minced lamb and cinnamon; grilled chicken with soy sauce and honey; mozzarella and tomato salad; bread in different shapes and sizes. A bottle of good Italian wine.

'Are we celebrating?' Sloane asked.

'I think so.'

They drank a toast in paper cups to Connie's recovery.

A little over an hour later, Rachel shook Sloane awake. 'You're snoring.'

'Sorry.' He stretched, rubbed his eyes and yawned.

'Go home.'

'Home?'

'Go back to my place, a real bed. Get some decent sleep.'

Sloane shook his head. 'I'll be fine.' And yawned again.

'Go on,' she said. 'Don't be so stubborn. I'll wait here.'

'Are you sure?' he said, weakening.

'Certain.'

'Okay, just a couple of hours.'

Rachel was on her feet, the keys in her hand. 'Go. Just go.'

◆

'You want this?' the security guard asked, waving the newspaper in front of Rachel's face. 'I'm off duty, half-hour ago.'

Rachel set aside the magazine she had been reading and took the paper from the man's hand.

'Keep it,' the guard said, walking away. Nobody came to take his place.

42

SLOANE SAT UP, IMMEDIATELY awake but uncertain, for the moment, where he was. Anxiety flooded his mind. The digital clock by the side of Rachel's bed told him he had slept longer than intended, almost three hours. Swiftly he slipped out from under the covers and began to dress.

There was a cab, loitering on the edge of the Square. Sloane gave the driver the name of the hospital and, promising him a ten-dollar tip if he got there fast, sat on the edge of his seat, being bounced this way and that, until they drew up outside.

Too impatient to wait for the elevator, he took the stairs, running, two or three at a time. At the beginning of the final corridor he stopped, leaning sideways against the wall to catch his breath. Someone coughed and then was still. The guard's chair at the far end was unoccupied.

The door to Connie's room was slightly ajar and Sloane's breathing stopped. His skin was glass. He began to ease the door open slowly, then pushed it back. Everything was as it should be, as it had been. In the muted light, Connie's shape on the bed. The same tubes and wires. Of Rachel, there was no sign.

Released, Sloane's breath escaped him in a sigh.

'Knight to the fuckin' rescue,' Delaney said and Sloane spun round. 'Shame your timing's fucked too.'

He was standing over Rachel, her arms bound behind her as she knelt before him, tape across her mouth, the barrel of a Smith and Wesson .38 pressed against the side of her head.

'One move,' Delaney said, 'and she's dead.'

Sloane's guts twisted tight.

Delaney's hair was blond, cut shorter; he was wearing casual clothes, dark chinos, a leather waist-length jacket. He looked younger, slimmer.

'Now stand straight,' Delaney ordered. 'That's it. Turn around now, all the way around. But slowly. Hands by your sides. Good. That's very good.'

Sloane sensed Delaney stepping away from Rachel and into the center of the room. Towards him. Towards the bed.

'How's she doing?' Delaney asked.

'What do you care?'

The tip of the gun barrel prodded Sloane in the back. 'How's she doing?'

'Getting better.'

'A pity.'

Sloane jabbed an elbow towards Delaney's chest and swung round—an aimless, instinctive move—and, stepping smartly to one side, Delaney raised the gun and brought it raking down across Sloane's face, gouging blood.

Sloane stumbled to his knees and Delaney brought the gun to bear, resting it on the flat plateau of bone and skin above the nose, between the eyes.

'Next time I'll kill you.'

'I doubt it,' Sloane said.

'No?' Delaney laughed.

'Use that in here,' Sloane said, 'and you'll have half the hospital awake. Not what you want at all.'

Delaney cocked the hammer back. 'Three shots,' he said, 'that's all I need. In a couple of hours I'll be out of this country for good.'

He smiled and as he did so Sloane threw himself sideways and back, his right foot coming up fast and catching Delaney hard and high between his legs, Delaney, doubled up, staggering back even as the gun went off, a single shot that tore through the ceiling above their heads.

Sloane hurled himself forward, head driving deep into Delaney's solar plexus and they caromed off the bed, the gun slithering from Delaney's grasp across the floor. Sloane closed fast, hands out, fingers spread, Delaney feinting with a punch and ducking low, landing two blows before jabbing his fingers at Sloane's throat. Sloane leaned away, choking, half turned and unleashed a knee into Delaney's kidneys with all the strength he could.

There were sounds from outside now, a distant alarm.

On one knee, Delaney saw the gun in the far corner of the room and swivelled towards it. Sloane started after him and slipped: the room had started spinning round.

Feet running in the corridor, getting closer.

'Good try,' Delaney said, grinning, raising the gun, finger fast against the trigger, beginning to squeeze back.

The door swung open and a uniformed security guard burst in and Delaney, swivelling, shot him from close range, jumping over his falling body as he ran.

◆

Cherry was at the hospital in under thirty minutes, still rubbing sleep from the corners of his eyes. He listened carefully as Sloane, face bandaged, told him what had happened. Sloane's head hurt, despite medication, and his mind was dull and slow, a result of the painkillers he had taken.

Rachel, who had suffered little more than surface bruising, was on another floor, being treated for shock.

Miraculously, a few scrabbling movements aside, Connie seemed to have slept through it all.

'What about Delaney?' Sloane asked.

'We'll catch him,' Cherry answered, face drawn.

'You said that before.'

◆

The limo was waiting alongside a patch of wasteland in the lee of the Triborough Bridge. Smoked glass windows. Bodywork that had seen better days. First light spreading across the East River. Delaney crossed the street on a steep diagonal and as he did so, the window wound part-way down.

'Get in,' Marchetti said, his voice thick with phlegm.

'No need,' Delaney said. 'Let's do it here.'

Marchetti pushed the rear door open. 'Get in,' he said again.

Delaney could see the wall-eyed kid behind the wheel, grinning his off-center grin. He climbed in alongside Marchetti and pulled the door closed.

'What happened to you?' Marchetti growled. 'You look like shit.'

'And that's just your hair,' the kid said.

'You've got what I need?' Delaney asked. 'What we arranged?'

Marchetti nodded. 'New passport, ticket, visa.'

'Good.' One eye on the kid, he said, 'What I'm doin' now, gettin' you your money.'

The kid looked at Marchetti and Marchetti nodded, go ahead.

Delaney slid a fat envelope from the inside of his leather jacket and held it out towards Marchetti.

'The girl,' Marchetti said. 'Connie. How is she?'

Delaney shrugged.

'You're a cold bastard, Vincent, you know that?'

Delaney looked him square in the eye. 'A cold bastard with a plane to catch. Here, take this.'

Still Marchetti didn't take the money.

'How much you stiffin' me for this time, Vincent? Fifteen per cent? Twenty?'

'Count it, for fuck's sake. Count it, you don't fuckin' believe me. All that other stuff's bullshit an' you know it.'

A smile crossed the yellowing corners of Marchetti's eyes. 'I tell you, Vincent, who to believe these days, it gets harder and harder to tell. But you . . .'

He reached forward to take the money but his hand shot past the envelope and grasped Delaney's wrist instead. For an elderly man he was fast, his grip surprisingly strong. Before Delaney could free himself the wall-eyed kid had brought up a plastic-bodied Glock from beneath the seat and stitched half a dozen bullets through the side of Delaney's head.

Blood smeared Marchetti's hand and arm, and he took a clean handkerchief from his coat pocket and wiped it carefully away.

'You know what your trouble was, Vincent,' Marchetti said, 'no matter how hard you tried, you were always second-rate. You were always your father's son. And the girl, you should've left the girl alone.'

Climbing out of the car, he began to walk slowly away, enjoying the warmth of the first rays of sun on his skin.

◆

They found Catherine Vargas around an hour later, back inside the boiler room of a nearby building, bound and gagged and left to die. She had been badly beaten, raped and sodomized, but she was still alive.

43

IT WAS A PERFECT autumn day. The light bright and clear, the sky an undisturbed blue; the warmth of the sun such that they could sit outside with their coffee, Sloane with a paperback open on his lap, Rachel, a towel twisted around her hair, damp still from the shower. On all the hills, rising deep into the Garfagnana, trees were changing their colors, russet and gold, beginning to shed their leaves.

'You know,' Rachel had said earlier, rolling on to the side of the bed, 'for an old man, you're not a bad lover.'

Sloane had smoothed his hand down her ribs, over the curve of her hip. 'You know why, don't you?'

'Tell me.'

'Each time, you think it might be the last.'

Rachel had laughed and caught hold of his hand. 'It better not be.'

They had rented the same house where Sloane had originally stayed, a week in which to relax and wind down, walk, eat and drink wine and little else. There were things to resolve with Valentina and Rachel, of course, had brought her laptop and was in daily communication with her gallery in New York, but for the most part it was a holiday, a chance to see how they fared when restricted, pretty much, to one another's company.

So far the signs were good.

Valentina had proved more amenable than Sloane had feared, chastened, perhaps, by the close call of her liaison with Robert Parsons, which now seemed foolhardy at best. Officers from the Arts and Antiques Unit had been out to interview her and had taken a deposition, choosing to believe her statement that whereas Parsons had indeed suggested faking the addition of several works to Jane Graham's collection, this was never anything she had agreed to in any way. The officers had gone away happy, having persuaded Valentina to return to England and testify at the trial: another brick in the wall they were confidently hoping to shut Parsons behind for the best part of ten years.

Valentina, who despite everything else had been working hard to pull together an impressive Board of Trustees to administer the Foundation and its student scholarship scheme, surprised Sloane by asking him if he would like to be a member and was perhaps a little relieved when he declined. What he did urge was that she might like to invite Connie in his place and, in just a few weeks' time, Connie was flying out so that she and Valentina could talk things over.

◆

When Sloane had last seen Connie in New York, two weeks before coming to Italy, she had looked thin but strong, determined.

'You know how close I came to dying?' she had said, the two of them on a bench in Central Park, near the Hans Christian Andersen statue, birds skimming the small lake before them.

'Don't think about it,' Sloane said, remembering, but Connie had disagreed.

'I should think about it every day. What I'd come to. What I owe.' Reaching out, she squeezed his hand. 'The ugly duckling, right. That's me. Thanks to you I get a second chance to turn into a swan.' She kissed his cheek and said, 'I am grateful, you know.'

And Sloane had laughed and said, 'It's what fathers are for, didn't you know?'

Childlike, she had put out her tongue. 'Come on, then, Dad. Race you to the other side.'

But they had walked, Connie slipping her arm through his, the most natural thing to have done.

Connie had joined a voluntary dependency group for drugs and alcohol, and was having therapy sessions twice a week to help restore freedom of movement to her face and jaw. As Wayne had put it, 'Once you can get that mouth of yours open enough to do more than squeak, we'll get back into rehearsal.'

They had received a postcard yesterday, Rachel and himself, a black and white shot of Billie Holiday. *Wayne's got a gig in London this November and I might come over with him. What do you think?*

'She's going to be all right, isn't she?' Rachel said, setting down her coffee cup.

'Yes, I think so. I really do.'

'Proud father,' Rachel teased him.

'Balls!' Sloane replied, unable to prevent himself from smiling.

◆

Catherine Vargas took a month's sick leave, which extended to two. When the worst of her injuries were healed she flew out to Denver to stay with her parents, but rapidly her father's questioning looks, the things he had no way of putting into words, made it impossible and she went back to New York. Friday evenings she and John Cherry, and sometimes Cherry's lover, would take in a first-run movie and then have dinner.

By the time she returned to duty she was still seeing a counsellor, still suffering from migraines, still sleeping with the lights on.

When the lieutenant suggested she might confine herself to desk work for a while she didn't complain.

Out of the blue she received a brief letter from Sloane in London, asking how she was, hoping she was on the mend. She kept the letter, but didn't reply.

◆

As part of their American Piano Festival, Wayne played three nights at the Pizza Express Jazz Club in Soho, just up the street from Ronnie Scott's.

'Next time,' Wayne said to Connie, pointing across to the Scott Club, where Georgie Fame was the main attraction, 'that's gonna be your name up there, right?'

'Is that above yours,' Connie asked, 'or underneath?'

Wayne grinned his wicked grin. 'Whichever way you like it best.'

'That'll be on top then,' Connie said and gave his arm a playful punch.

After Italy, Rachel had suggested to Sloane that he might like to fly back to New York with her and stay for a while, but by then he was itching to get back to work and opted for London instead. In less than six weeks he had three more finished canvases, and was hoping to persuade one of the smaller galleries to offer him a show the following spring.

When he phoned Rachel to tell her this and she asked if she could handle him in New York, all she got was a dirty laugh and a promise that he'd see.

So it was that Rachel came over for the last night of Wayne's brief London residency and ended up sitting at the table in Sloane's place the following evening—Wayne, Connie, Dumar, Dumar's daughter, Olivia, and her friend, Nicky, Rachel and Sloane himself—all there to celebrate Dumar's successful application for asylum and to enjoy the feast he had spent the last day and a half preparing.

Two-thirds of the way through dinner, amidst much laughter and many conversations, Sloane excused himself and went outside, which was where Rachel found him ten minutes later, leaning back against the wall and staring up into the faint orange glow of the sky.

'All that happiness getting to you?' she asked, sliding her hand in his.

'Yeah. Not sure I can stand it.'

Pivoting smartly, Rachel kissed him on the mouth. 'Try,' she said. 'Just try.'

Acknowledgements

For background information about the heady mix of art, poetry and jazz in New York City in the 1950s I am indebted to the following books, the nucleus of which was suggested by the poet and commentator, William Corbett, to whom go especial thanks.

William Corbett, *New York Literary Lights* (Graywolf Press)

Brad Gooch, *City Poet: The Life & Times of Frank O'Hara* (Knopf)

John Gruen, *The Party's Over Now* (Viking)

David Lehman, *The Last Avant-Garde* (Anchor Books)

Fred McDarrah, *The Artist's World* (Dutton)

——, *Greenwich Village* (Corinth)

S. Naifeh & G. White Smith, *Jackson Pollock: An American Saga* (Potter)

Frank O'Hara, *Art Chronicles 1954–1966* (Braziller)

Lisa Phillips, *Beat Culture & The New America 1950–1965* (Whitney Museum/Flammarion)

——, *The American Century: Art & Culture 1950–2000* (Whitney Museum/Flammarion)

Larry Rivers with Arnold Weinstein, *What Did I Do?* (HarperCollins)

James Schuyler (ed. Simon Pettet), *Selected Art Writings* (Black Sparrow Press)

Dan Wakefield, *New York in the 50s* (Houghton Mifflin)

One of the great pleasures in writing this novel, has been the excuse it has given me to spend more time than usual enjoying the paintings of many of the women artists who first came to prominence in America in the 1950s, notably Helen Frankenthaler, Jane Freilicher, Grace Hartigan, Elaine de Kooning, Lee Krasner and Joan Mitchell. For particular insight into their work and the process of painting, I am grateful to the following:

After Mountains & Sea: Frankenthaler 1956–1959 (Guggenheim Museum)

Judith E. Benstock, *Joan Mitchell* (Hudson Hills Press)

Robert Doty (ed.), *Jane Freilicher* (Taplinger)

Eleanor Munro, *Originals: American Women Artists* (Da Capo)